Boxing Day

PAUL BULLIMORE

Copyright © 2017 Paul Bullimore

All rights reserved.

Cover design by Nik A. and Tom J. at www.bookbeaver.co.uk

ISBN-13: 9781549744891

DEDICATION

To everyone who feels sad when their team loses and happy when they win, no matter which league they plan in and from where they follow the match.

Especially to all those who volunteer their time and energy to organise things for others. The silent people without whom nothing would ever get done.

CONTENTS

	Acknowledgments	i
1	The Battle of Cherry Lane	1
2	When Saturday Comes	11
3	Shit, We're on Telly	19
4	I Don't Like Mondays	31
5	Made in the UK	37
6	Monday Night 5-aside	42
7	Statto's Challenge	49
8	The Great Escape?	53
9	Advantage Blues	60
10	Trials and Tribulations	68
11	No Room at the Inn	77
12	The Battle of Lovers View	80
13	Four Calling Birds	89
14	Snowball	92
15	The Secret Garden	100
16	Practice Makes Perfect	108
17	The Wheelwright's Arms	116

18	Getting the Band Back Together	124
19	Elf and Safety	134
20	The Night Shift	143
21	The Three Wise Men	150
22	Calling All Hands	159
23	O Come All Ye Faithful	168
24	Brass Bands and Reindeer	180
25	The King's Christmas Message	189
26	The Big Day	199
27	Match of the Day part 1	212
28	Match of the Day part 2	218
29	Match of the Day part 3	225
30	The Six O'Clock News	228
31	What Are You Doing New Year's Day	238
32	I Don't Like Mondays	246

ACKNOWLEDGMENTS

Many thanks to my wonderful wife and children for their patience whilst I was writing this book. Also to all of the people who provided feedback, insults and inspiration in the months that it took to create.

Characters in works of fiction come from experience and observation. I have been lucky enough to meet a lot of wonderful people along my particular journey and I hope that none of you mind if I took a little part of you and put it on a page somewhere.

1 THE BATTLE OF CHERRY LANE

Cherry Lane.

An unremarkable thoroughfare in an orchard of fruit themed passages hanging off the main road into the town centre. Camouflaged amongst the mixture of terraced houses and old shops, where you could buy everything from mobile phones to spectacles to electronic cigarettes to mobile phones. The typical family of shops that now make every town in the country seem the same.

Why anyone had decided to name the group of streets after fruits nobody could remember. They may just as well have been named after Indian princesses, or breeds of parrots, but fruit it had been. And Cherry Lane became the most famous of them all, probably the most famous Lane in the town.

It was there that, over a hundred years before, someone had decided to build a football stadium. The football stadium that supporters of The Whites had been visiting ever since. Ignoring the depressions and the World Wars, the Winters of Ice and the Winters of Discontent, and focussing on the one thing that bound them together. Their love for the game, for their team and for their town.

It was into Cherry Lane that Danny and his friends walked that Friday evening, a strange day to be visiting the ground for a team that was rarely troubled by the TV fixture selectors. It was the evening that followed the day when The Whites had followed many other teams, out of money, out of luck and out of business. Their shift at Marshalls finished, they walked past the King's Head and started towards the ground, late replacements for a battle that they'd already missed.

A light fog was just visible above the dim street lighting, the condensation from eager conversations rising to meet it. The rumble of a large group of people in front of Danny competed with the crunching of the rubbish beneath his feet, broken plant pots and other left overs from the trouble that afternoon. Nearing the ground the lighting got brighter, the noise becoming less important as Danny's eyes took over.

"Well there's still quite a few here lads. They say there were hundreds this afternoon," the four friends pushed into the group, looking patiently on with the rest.

"Charge the bastards!" Danny heard the shout from his left and his muscles tightened as it was accompanied by the sound of breaking glass. Glancing quickly he strained to make out what had happened, but saw nothing to tell if it had been broken on purpose or by accident. The two policemen at the end of the line in front of him continued their conversation, apparently no longer worried by the empty threats coming their way. Well at least he called it a line, there were eight of them.

The noises of the group around him kept him on edge. Shouts, chants and threats born of anger and sadness, two emotions that had brought them there without having the decency to tell them what to do once they arrived. Behind the main crowd were the older men and women, some staring in disbelief, others wiping tears from their eyes as the home of their childhood hopes was taken away from them for ever.

Catching a flicker of movement he turned, the adrenalin again kicking in. Nothing, just an officer moving to the side to take a call. The rest of the line remained motionless in front of the newly locked gates, a padlock shining out like a taunting star.

"Round the back, there's a door open round the back." A breakthrough? The fastest were already past him as everyone set off, hoping to be first to find the weakness and their way into the stadium. That is everyone except for the still line of police, unworried by the new information. Legs pumping he joined them, glad at least for the warmth it brought him on the cold night just a few days before Christmas. Where were the others? Despite the darkness he could clearly pick out Richo in front, the hare, bursting to be the first to get to the open door. He didn't need to look to know that Statto and Al were behind him, the tortoise and the turtle. There was no shame in being last through the door as long as you got through it. Of the others there were none that he'd have called a friend, but today they were brothers.

He turned the corner, taking large gulps of damp air.

"There's nothing here Danny, no doors, nothing," Richo was shouting at him, urging him to stop. They quickly stepped aside as the rest of the crowd arrived, eager to avoid the crush that inevitably followed.

"Statto, Al, over here," they were all together again.

"What're we doing Danny?" Statto squeezed the words out between gasping breaths. Al was behind him, looking as though he felt the same, but unable to speak to confirm it.

"We're doing something Statto, we're here. We're protesting, we're doing anything but sitting on our arses and letting them win." The rest of the crowd milled around them, giving them time to catch their breath.

"But they have won Danny, the doors are locked and

will be forever. You saw them, just like me. The place is empty now. No money, no football. That's the way it is." It had been better when Al was still breathless. "We're team fifty three, like Statto said. The one between Peterborough and Brentford." It would never be a quiz question, but to them it was important. The trickle of failures had become a wave and the Whites had been washed away, just like the others.

"No, there's always something we can do. We won't give in, we'll fight. They'll have to listen to us." Danny saw nothing but resignation in the faces that looked at him, no fight at all.

"Al's right Danny, we're wasting our time here. There's no way in and nothing to do even if we get in."

"Not you too Richo? Go on then, piss off both of you. Go and join the old men at the back and cry like you're at a fucking funeral." Their hesitation was momentary but clear as they looked at each other for clues. The steady stream of others passing by quickly made up their minds.

"We've already been here long enough Danny, you can't blame us. We'll be back tomorrow too, if there's anything organised. Come on Richo, let's go." That just left him and Statto.

"Leave them Danny, they've done their bit today. Let's get back round the front."

What was that? He heard it as they walked back through the thinning crowd, the sound of music, the sound of a heavenly choir.

"You are my sunshine, my only sunshine…." His lips started to move too, with no apparent prompting from his brain.

"You'll never know just, how much I love you. Please don't take……" There they were, in front of the gates. A choir, arms and scarves raised, repeating the words in a loop as only football supporters can.

"You make me happy, when skies are grey….." The line of policemen packed up and marched off. The castle was empty and the King had pissed off with what was left of the gold. The knights in shining armour were no longer needed.

"Please don't take, my sunshine, away….."

The Herald Angels finished their lament. Could Al be right? The Whites were dead, as dead as a coffin nail!

"Come on Statto, I need a drink," his friend joined him and they walked silently towards the end of the Lane. Even as they approached it was clear that the King's Head was full to the rafters, more match day than quiet night just before Christmas. Better to do the wake with brothers than face it alone.

"Here, there's a space," Statto called him and they squeezed into a corner. The pub was a mass of noise and colours as bodies quickly adjusted to the warmth and frustrations were vented. Beer, condensation and the smell of people who'd spent the afternoon running around aimlessly filled his nose. In the background some Christmas song or other filled in the rare silences when everyone decided to breathe at the same time.

"I thought we'd at least see the season out, have a chance of joining a new league or something for next year." He leaned forwards, struggling to hear Statto's words. "There must be something else planned, that's it. Save some money until we start up again?" You're dreaming Statto, it's over. Danny drank, big gulps. "Come in number fifty three, your time is up," their laughter was borne of desperation.

"How could it all go so wrong Statto? One minute everything's fine, the next a "World Series" tournament replaces the cancelled World Cup and then this? The World Series carries on whilst everything else dies. Two years to kill fifty three football teams."

"It was the Brexit. That plus Trump. That's the problem," the answer was to his question, but the voice wasn't Statto's. In front of him was an older man, thirty or so and shivering in just a Whites shirt. Next to him sat a friend, ready to shout out his thoughts.

"Don't be soft, they blame everything on those two these days. It was before then, when the Champions League started. That gave them the idea. Lots of games and lots of money, at least for the top teams, and we all picked up a bit of the left overs. People spent a hell of a lot of money trying to catch that pot of gold, and now the pot's gone there's nothing left." Whites shirt nodded in agreement, Brexit's innocence accepted.

"I hate to disagree, but I think it all happened a long time before then," Statto was woken from his sadness, alive to an opportunity to opine and orate. "You remember Danny, the documentary we watched? The Last Champions, how Leeds won the last ever First Division title, the year before the Premier League started." How could he forget? His head nodded in agreement. "That was the start point." Danny saw the face, smarmy and greasy. The beard and the awful cockney accent. Sir Sugar, or something like that, positively crowing that it was all down to him. Him who'd told BSB to pay whatever it took to get the deal. Praise him, praise him he'd said. Fuck him, more like. Whites shirt's friend butted in.

"But that was almost thirty years ago now, you can't honestly blame that?"

"I can and I do. It all changed from then on. Satellite dishes started appearing on houses like sores on a leper. More and more matches were shown on TV and the money got shared out amongst the best teams. With the money they brought great payers and great managers over from the continent and showed even more matches to generate even more money. With it went the loyalty, and the need to engage with us, the supporters. And as things got bigger the madness set in." There were more nods, not necessarily ones of agreement, but surely of approval.

"They called them the "big five" didn't they?"

"They did indeed, though they're just as big as us now.

The World Series didn't even want the trouble of choosing which teams to keep on, so they just franchised out brand new teams. Those big five are now just flecks on the shirts of the Northern Wildcats and the London Monarchs, disappeared like the rest."

Danny drank, happier when he could listen and didn't have to speak. Around him tens of similar conversations were in progress. Questions and comments shouted out above the noise, only adding more noise and making the shouts louder again.

"And then with Bosman all of the money started going to the players."

"Exactly," Statto retook the floor as the friend took a breath. "Players and agents to be exact. And both guaranteed to take the money out of the game for good. Nothing to the lower leagues and nothing to the grass roots. The bastards." More nods of approval and more beer. The pub was starting to thin out. "We all remember the stories of entire teams worth of millionaire players who didn't kick a ball in anger all season. And Chelsea having over thirty players out on loan one season. There was one guy who was on loan every year for five years. He never played a single game for them." The friend was keen to interrupt.

"And in 2017 Chinese teams spent over two hundred million on players who were coming to the end of their careers. And guess what, they all had the same agent. He must've made a killing that year." Two Statto's on one night. Could Danny take it? A song started up in the corner, giving him a break and the opportunity to get a round in. By the time he returned Statto was on his own, singing along and banging the table in time. As the last bottle accidentally fell some peace was restored. The faces around him were strangely happy, a defiance brought about by the song's memories. Someone in the opposite corner took advantage to shout out.

"In any case, at least we lasted longer than those Blue

bastards. They went at the end of last year they did. Number thirty three or something weren't they?" A cheer was accompanied by banging on tables, stamping of feet and sloshing of beer as celebratory toasts were drunk. A younger boy got to his feet as if to propose a toast.

"Yes, but that was all thanks to Big John that was. You all called him when he left us to be their manager, but I knew he was just going to sabotage them. And what a cracking job he did eh? Big John!" His glass was raised, spilling beer onto a neighbour who didn't seem to care.

"Big John!" The whole pub joined in now, the happiness of old memories slowly replacing the despair of a few hours previous. Fucking unbelievable Jeff, as Big John would say.

Would they see his embarrassment? Statto was staring at him, a broad grin under his beard.

"You see, he's still a hero. You needn't worry, no one knows you're his son." Knew or cared, except Danny. "Big John!" Statto repeated the toast and gave it his best Cheshire cat as everyone joined in again.

"You bastard," Danny's grin wasn't the same as the ones on the other faces in the pub. More forced, hiding a deeper hurt. Or so it felt. "But come on, it can't be over. Not for good surely?" Statto positioned himself to deliver his verdict.

"The money's still there, that's for sure. Trillions of pounds, euros, dollars and every other conceivable currency are still spent on the best players, the most successful coaches, the richest agents and the top presenters and pundits. All greasing the wheels of commercial reality and entertaining the masses. But it's now just for the TV. Us supporters have been eliminated from the equation. Pride of place has been taken by the endorsers, the sponsors, the global partners, the betting companies and the billions of world-wide consumers. You know as much as me that a hundred and fifty thousand people go along to the Wildcats stadium to watch them play, them and the other teams that play their traveling games there, but they don't need us. I can't see that changing any time soon, so the leagues as we knew them are finished." Speak words of comfort to me, please.

"But at our level, the lower leagues. Surely we can regroup and get things going again?" That frown of Statto's, more bad news.

"Who knows? They tried last year and will probably do it again, if there are any teams left to play. The problem's that they just try and reorganise to the old model. And that's too broken to put back together. The money's gone, the players are gone. To some extent the interest has too. God knows it was quick, but the number of pricks you see with the new shirts on and all, even round here, is frightening. Something must happen though. There's thousands of us who are used to watching matches. Millions of us who are used to checking the results on a Saturday night and talking things over on a Sunday lunch time."

"Yes, and taking the piss at work on a Monday morning and worrying all week about injuries and suspensions. The old, the young, everybody." Of course it'll come back, how could anyone let all that die?

"But didn't we have some fun eh. The run to the FA Vase semi-final."

"Ooh yes. That looked good on the old mug didn't it, FA vase semi-final losers 2006. It pales Arsenal's FA Cup wins into insignificance." Did he just make a sort of a joke? Statto remained serious.

"Steady on now. I know we lost, but the town talked of nothing but that game for weeks before and days afterwards."

"You're right, it's stupid. They can't just rip a hundred and so years of history out of society, just like that, and expect no-one to react, to fight back. It's not just us who go to the matches who care, the whole town does. You can tell by the faces after the matches that everyone follows the results, they know if we've won or lost. They'll never let it happen."

"Do I sense the old Danny coming back?" Statto knew him better than he knew himself. Seven years at Tech and then work together and even longer on the terraces. Now that's worth a smile.

"Of course you do. So are we coming back tomorrow then? I can call Richo and Al, let them know what time."

"Yes, let's do that. After all, it's Saturday and we've got nothing else to do."

Walking out again into the cold air Danny regretted his last pint. That night he knew for sure that someone, someday, would save them. They had to. He just didn't realise that it would take so long and that destiny had decided that he would play such an important part.

2 WHEN SATURDAY COMES

A nice walk in the fresh air, what could be better? It was neither hot nor cold under the pale autumn sunshine that late October had decided to bless them with. The leafy lanes of the new estate where his parents lived accompanied Danny on his walk towards the main road into town. Perhaps the bus today? Saturday morning with Big John and Mary never changed, and for that he was grateful. The combination of stories and rumours from the sports desk at the local radio station and the secret rooms at the local WI always kept them well entertained, as they drank their tea and nibbled on digestive biscuits. He gave his head a little shake of disbelief at the memory of that morning's laughter. His parents laughter, just like his parents, married together perfectly. They must surely have met at the prize giving ceremony of some laughing competition all those years ago. They'd spent the morning looking back thirty years at old wedding photos. Savage, with his long hair, smart suit and grumpy face being the star turn and the source of the majority of the laughter. John had mixed with many promising young players in his day, they all having been sorted the chaff from the wheat, eventually being forced their separate ways.

The bus stop. Next bus in five minutes, according to the electronic display. Were they ever right? To be honest, the traffic into town on a Saturday lunchtime was hardly going to be too much of a problem.

"Hi Danny, your Dad okay?" Danny nodded a quick yes. He didn't recognise the man who'd asked, but from an early age he'd got used to being stopped by people in the street when he was with his Dad. He'd not realised that his Dad had been special, the local boy come good. Tough tackling midfield general and overall nice guy. How was he to know that his Dad was different? He took his place in the queue.

"You seen the fixtures for today? The Wildcats'll massacre the Bangkok Tigers. And later there's Austro-Hungary against Tokyo Blast. Pogba will be playing in that one." Danny looked at the two youths next to him. He quickly turned away, not wanting them to see the disgust on his face and mistake it as being personal.

"Pogba's way past it. He'd be at a better team if he was still any good."

"He still cost two hundred million quid though. He may have lost his pace, but he can still tackle." Lost his pace? He never had any. And everyone cost at least two hundred million these days. Oh well, they'd probably never known any better.

"Is your uncle going to the game tomorrow, at the Wildcats' stadium. Its Mexico City against Polska Reds isn't it?" Bloody travelling circus. Everyone playing everywhere at all hours, and young kids talking about it as if it was normal. Well, for those who were interested it was becoming normal, after over six years of the World Series.

"No, he got tickets for the under 21s and the ladies games today, but missed out on the main ones. His luck eh." The youths carried on, the rest of the line waited patiently in silence.

Ten minutes later and he took his seat on the bus, fortunately far enough away to no longer hear the youths' conversation. He would have almost been as quick walking after that wait. His eyes fixed on the roadside buildings, but he quickly floated off to another time. The bus approached Pear Street and he started to hear the noises. Turnstiles turning, programme sellers shouting, greetings between friends being exchanged. Apple Lane, he could start to smell the hot dogs and burgers, the stale ale coming out of the King's Head and the smell of the smokers huddled in the car park. Cherry Lane, he could see it. Not as it was now, boarded up like an unwanted Christmas present, but as it was in its glory. The colours, the people. Himself inside, his white scarf around his neck. Ollie the Ostrich warming up on the touchline, making the children laugh and being abused by the older boys. The boom of the drum as Fat Frank and the band started up on yet another song, cheering their team to glory. The Fist and his gang were always at the back of the stand, threatening trouble but never finding it and turning into excited boys themselves as Dick Sparrow scored another goal. The joy, the excitement. The past.

An oversize shopping bag brushed his elbow, waking him up just in time for his stop. He quickly crossed the Elizabeth Park, once home to at least ten pitches that were all full on both Saturday and Sunday, but now eerily empty. Then it was onwards past the fire station and the swimming pool, finally arriving at The Bell.

It was an old pub, probably Victorian, and was where Danny and Richo had drunk their first pints as young fourteen year olds after midweek games of cricket. It was strangely placed, just far enough out of town to not be a town centre pub, but with no housing around it to make it an estate pub. This was one of the qualities that made it their ideal choice, the place where they met and where all their plans were made.

Breathing deeply, as he always did, he pushed through the dark blue door. A quick glance around comforted him.

Nothing inside had changed. As a child on long journeys his Mum had made him do his puzzle books, two pictures side by side with seven differences to spot. He played the game now. Between this and his last visit some things were different, what could they be? He laughed, happy as ever that at least here things stayed the same.

On receiving the signal from the door, either by sound or change in temperature, Statto looked up, nodding acknowledgement and then looking back again at his phone. The processor that was his brain had possibly paused for a millisecond as it continued to absorb the information it had no doubt been searching. Years before he'd have been reading a book or a newspaper, but those days were long gone. The modern day anthropologist, piecing together the football tribe as it meandered from the end of the last century into its inevitable destruction. His information would never find its way into a bound thesis as he was far too fond of communication of the verbal type, especially after a few pints. There was no difference there.

"Hear this lads, he reckons Brunhilde fancies him," Richo was moving in short, animated bursts, clearly enjoying the argument.

"Her name isn't Brunhilde, it's Gesine, and as it happens she's mad for me," Red Al was playing more a game of defence with silences followed by large gestures as he fought back.

They both looked up and a feeble 'Hi Danny' gave them chance to breathe before they started off again.

"Fond of you? Fuck off. How'd you know if she was?"

"She talks to me, in German. She's got this amazing way of making things sound so sexy with her German accent." Al's interest in the fierce German girl, left behind when her company went bankrupt, was almost as famous as her resistance to his clumsy advances. No difference there.

"No sign of the girls?" It was his turn to speak.

"Shopping. Apparently the Diwali dresses can't double for Christmas, so they're off out for more." Statto had answered without raising his head while Richo and Al continued their argument. Annie and Geeta would have to wait until later.

Danny bought a drink and settled at the end of the empty bar. Al and Richo had finally decided to agree to disagree, Al going to annoy Statto while Richo walked towards Danny. It was difficult to think back to the day that the two four year old Jedis had met out in the street. Matching brown cloaks, but Danny armed with a proper plastic light sabre and Richo with a cut off broom handle. It had at least been a red broom handle. From that day their paths had been the same. Spending their early years in the same street, studying at the same school, getting into the same fights and always with the same one love. Football and the Whites.

"Hi there Danny boy. Saw my uncle Mick this morning," the sentence needed no finishing, both of them breaking into broad smiles.

"Still doing well is he?"

"Not half. My Auntie's the only person I know who can afford to wear that clobber we knock out at Marshalls. Looks the dog's it does. Mick's just the same, banging on about that goal your Dad scored against Villa in the FA Cup all those years ago." Had Richo seen the Danny smile slip then, just for a second?

"Not that one again. Everyone wanted to talk with him that week. You remember how he lined all the other kids up, giving them names and positions, and put me in goal? Mark Bosnich I think I was. Then he got the ball and did a re-enactment that had everyone rolling around with laughter, with his silly commentary voice. All the dads were cheering him on from the sidelines as the kids tried to tackle him, but just like in the match he bravely fought through them all and tucked it past me in the goal. I thought he was going to die laughing afterwards."

"Especially after my Uncle Mick tried that last gasp slider and split his new suit trousers." They both laughed now, old Danny almost forgetting the disappointment that young Danny had felt when he'd had to share the moment with the whole park.

Seemingly attracted to their laughter Statto and Al came over to join them.

"So then, just the four musketeers today?" Red Al always liked to think of them as some romantic group of heroes, instead of the four non-descript people they were. "What've you been digging up this time Statto?"

"Francis and Pogba," came the reply. Richo fixed him.

"Not another one of your scary ghost stories Statto? Boo!" Typical Richo, always bored quickly. Statto remained determined and focussed.

"If we forget these stories Richo, what hope will we have for our children?" Richo now looked bored and confused. "Just under forty years between the first one million pound transfer and the first one hundred million pound transfer. That's a one hundred times increase, while at the same time a pint went from seventy five pence to three pound eighty." Al was just as entranced as Danny, Richo played with his four pound fifty pint. "For Francis, Forest paid a million, Birmingham received a million and there were probably a few bags of notes lost here and there somewhere between the West and East Midlands. All straightforward and a million quid's left to circulate in the game. Pogba signs for Palace for a hundred million. They say they paid that much, but where it all went who really knows? It probably included the millions needed to cover his contract, money for his agent, money for his image rights, all sorts of cock. What United had left to invest in the game, nobody knows."

"And do tell me again Statto, why I should care?" Richo was never going to get it, Statto looked hurt.

"It's just a reminder of why we no longer have a team to support, that the world went mad. We should teach it to the next generation, so they never forget. We've no idea how much of the TV money actually went to the clubs, actually got spent on new players, or ground improvements or youth development. The one certainty is, that not all of it did, and therein, brethren, was the heart of the problem," Statto finished his sermon and they stood in silence. A gulp of beer and a shuffle of feet, as though waiting for the collection box to be passed round.

"So then, what to do this afternoon?" Richo broke the silence. "We could go to the rugby, the Braves are at home?"

"Fuck off." Danny's reply was echoed by Al and Statto.

"Just because they use a ball and have grass and a stadium and all that, it isn't the same," Statto was always animated when rugby was mentioned, as if it had been a bad medicine that he was force fed as a child. There was singing and chanting and you could almost smell an atmosphere, but it would never be the same. "They're not even pros now, it's all rozzers and school teachers again." Richo only proposed the rugby from time to time to piss Statto off.

"So then," Red Al took the floor. "I'm assuming that we're not looking for party dresses and that there's nothing special on at the cinema?" nods all round, "so, how about the Sky Bar?" Why, oh why Al?

"Give it a rest. The place is full of tossers, you can't hear a word people are saying."

"But there'll be a game on. I think it's even the Wildcats this afternoon." Not you too Statto.

"An even better reason not to go there. Not only did they take away our team but they even wear their fucking white shirts, the bastards. Come on, there must be something else we can do?"

"Laetitia will be there, at least there'll be something to look at." Cheers Richo. As if he needed reminding. There's nothing better than seeing your childhood sweetheart, newly returned to town and shacked up with her new bloke. Especially when that bloke's Ted Holmes, the smarmy bastard owner of the Sky Bar. A sneering Ted, but a radiant Laetitia.

"Fuck it, the Sky Bar it is."

3 SHIT, WE'RE ON TELLY

The large brick building in front of them was imposing and refined, a throwback to times when looks were as important as cost. For years it had been BHS, the department store. Anything you wanted could be bought from there, and with a quality better than anything else available in town.

"I remember your school jumpers from here," Richo said from behind him. "Come winter, when mine were all worn out, yours were always still in top condition." Danny smiled. Lord Green screwed it up of course, just like his friend Sugar. They really did sound like characters from Cluedo. Sir Sugar in the studio with the lead piping. Lord Green in the pantry with the candlestick. Who'd really killed her? BHS had gone, despite the rich trappings of its owner, and this town, like many others, had been left with another abandoned building to be converted into a pub.

"And to think that it all belongs to Ted the Trainer eh. Now there's a lucky sod who knows how to find himself in the right place at the right time." You're so right Al. "He caught the fitness craze with that old stuff he bought and then fell into this."

"Always a weasely bastard though, even at school.

Remember he could open a packet of biscuits in his blazer pocket and eat the lot without anyone noticing. I bet it used to take his mum ages to clean the crumbs out of those pockets." Now that's the boy Danny remembered so well.

"Come on then lads, that's enough of jumpers and Ted, let's have a pint. And you Danny, take no notice of Holmes, don't let him wind you up. And enjoy yourself." Of course he would, with Statto around how could he not?

They climbed the stairs. Four floors of bars, with open areas, exclusive seating areas, intimate group areas and wall to wall television. All provided for one purpose and one purpose only, to show around the clock the matches of the World Series.

The names of the teams flowed off Red Al's lips as he read out the day's fixtures.

"China Reds, Baltic Vikings, Bombay Spice, Southern Kangaroos, All Blacks, Red Bull Deutschland, Joburg Boks, Sao Paolo Carnaval, Russian Federation, Mexico City," Breathe before you fall over Al, "Iberian Fury, Ontario Storm, Northern Wildcats, Austro-Hungary, Tokyo Blast, Paris Bleu Blanc Rouge." Who could ever take all of that in in one day? And then there's tomorrow to come. All of those time zones to please a worldwide audience of billions. Convert old buildings into mega venues to attract the crowds and play the games all day long. The advertisers loved it. One source of coverage and a relentless pursuit of anyone who tried to pirate the images or break the rules. And with all that who needed the old teams, the ones that had nothing but history and a place in their local communities?

"Come on, to the second floor. It's quieter there."

The 'zen' floor, whatever that meant. Statto and Al were advancing towards a neatly polished bar that was a good twenty yards long. To the sides were smaller viewing areas, each with its own array of TV screens and seating, most of them still empty that early afternoon. There was a match visible to his left, the familiar red and yellow of Iberian Storm building a patient attack as the Canadians retreated on a large screen in the corner. This had replaced the life of a real match on a Saturday. How could it have been allowed to happen?

"Go on, out left," he was muttering under his breath. "Good, overlap, cross it early, cross it early. Idiot." He balled his fists and raised himself on tip toes. "Come on then, second time, second time. Cross it. Now, get it in there. Attack it. Yes, goal, goal," his heart thrilled as the ball went in, still programmed from years before. Immediately the image changed. A dark room somewhere else, South America judging by the faces.

"Fuck me, there won't be anyone playing pan pipes down the market tonight," it was Red Al, never one for tact, despite his lefty leanings. "You know what, I don't give two hoots about the goals, but the Golden Camera makes my day."

Now there was a master idea to get the global juices running. After every goal the coverage switched to one of the thousands of cameras present on every screen in the whole Sky Bar chain. The viewers were almost always rewarded with jumping, enthusiastic crowds from all over the world, representing the World Series and its global touch.

"Remember that time there were all of those pissed up Aussies fighting, when Southern Kangaroos played the All Blacks? Priceless it was." It had been funny, but would never replace Fat Frank and the band, with The Fist and his crew jumping around in adulation. Why on earth would you want to see a load of smiling strangers whenever your team scored a goal?

"Hey up, hey up," a new voice, clearly male but high pitched. A dark haired man in a suit had left the young girl he'd been talking to in the far corner of the bar and slowly moved towards them.

"Sorry gentlemen, but the Halloween Blast isn't until

next weekend," he didn't even try to disguise his sneer.

"Piss off Holmes," their ability to talk in unison sometimes was amazing. Could they be some strange form of unrelated quadruplets?

"Oh, sorry, I didn't realise. You're collecting early for the Guy. Which one of you useless bastards is getting burnt this year? The big one with his head stuck in his books? He should at least burn long and well."

"Piss off Holmes," this time it was louder.

"Oh come on boys, it's just me having a joke. Welcome to The Sky Bar, where things happen, where dreams are made," Holmes waved his hands around, showing to anyone who could be bothered to follow them his empire.

"You sound like Willy Wonka Holmes," they laughed.

"Thank you Al, for your wisdom. Now, if you're staying around then please do me a favour. Try and stay away from the rest of my customers. I wouldn't want any of them being frightened off. Ha ha." The boys took their drinks and turned to walk away. "Oh and Danny," he met those eyes that he so detested. "You see that adorable creature at the end of the bar? Try and stay away from her, you'd only bore her. Again. Ha ha." Why had they come here?

He followed Al to an empty booth and they sat down.

"One thing I can't stand. Bright green sofas and plastic tables, in a pub. And in a pub that's sole purpose is to show football matches. How on earth did that happen?" Red Al mused between sups of his pint. "It's all for the money people. Food and a day out"

"They need to be able to pay all of those extortionate transfer fees somehow," Richo gave Al his answer. "Advertising brands to people sat on green sofas costs quite a bit more than hoardings around the side of the pitch. And let's face it, around the world at the moment there are a hell of a lot of green sofas. What do you think Danny?"

They were talking to him, but it was all noise, no words. Holmes, the bastard. Him and Laetitia together, laughing and flirting and doing all of the other things that young couples do.

"Forget him Danny. It won't last, it can't, and when it does all go tits up he'll be back where he belongs and Laetitia won't be seen for dust." They could obviously see in which direction he was looking.

"I'm not so sure Statto. Perhaps there's more there than meets the eye. Perhaps he's got deep hidden secrets invisible to our eyes."

"Leave it out Al," Richo jumped in and Danny sensed his stare. "There's nothing serious there and it'll all be over when she wakes up to what a twat he is." If Richo was still staring he'd be looking at an empty space. Holmes had gone and Danny's feet were taking him in unsteady steps in that direction. Now just don't do anything stupid Danny boy.

She was still the girl he remembered from their teens. She'd always been pretty and had been lucky that the prettiness had stayed. But she'd also understood. Especially the pressure he'd always felt to be someone else, to be more than he was. There was an empty seat and space for a glass on the bar and he took advantage of both.

"Not too much grief I hope?" Great, she started. "He does have his moments I know, but he can be really fun." Yes, right.

"Just some kids' stuff, that's all. Nothing we can't cope with." Silence. "Everything going okay with the job?" Surely he could do better than that?

"Yes, great thanks. I'm starting to settle in. It's strange after all those years studying, to finally get a job. It's really rewarding working for the Council in my home town, helping the people I grew up with."

"I don't remember you talking about it much at the time." Too quick, don't jump in, take it easy. Her face turned towards him, beautiful but serious.

"Danny," why had she sighed? "It was a long time ago, and as I remember you didn't hear a lot of what I said at the time. I'm sure I told you I was pregnant once, just to see if you were listening, and you didn't react at all." Harsh but friendly all the same. "All of that first love stuff eh. Great memories, but it wasn't meant to be. Me going away to Uni just saved us finding out later." First love she'd said.

Bristol had been a new place to visit, but with all of her new friends it had been difficult. They were never his type. Believing deep down that it would work he'd carried on for a while, but other things, bigger things had got in the way. It had been easier for him to let it go, to walk away. At the time he'd thought that he'd get over it, that he'd find someone else. The face he was looking at in the mirror behind the bar told him otherwise.

"I saw Annie yesterday. She's looking great. Surely you can find her someone to make her happy?" he nodded. "And how are your Mum and Dad. Are they keeping well?"

"They're fine." She was talking to him like an old cousin. Why had he come over?

"So you left the rest of the wise monkeys to go solo did you? Managed to walk all the way over here on your own?" Was he pleased that Holmes was back? "Wise monkeys eh. The four wise monkeys and they're all in my bar. Ha ha."

"So then Laetitia, I'll perhaps see you later. Pass my regards on to Winston and Edith," what a look of surprise she had. She was quick too though, already realising that he was just trying to wind Ted up. "And by the way Holmes, there were only three wise monkeys, not four, so I can't have left the others behind. There were four amigos and four fantastics, but only three wise monkeys." Steering himself back towards the green sofa and the monkeys he'd left behind he allowed himself a little smile.

"Was it worth it? All that way and you didn't even get a round in. Come on, the Wildcats are on next, get 'em in."

Putting the four fresh pints down on the table Danny looked up at the TV screen, just as the teams for the next game were displayed. The Northern Wildcats vs the Bangkok Tigers. Another 'home game' not actually being played at the home of the Wildcats, the league preferring to mix the games around in order to get more global interest.

"There's a game at the Wildcats Stadium tomorrow," Statto was always in the know. "It's the lot from Mexico playing against the lot from Poland. The juniors and the ladies play today. Tomorrow it's the reserves and then the main event."

"Main event? A Mexican team with no Mexicans playing against a Polish team with no Poles, all taking place in the North of England. Do me a favour," Richo joined the conversation. "And before you say it Al, yes, at least the Poles will have a lot of supporters and yes it will be difficult to get hold of a plumber," they laughed in unison, Al's hurt look showing his disappointment that his joke had been stolen. "But they're forced to have lots of home country players in the junior teams though." Was Richo turning into Statto? "Without that the Internationals would've died." Football talk was easier.

"That last World Cup did die. Sixty four teams and eight weeks of matches played across four countries. They really know how to keep the tension going. And with us knocked out after the second group stage, by the time of the final I'd forgotten there was a tournament going on." They all had. The line ups for the match flashed up on the screen.

"Well look at that, boys. I think it's the first time the Wildcats have ever started a game without a single British player. Not even one." Despite his disinterest in the team Red Al sounded genuinely sad. "When it starts happening to the British teams it's a sorry state." Statto was shifting eagerly in his seat. A tell-tale sign he had something he wanted to share.

"Boxing Day," he stated matter of factly, "that's when it happened."

"What?" answered Richo. "Good King Wenceslas last looked out?" Statto was unmoved.

"The Premier League had been going for about 6 or 7 years, when on Boxing Day 1999 Chelsea put out the first ever Premier League team without a single British player. There'd been over one hundred and eleven years of football history before, but their Italian manager decided that his best formation didn't contain a single British player. Interesting for everyone at the time, but perhaps fatal for us all in the long run. Global players lead to global appeal lead to there being no need for us bums to turn up at Cherry Lane anymore on a Saturday afternoon." And the rest was history.

Kick off and silence, helped by the few pints they'd already drunk. For all he disliked the set-up, a game was still a game and when it was in front of him watching became easy. The noises of the Sky Bar weren't the same as the noises of the stadium, far too polite and organised, like background conversation at a wedding. It was the same for the colours and the smells. On the screen though, the movements of the players didn't change. Two teams with big budgets and players of the highest level. The first fifteen minutes passed with nothing more memorable than Al getting another round of beers.

"I think it's going to be one of them games again lads. I know it's early, but has anyone got any ideas for the Christmas party this year?" They all gave Red Al a surprised look. "I was thinking we could try and book the back room at The Bell and try and get a bit of a disco on? Everyone would enjoy that and all the management would stay well away. We could…"

"Goal!!" came the cheers from around the floor. "Shit, we missed it," came Richo. Looking out from their booth Danny saw that The Sky Bar had filled up considerably since they'd arrived. People dressed in their Saturday best were cheering and congratulating each other as the goal was celebrated. On the screen there were scenes of jubilation as hundreds of fans packed into a Sky Bar in a far off location joined in the celebrations. Danny could just make out that the Sky Bar in Milan had been chosen for the Golden Camera for the eighteenth goal of the weekend.

"Well what do you think? I could get my mum to put on a spread and Marlon's brother could do the disco. And we could ask Geeta if her family could organise some food for her lot. They'd have to dance to our music though, I don't think Marlon's brother's got any of the stuff that they'd like." The spell was broken and the football was forgotten. Statto and Danny slowly joined in with the conversation. Discussing something as important as the Christmas party was better than talking bollocks. Richo got another round in.

"Goal!!" came the cheers. "Shit, we missed it," came Richo. Looking up they were now seeing a Sky Bar in India. The Tigers' equaliser had obviously gone down well, even though most of the cheering people seemed to be wearing Wildcats shirts. That was the way it was. Half time came and went and the Christmas party developed. The food was organised, the playlist chosen, bouncers were on, then off, then on, then off and tickets would cost a tenner.

"But we've got to sing carols, just a few."

"Carols Al, do piss off."

"But it's tradition. As long as people can at least hum along to Hark the Herald we know we're still in a Christian country at Christmas Time." Now he's started singing we're done for. How many carols does he know?

"Al, somewhere this evening there's a village surviving without its idiot and we're putting up with him on their behalf. The Christmas party's for drinking and trying to pull. Just look around you, at the effect your God Bless You Merry Gentlemen is having on everyone else." Their corner was becoming less and less populated, everyone moving towards any of the other screens with a space. Statto took advantage and went for another round.

He was soon back, a tray in his hand containing four fresh pints, some crisps and his change. Seeing the table in front of him full he tried to move some of the empty glasses to the side and make some space for the tray.

"Don't worry Statto, I'll get the beers," Richo lurched forward and took two of the pints, but Statto was caught by surprise and the tray, now a couple of kilogrammes lighter went upwards. What a mess. There was a big pile of change rolling about on the floor and two upended pints rolling about the tray, the dark brown liquid that had been in them gently rippling over the tray edge and onto the floor.

"Bloody hell Statto, that's all over my shirt," Danny wasn't happy.

"It wasn't my fault, I had everything under control until Richo decided to help out." Tensions were rising. Danny had his hankie out and was vigorously rubbing at his shirt.

"That's right, blame me you lummox."

"Don't worry about the empties, I'll sort them out. Do you remember that bloke we saw at the cricket once, he must've had over fifty pint pots all stacked up. It was wonderful."

"Yes, but watch out Al. His were plastic, not real glass. If you put too many real ones together they'll get stuck, or break," Statto even had time for facts in an emergency.

"Has anyone seen my change? There were at least three five pound coins on there. Shift your legs Richo, I can't see under the table."

"Goal!!" came the cheers. Pause. "Shit, we're on telly," came Richo. Not understanding Danny looked up at the screen. Gone were the throngs of cultured Milanese, gone were the eager Indians cheering and showing their appreciation. In their place was the sight of Statto's builders' bum cleavage wiggling away under the table.

Stood up behind him was Al, his beer glass tower in hand, raising it towards the ceiling. There was a strange guy, who looked just like Danny did, agitatedly rubbing at a large brown stain on the front of his shirt, just like Danny was. To finish there was Richo, the look of a madman on his face as he rolled about the green sofa, almost brought to tears. Statto's face looked round to join the scene. It was there before him, framed in gold. Four disbelieving faces, plus one bum crack, all caught on screen like rabbits in a spotlight.

"Shit," said Danny. "The bloke choosing the Golden Camera won't be getting much of a bonus today."

The usual cheers for a Wildcats goal had been replaced by laughter, a laughter that got louder and louder. It was then displayed that the home of the scene in front of them was their Sky Bar. Heads were turning, looking around for the culprits and finally resting on the carol singing corner. Yes, it was them.

"What the fuck," Ted Holmes' already high tenor tones had gone up at least another octave. There was a commotion around them as people pushed through the crowd on the floor. "You bastards, you bastards," Ted screamed. "Three years and god knows how many goals without a Golden Camera, and when it comes…" Holmes breathed deeply, his high pitched scream taking more breath than he'd imagined "..And when it comes, what do I get? No joyous happy fans showing that my Sky Bar's the best. No singing, dancing people having a good time even. No, I get the four wise monkeys bang in the middle of a fucking Monty Python sketch re-enactment."

"There were only three wise monkeys." Did Holmes not get anything? All four of them burst into fits of uncontrollable, drunken laughter. If they'd believed earlier in the day that they'd have such an opportunity to embarrass Ted Holmes like this, in front of the whole world, not just his friends, they'd surely have grasped it with both hands. Several pints in to a Saturday afternoon it was beyond their wildest dreams. Laughter was clearly not what Ted had expected or wanted.

"Go on, get out you bastards. Get out and never come back. You wasting scumbags, enemies of the people, saboteurs, bastards….. Just get out." Any redder and he'd look like a tomato.

As everyone looked on they became a mass of movement, jackets were put on and drinks were drunk up. Out they bundled, followed by a flustered man and his high pitched wailing.

"Good bye Laetitia, enjoy the rest of your afternoon," Richo shouted out as they passed. Danny glanced at her quickly, catching her eye. Was that a wicked glint within it? It was cold and dark and he needed the toilet, but his heart raced and he smiled like a madman. He talked, but no one could possibly have made out what he'd said amongst the excited words of his three companions, each one wanting to tell how they'd appeared on world-wide television in front of billions of viewers.

"I just hope someone's got a copy somewhere," said Al. "I just have to see Statto on his knees, looking for that money."

"At least he looked round and showed us his real face, otherwise he'd now be known all around the world simply as 'arse face'. Come on, let's get back down the Bell. We can tell Geeta and Annie all about it." A spring in their step, they made the short walk back to base.

Saturday had come and gone and it was one of the best they'd had in a good five years. Unbelievable Jeff, as Danny's Dad would've said.

4 I DON'T LIKE MONDAYS

Monday morning at a quarter to eight. Never a problem finding a parking space at Marshalls, the site having been built for hundreds more employees than it currently had.

Danny squeezed his car in next to Statto's old Vauxhall and he and Richo got out, walking quickly across the car park to the back entrance and the changing rooms. The memories from Saturday in the Sky Bar had kept them busy for the drive over from the White town and Danny was feeling good and all ready for another week.

"Another day producing good quality Made in the UK clobber to keep us entertained," Richo was all talk as usual. "It needs to be good mind. Without that quality we'd be in the call centres with the others, and it'd all be made in China or India like the rest." Technology versus cheap labour. People had called it progress for over half a century, but exactly what were they progressing towards?

He was quickly changed and took his normal place near the back of the floor. Next to him a couple of young lads were arguing over the weekend games, a chattering sound above the general air of silence.

"Get out, Paris would've battered them if it wasn't for

their keeper. He had a blinder."

"Well of course he did, that's what he's paid to do. If you can't score you don't win, everyone knows that. And the All Blacks were rubbish yesterday. Ronaldo can't hit a cow's arse with a banjo at the moment."

"Well he's getting on a bit now. I'm surprised he still gets a run out." Danny's face turned into a large, ironic smile. Years before the whole shop would have been a hive of discussion on a Monday morning, everyone poring over the weekend games. Now?

The silence became absolute as the Monday meeting began. Looking around he picked out Richo, Statto and Geeta. No sign of Red Al. Benjamin, the site director, stood at the front looking around, clearly waiting for something. Hoping not to get noticed Danny looked quickly up. Damn! Their eyes locked momentarily, Danny's burnt by the contact. Benjamin's face transformed into a warm, satisfying smile. Hearing a small disturbance to his left Danny looked around. Al had finally made it and Benjamin wasted no time.

"And at last we're joined by the fourth Horsemen of the Apocalypse," as ever Benjamin's voice was clear and energetic. A mild laughter accompanied it. "Nice of you to finally join us Al. I must admit these past years I've really missed our Monday morning get-togethers. It was always a good time to reflect on the events of the weekend. How the White shite from over yonder had inevitably been beaten, while the magnificent Blues had surely taken another scalp and the associated three points," more laughter. He was right though, Benjamin was. Danny's mind ran back to those Monday mornings, everyone discussing the weekend's results and reflecting on the differing fortunes of their teams. Not just the Whites and Blues, but all the other teams supported by people who'd grown up elsewhere but found themselves in this corner of England. The next few minutes weren't going to be much fun. "So imagine the horror I felt on Saturday afternoon," he was a fine speaker Benjamin, almost as good as Statto, "as I was watching the Northern Wildcats match, when I saw this."

"Shit," Danny muttered under his breath. The large display screen behind Benjamin was no longer displaying the figures and graphs of a normal day. Those had all been replaced by a crystal clear view of the Golden Camera image. The loud gasps suggested that many were seeing it for the first time. A surprised silence was broken as sniggers rang out, finally followed by full blown laughter. Beneath his overall Danny's shirt clung clammily to his back. He ignored the looks coming his way, focussing his thoughts and eyes firmly on Statto, who was himself defiantly staring directly at their tormentor. Benjamin continued.

"I must admit that when the one on the floor turned around to show us all his face I was relieved. At least it avoided us having to have an identity parade to name him." He was now in full oratory flow, just like the barrister for the prosecution. "Consider then my surprise, no in fact my horror, when I realised that these four people were not only people that I knew, but also people that I employ." His fine voice grew in volume, rising above the increasing laughter. "The four Horsemen of the Apocalypse, in front of me in full technicolour. Representing my town, representing my Sky Bar and representing my factory."

"Bastard," just quiet enough for no one to hear. His eyes searched out Richo, quickly dropping as he saw his friend just laughing along with the rest.

"Anyhow, Marsha's informed me that as the offence happened off site and out of work hours there's nothing that can be done officially," Danny caught Red Al's pleading look towards him, his lips tight and motionless. "But at least we can all have a bloody good laugh and never let them forget what a bunch of muppets they looked like." More laughter, quickly calmed as Benjamin raised his hands to bring about silence. He milked his pause and finally continued. "I'm sure that you're all pleased to be reminded that these people are also the organising committee for this year's Christmas Party," Danny no longer heard the laughter. His eyes tried to make sense of the people before him, their faces a mixture of sympathy and contempt. Which one did he dislike most?

"The arsehole. His day'll come, don't worry," Statto had moved round to join him.

"Anyway, on a more professional note," Benjamin brought them again to order. "There's not a lot to tell you on new orders. We've taken nothing new since last week, though we've sent out some very strong and competitive offers. The order book's nicely full for the next months, so we'll have time to focus on the jobs at hand while we wait to see how they go. Now Dave'll fill you in on Production for the week."

He should've been a football manager, Dave. Hardly a modern day coach or tactician, but a good old fashioned manager from the late 90s. Not because he was a good organiser of people, or because he could motivate them to go above themselves. There he was a dead loss, only in his job because he was Benjamin's oldest friend. No, he should've been a football manager because he spoke just like them, cliché after cliché coming from his boring, downturned mouth.

"So then, production this week," he was no Benjamin or Statto, revelling in the opportunity to speak in public and taking pleasure holding the ears of their audience. "We've got a lot of small orders to get through, so we should really focus and just take it one order at a time. There's a lot to get through, but if we all give it one hundred and ten percent and make sure we play for the full ninety minutes then we should be okay. Pay special attention with the order for Spain today, you can't win your week on Monday but you can certainly lose it, and just make sure that everyone knows their job." Finished and back in his position, no waiting for questions, no extra detail, a poacher's tap in from two yards if ever there was one.

"Better than the one just after the holidays," Statto sounded calmer. "Not just the number of clichés but the way he intertwined them to make a coherent sentence."

Finally Marsha. She must be the only person Danny knew who might wear the expensive, flamboyant clothes that they made in the factory. Her fine blue trouser suit was proof. Super-efficient and super organised she almost kept the world turning on her own.

"So then, just to finish, one new item that everyone needs to be aware of. We've updated the paternity policy to bring it in line with the new laws that I told you about last week. It's good for you all to know that there are an additional two days paid leave for fathers to take after the birth of the first child. This is the last of the modifications made following the post EU changes to the parental working time policy directives." Everyone looked pleased except for Benjamin, surely seeing yet more days paid for no work. "So are there any questions?" as these last words passed her lips her eyes toured the room, finally settling on Red Al.

"Not a question as such, just some clarification for everyone," Red Al, deliberate and measured as always. "The paternity policy changes were discussed at District level and have now been approved and inserted into the collective agreement policy for the Area. We should all thank Mr Corbyn for his tireless work in this area, despite the many obstacles that he faced. And just one final reminder that new members for the Union are always welcome. You can all …."

"Yes, thank you Al," Benjamin burst in. "If there are no more questions, let's get those machines running."

All around Danny the bustle erupted, everyone

moving back to their positions on the lines. Within minutes the first production orders of the week were rolling across the machines. He was calmer with the whir of the machines around him. How could things have changed so much in such a short time? Where were the hives of people and the noise and chatter he'd known when he started? Now there were just automated machines that printed and cut, the synchronisation of those two tasks being the factor that distinguished them from their competitors and kept them in business. The people around were no longer valued for their skilled hands, and eyes that could detect detail. They were now simply loading and unloading, making sure that the material continued to move. And running one of these lines made him lucky?

A ringing alarm and a flashing light. Shit, already? He turned to see that it was the cutting machine. Richo was already knee deep in cloth.

"What's up Richo?"

"Same as before, whatever should be keeping it in place isn't doing its job, so we're cutting across the pattern," Danny examined the offered example. "Everything seems fixed underneath, so I don't think it's mechanical, but I haven't got a clue what it could be." There was no change there then.

"Okay, follow the debugging process and I'll give Statto a call." Richo left him, troubleshooting guide in hand. Danny got out his walkie talkie. Marlon and Geeta were already hovering around, eager to get stuck into their first call of the day, their cuppas still warm.

"In you go then you two," Danny gave the okay as Richo shook his head. "Troubleshooting complete and nothing found, Statto says that all the traces look just as normal. Let's see what you can find. The rest of you," as Geeta and Marlon moved in he turned towards the rest of his team, "get everything prepared for the next order. It'll soon be with us once the grease monkeys have finished."

5 MADE IN THE UK

"Come on gentlemen, what's the problem?" a shouting Dave was added into the flashing lights. "It's been over half an hour that we're down now. This would be a very good time to score." Danny looked over towards Geeta. Ladies and gentlemen Dave, surely? Geeta rewarded Danny with a cheeky little grin as she walked over.

"And he thinks that shouting louder will help?" Her thick local accent never ceased to amaze anyone who saw her and expected a more traditional Indian sound. "After my folks having a go at me over arranged marriages and Technical colleges, he's got no chance of getting me flustered," she turned now to Dave. "Don't worry boss, we're on it." A wink and she was back on her way towards the machine, Dave following closely behind.

She'd always been tough, Geeta. From the first day she'd joined them at Tech, blowing Danny and Statto away with a knowledge of the Whites gained from her brothers, and a knowledge of repairing things that she'd inherited herself. With nothing better to do Danny wandered over to where she was now standing.

"Come in Marlon, your time is up," she spoke clearly into her walkie talkie and the crackle in return suggested that Marlon had heard her. They both looked down as Marlon's thinning hair appeared, finally followed by his whole body.

"Found anything yet Marlon?" the look on her face wasn't one that expected good news.

"The transfer mechanism's alright here. I'll move down to section four," Marlon's typical Caribbean twang gave the reply that Danny knew she was expecting. How many times had she told him that there was nothing there to be found? It was all in the programming she always said.

"That's not the answer I wanted. Where's The Bloody Problem?" Dave was getting stressed.

"We're doing all we can," Geeta almost pleaded. "Sometimes things just take time." Dave stared at her, a look of childlike surprise on his face.

"Geeta, I can see that you're giving one hundred and ten percent, but at this moment in time we just need a little bit more."

"Danny," this time it was the not so calm voice of Benjamin. What's he doing creeping up on us? "What's going on? This is your line yes? Thirty five minutes down and counting, why is it always you?" Just ignore him, make him ask again. That sounds like a plan.

"I think I've got it," saved by Marlon. "Geeta, over here. Have a look at this." Geeta moved quickly to Marlon's side, examining the part that he was expectantly offering. Next to them Benjamin and Dave were exchanging furious looks. Danny could only admire her as she talked slowly and calmly into her telephone and a few minutes later Bob from maintenance arrived with a brand new shiny box. Within another five minutes the safety mode was disarmed.

"Go Statto, start her up," Danny gave the long awaited order. Seconds later line 3 was moving again, slowly accelerating up to full speed. All around were expectant glances as the rhythm settled, and with a high five here and there Danny and his team were left on their own. Well almost.

"Danny, for Christ's sake keep control of your line. That's what we pay you for. We can't afford to have all of these problems and you know it," Benjamin was giving one last blast. How could it be Danny's fault if Benjamin's bloody machines didn't work?

Again he decided not to answer, turning back to supervise the loading. A movement high up caught his eye, a blind in the office upstairs giving away the fact that they'd been watched. Winston, stuck up in his glass tower, as usual. No doubt still lamenting the loss of his beloved Blues, with a few glasses of whisky in crystal tumblers. He should've spent more time worrying about his factory, instead of playing at owning a football club. A lot of good it had done him. With the Blues gone like all the rest, his factory was now his only choice.

Three major stops, all on the same day, plus the horror of the morning meeting. Could things get any worse? He closed his locker and started to leave. A faint noise stopped him, quiet voices in the tea room. Geeta, Al and Statto were huddled in deep discussion.

"What's up now? Are you taking bets on tomorrow?" their reactions said it all. It was no normal conversation.

"Danny, glad you're here. We've sort of got some, news," Al took the lead, but quickly passed it over. "Tell him Geeta, it was you who heard it." This wasn't going to be good.

"It was this afternoon," there was no hesitation in her voice. "I was up in the archive room, looking over the drawings for the machines."

"Not a lot of good that'll do you. You've looked at them enough times."

"Thanks Statto, I'll ask you if I need help. Anyway, the archives are next to Winston's office, and I sort of overheard him talking with Benjamin." Not a normal father and son chat, Danny was sure. A nod of his head encouraged her on. "It seems that we're finished. From what I could make out we've got orders but we make no profit. The costs are too high and it's all down to those bloody machines that are always breaking down." A violent bang shook him, Al's hand having banged into the side of the fridge.

"Typical bloody management. Him off playing with his football team and buying his shiny new machines. Playing around and gambling with the lives of us workers. It's always us workers who pay in the end." Danny's head was racing, trying to process the new information as fast as it could.

"Wait a minute Geeta. So he said we were finished? That the factory's closing?" Statto had pushed in, uninvited. "As I understood it, you said we had until Christmas and then they'd have to make some plans?" Danny saw Geeta nodding silently.

"Bloody Ebeneezer Scrooge, that's who he is." Calm down Al, calm down. Statto talked again.

"Look, it's true that ever since we had the machines there's been nothing but problems." That was the understatement of the year. The German company that delivered them went out of business almost the next day, leaving behind a set of incomplete instructions and Gesine, the subject of Al's desires who'd surprisingly decided to stay. "But we all know Winston. This'll be hurting him just as much as us, with all of the work he's done to keep us going over the years. What do you think Danny?" What did he think? Why were they all looking at him like that?

"Me? Well let's not get carried away yet. It was just something we overheard, and there's still a couple of months to Christmas." Think about it, let's not panic. "We'll just keep our eyes peeled and wait and see. Geeta, keep reading those manuals and see what you can find." No-one looked convinced, not least Al, brooding at the back. But what was the point in causing trouble when they had no real facts? He needed to close the get together and move them on.

"Anyway, It's Monday night. Come on lads, or we'll be late."

6 MONDAY NIGHT 5-ASIDE

His muscles stretched back into life and the cold air filled his lungs, as Danny prepared to actually do something physical and useful. Gone were the factory walls, the shouts of Benjamin and Dave and the rumours. In their place the green surface, the floodlights and the iron fences of the five-a-side pitches at the Memorial Ground. What a day it had been.

"So, it's six against seven then," Red Al, resplendent in the full 2006 FA Vase semi-final Whites strip was last out of the changing rooms. Behind him, Danny saw hope. Towns on a Saturday afternoon were boring and bland. Either the pale shirts of the Northern Wildcats or the harlequin colours of the London Monarchs, or an occasional mixture of the two. Behind Al though were people who remembered, people still wearing colours from the old times, like Native American Indians wearing headdresses in Vegas. The twelve closely packed pitches were full of the colours from his youth, each colour a personal memory from earlier days. The yellow and green of Norwich and the proud gold of Wolves. Blue from Ipswich, White from Port Vale and Red from Nottingham Forest. Claret and blue of Scunthorpe with hoops from

Doncaster, stripes from Plymouth and the heraldic quarters of Bristol Rovers. Every colour and pattern imaginable was there, each one born in a boyhood dream and maintained ever since by the desire to see their team do well. Colours and hope.

"So who's got seven then, us or them?" Statto was doing his goalies stretches.

"Us I think. Me, Danny, you, Richo, Dev, Harish and Marlon," Al counted them off deliberately.

"But Marlon doesn't play for us, he plays for them. He has done for the last five hundred games," Statto made one of his least factually correct statements.

"Yep, you're right. So it looks like they've got seven and us six. It's going to be tough tonight." Al wasn't joking, but they'd be okay.

"Don't worry about them. We finished really strong last week, just carry on like that and we'll give them a good game," no worries. Dev and Harish made a great combination on the left and Richo would score more than he missed. Al on the right and Statto in goal. Danny would stay in the centre, shoring everything up. Each one was in white. Not the new white, but the old white, the one they'd grown up loving. They were as ready as they could be.

"Look at that," he followed Richo's finger to the other end of the pitch. Ted the Trainer had the Blues going through a warm up routine, all rolling on the floor and stretches. He was no doubt squealing to them about how important it was to be warmed up fully before the game started. Had they all forgotten that he'd no qualifications or experience in sports? He'd just been in the right place when it came to buying some old gym kit and he'd never looked back since. It promised to be a good competitive game.

"Come on then you Blues, don't forget that it's a game of two halves, so don't get too down if things don't go how we'd want from the start," the unmistakeable sound of Dave announced the end of the Blues warm up.

"Yep, we're the Magnificent Seven tonight, so we should give these White Shite a bit of a seeing to," Benjamin joined in, the others just looking on silently. How had they ever come to play every week? Management versus workers, Blue versus White. It was a game that managed to stretch the unwritten rules of sportsmanship to the limits, but those rules still held. In front of him he saw five blues, red hoops, and Ted in Manchester red. No colour clashes tonight. At last he felt good.

Four minutes gone, skipping run down the left as Holmes avoided a scything challenge. Cross shot parried out by the keeper, defender misses the clearance.

"Goal!"

Seven minutes gone, moving calmly out of defence, takes aim, shoots. Thunderbolt into the top corner.

"Yes, two nil!"

Nine minutes gone, one two in midfield, and Holmes falls to the floor as he's challenged late. Play goes on as Danny smiles. Pass up to the forward with his back to goal, lay off to the right, defender slips and the goalie goes down too early. The ball rolls into the back of the net.

"Three nil! Here we go, here we go, here we go."

"Fucks sake," how could they have started so badly?

"It could be a cricket score here." Fuck off Dave.

He felt it happening again. The rage that left him feeling like an impotent viewer transforming itself into an anger that gave him energy and control.

"Right then, plan B," they huddled around him. "Dev, you switch to the right, put pressure on Rodney. Al, get in Ben's face and stay there, don't give him any time and if he moves kick him. Statto, just stand up. You don't have to dive, believe me. And all of us, let's toughen up a bit." Muffled claps warmed hands and brought them back life.

Straight away the passing got crisper and the movement better. Danny to Dev, Dev into Al, quickly up to Richo. Dave would've said that he turned on a sixpence, but it was just speed and power and a wonderful finish. 3 –

1. Al pressuring Benjamin, a misplaced pass, interception by Harish, who crumpled under a late challenge from Holmes. The ball rolled on to Richo and another great finish. 3 – 2. Danny moving forward, crack.

"You bastard!" he rolled on the floor, Holmes smiling down at him as Benjamin restored the two goal lead. A quick restart and Richo straight away adding his third and bringing the Whites back to within a goal. Al and Dev with an overlap, sweet cross and what a volley. Harish was on the scoresheet and even stevens. More tough tackles from both sides, neither giving an inch and doing everything to take the prize. Disaster struck. Harish limped out of a cruncher with Holmes and two quick-fire strikes from Arnie seemed to have taken the game away.

"Time out, Harish is injured." A breather for everyone to take stock, but the clock was ticking away. "Come on lads, we can do this. We may be a man down, two now, but we're fitter than them and we're better than them. Al, you're having a great game," Al's boyish smile was a picture. "Richo you can't miss tonight. Statto they need miracles to beat you. Dev and Harish, I haven't seen you play this well all year. So come on, keep doing what we're doing and we'll win this."

Where did they come from? The words he found only when he needed them. He tried to remember where he'd heard them before. His Dad perhaps? Wherever they'd come from he was thankful that here, and in the factory, he could call on them when he really needed them. Looking into the eyes of the team he could see that they all believed. They knew what they were capable of achieving and that they could win.

"Come on girls, I can't believe you're playing for the 6 – 4 draw," who else but Benjamin? "Much as though I don't mind winning like that, I do admit that I'd quite like a bigger margin. Oh, and there are ten minutes left. Just like you lot don't appreciate staying behind at work after time, unless of course there's bloody extra money in it for you, I don't like overtime on the footy pitch either, so best get on with it and get it over. Come on you Blues."

Restart with the Whites. Flowing football, but less movement now. Playing with a man down all game had made them tired. Dev to Harish, who dummied and let it run.

"Yes, four for me," Richo had another. The clock ticking down and few chances for either team. Danny received the ball, rolled out to him by Statto. Starting forward with a dribble, round one, round two. Through Dave's legs, his body swaying left and the ball going right. Through on goal now, he dropped his shoulder and shot. No! Heart in his boots as it rebounded off the bar. His look behind was desperate as the Blues broke, seeing that no one was covering. Holmes against Statto, one on one. Stand up Statto, hold your ground. Holmes checks his options as he approaches the D, deciding to roll it left with no real pace but on the ground. Get down Statto, please get down, the silent words in Danny's head. The big frame takes advantage of gravity and heads downwards, but too late. The net doesn't ruffle, there isn't enough pace, but the ball's there, nestling in the corner. Damn. Another goal, the last goal. A 7 – 5 defeat for the Whites.

Jubilation from the Blues. It's like they really have won the cup, with handshakes and back slaps all round.

This was how they relieved the stress of work every Monday and everyone seemed to have enjoyed the thrill of the game. Around their pitch was a small crowd of spectators. Passing by to get to their own pitches they'd seen the action and preferred to stop and watch, the tension of the game pulling them in. He swallowed quickly, trying to eat the anger that had returned. Not even a victory here? Something small to talk and laugh about in the Bell later? No, just another defeat to add in to the day's tally.

"Danny," he looked round to see Benjamin. "This

must have been a bloody awful day for you". Take that smug look off your face. "Humiliated in front of the whole factory for your unforgettable TV performance at the weekend. Spending more time fixing your line than actually running it and then being pissed all over tonight by the mighty Blues on the field of battle. Just how do you manage to be so bloody useless?" Calm again. Everything so clear.

"You were just lucky. You had seven against six. We'd have beaten you if it was equal."

"You say that, but you never seem to beat us."

"Well here it's not serious, it's only a kick around on a Monday night. In a serious game we'd beat you easy." Two gun slingers facing each other across the pitch, the others looked on and listened.

"So what's a serious game then? Bigger pitch, more players, a bit of a crowd, a bit of an incentive? Yes, that's what we need a bigger game, with a bit of money involved," Benjamin was getting hooked. He was looking to humiliate, turn the screw on the Whites. Danny's pulse got quicker as his calm disappeared.

"Okay, sounds good to me. Eleven a side. We'll make it twenty a player. Two hundred quid says that we can beat you when it matters, at big boys football." Where's all of the sound gone? The Blues behind Benjamin were all tight lipped, content to let their captain do the talking.

"Twenty each isn't much. I guess you're just not very confident. What about a hundred each, a grand to the winners?" trust Benjamin to force it. And trust his own blind confidence and pride, risking money that wasn't his to risk. "Well then Danny, have we got a bet or not?"

He could feel every eye burning in to him as they waited for his answer. Five pairs behind him, pleading for him to come to his senses. Seven pairs in front of him, willing him to dig even deeper into his hole of despair. Nine pairs on the touchline, unaware of the details, but still watching anyway. Eight giant pairs of floodlights, simply there to throw some light onto the proceedings.

"One thousand per team. It's not even a hundred each, but it'll make a nice present, especially near the end of the year." Benjamin was making no attempt to hide his delight. How had he got here? He'd had a bad day, the alarms on the line ringing louder and longer than they had before. Then it was six against seven, never good odds against Benjamin and the rest of the management. They'd been three nil down before they'd even settled. Bit by bit he'd just lost it.

"Don't give me the silent treatment Danny, not after all the time we've known each other." The laughter from the rest of the Blues was greeted by a White murmur. He was sure they could beat them eleven against eleven. The lads would hate him, especially in late October, but he'd left himself no choice. In for a penny, in for a pound.

7 STATTO'S CHALLENGE

"Look, this is all wrong and we know it," Statto's voice cut in from behind Danny. In front of him the surprised look on Benjamin's face suggested that he at least didn't know that it was all wrong. "Be honest. What we're talking about's pride, and that's worth more than any money." Cheers Statto, you're saving my life. "And settling matters of pride takes something else, something special. Something that'll take us above what's gone on before." Benjamin seemed to have used all of his powers of recovery.

"Please carry on Statto, I'm intrigued to know where you're looking to take us, but try and be quick because the pub closes early on Mondays and we've all got work tomorrow." Typical smart arse.

"It'll take as long as it takes," Statto wasn't going to be intimidated. "We see here friends and enemies, managers and workers, but that's not what divides us. What's always divided us is the colour of our shirts, the White and the Blue. The signs of the two communities that the colours represent. Now that's all a question of pride, and it's for that pride that we must play."

"Well that's a nice lesson Statto, but you may've

noticed that no-one supports these shirts any more. No one gets out of bed on a Saturday morning dreaming of Harrod Road or Cherry Lane. They're all proud of something else now." Could Benjamin really believe what he said? Was Danny the only one who still dreamt of Cherry Lane?

"Benjamin, you say no one supports the shirts any more, yet you wear one every week. Look around these pitches and you see hundreds of people still clinging on to their pasts. It's for that, not money, that we should play."

"But how do we play a match for these people, how do we show them they still have something to be proud of? Let's be honest, not too many of them were showing a lot of pride five years ago anyway," the rest of the Blues joined in with Benjamin's laughter. The Whites remained still, silent and waiting for Statto to finish his work.

"You underestimate Benjamin. In the 2018 season the Whites had an average crowd of nine thousand four hundred and eighty seven people. The Blues, in a relegation year, had an average crowd of eleven thousand two hundred and thirty three people. You know as well as me that hundreds of others would've gone to watch if they'd had the money, or if they hadn't been working. Add to that the thousands of others who'd search for the results on a Saturday evening. It's for all of them that we should organise ourselves and play a final, deciding game." Amen. Now Benjamin'll tell him to piss off, they'll all forget about the bet and they can all go down the pub.

"The final deciding game?" it was Dave.

"Yes," Statto continued, "the scores are even. Since the formation of the league the Whites and Blues have played each other fifty seven times, forty eight times in the league and nine times in the cup. There've been nineteen victories for the Whites, nineteen victories for the Blues and nineteen draws. As things stand there's no winner. We need one last match to finally decide. Isn't that a lot more interesting than a few hundred pounds?" The look on

Benjamin's face showed that Statto had him. Whatever bait he'd used, Benjamin was taking it.

"So you're telling me that you took the time to find out all of this information and that, as things stand, after over a hundred and thirty years of local rivalry we're equal. There's nothing between us?"

"Obviously the Blues played more in the higher leagues, but head to head the scores are level. We need this final, deciding game." As Benjamin thought, Dave joined in.

"All very noble, but let's be honest. Tonight we had a handful of people watching us, but only because they had to walk past to get to their pitch. People struggled to get down to the grounds to watch the greats, who'd turn up to watch us?" Dave managed a full sentence without a cliché. Statto's look had pity in his eyes as he continued.

"Dave, you sang the names of the players along with the rest of them. But the players came and went and you kept singing. It was all because they played for the shirt, and that's what we'll do, fill the teams with people who'll die for the shirts. People will come because they'll want to see their team win this last game, see their team crowned as the local champions. Then they can all go away and talk about it, cry about it, laugh about it and annoy each other about it, just like in the old days."

"But what if we prefer to leave it where it is. To leave it even. Why does one of the teams need to end up better than the other?" Red Al sounded less than convinced.

"Come on Al," Richo joined in. "What could be better than beating those Blue bastards one last time?" Were they really falling for this? Danny wanted more than anything for the Whites to play the Blues again, and he wanted more than anything for the Whites to win. But it had to be with proper players. And it had to be other people, better people than them, organising it. They hadn't even managed to organise the Christmas Party. Statto, please shut up.

"Statto, you've sold it to me," Benjamin now, but a gear higher than before. "We organise a game and invite a few friends along. Put a few posters up, perhaps book a hot dog man, and then we beat you and the Blues are victorious forever. We don't need to bet any money, because it's not a case of me and the boys humiliating you, it's an opportunity for everyone who was ever a Blue to look down on you White shite for the rest of their lives. So, without further delay, where do we play?"

"There's a big pitch up here, at the Memorial Grounds, we could book that?"

"Dave, there's no parking and room for about twenty people around the pitch. Come on we have to think bigger than that."

"Then there's the old Works ground, out on the South Road. It's between the two towns and there's a stand on one side and everything. They still use it though, so it could be difficult to get hold of."

"Now that's better Dave, thinking big. A stand, good changing rooms, lots of parking and even a clubhouse for a party afterwards. I can get the champagne in the fridge now, ready. So that's where, now when?"

"There's only one day it could be," Statto gave no-one else a chance to speak. "Up until the 50s matches between local rivals were played over Christmas, the home leg on Christmas Day and the return on Boxing Day. The Christmas day game got dropped, but the other remained. The best game of the year, especially for the teams who had no titles or trophies to play for. A public holiday, the festive joy and the chance to play your local rivals. Boxing Day, it has to be Boxing Day when we play. One last game, winner takes all. The Whites against the Blues. A match for the towns and the communities."

"Done deal. Boxing Day it is!"

8 THE GREAT ESCAPE?

The Bell was quiet on a Monday night. In fact it was quiet every night. TVs in pubs had killed the traditional pub pastimes and the Sky Bars had killed TVs in pubs. There wasn't a lot left. Danny was sitting alone, desperately trying to understand what had happened earlier. Statto was quiet in the corner, the rest were stood around the bar. Looking towards them he caught another look from Al. The floor took on an interesting glow, the interest soon broken as Al's looks turned into words.

"A ton each, just coming up to the end of the year. Are you mad or what?" Danny had no answer, the floor still holding his attention.

"But what were you thinking of? Betting our money away," Al and his money. Still living at home with a dad who frightened him half to death and a mum who loved him half to death.

"I suppose you were planning on Big John bailing you out were you? We don't all have that luxury," Danny raised his head, their eyes fixed. What did Al know?

"My Dad would help me just as much as yours, so leave that one alone," as he fumed Richo timed his entrance perfectly.

"But come on Danny. What were you thinking of? I had a bad day too, but you didn't see me getting all wound up," Richo was right. He'd lost control and nearly got them all into a tight corner.

"I don't know Richo, he just got me going and I couldn't stop. Come on lads, we got away with it in the end didn't we?" Why's no one else smiling? Al turned back to the bar leaving Richo alone to try and lighten the mood.

"Well at least the big guy timed it to perfection. And what an entry it was." As the tension started to disappear, Harish and Dev also looked on with interest. "It was one of your best mate, the dogs," there was no acknowledgement from Statto and Al remained hunched at the bar. " 'As things stand there's no winner. We need to have one last match to finally decide. Could a few hundred pounds really be more important than that?' Could a few pounds be worth it," the Statto impersonation was good. Even Harish wanted to chip in.

"And the look on Benjamin's face when he mentioned something being more important than a few pounds. I thought we might have to pick him up off the floor," at least the three of them were enjoying the playback. What were they going to do now? Richo wasn't finished.

"Then there was all the stuff about White and Blue, communities and pride. One last game for the good of mankind," the enjoyment in Richo's voice was clear. Even Al turned round to take advantage of the lighter mood. "Honours even until boxing day," Richo bowed with a mock Shakespearean flourish. At last it all seemed forgotten in the new found laughter.

A shadow to Danny's left made him turn. Statto slowly stood with a strange deliberate movement. His first words were lost in the laughter and so he tried again, louder.

"The one that you're talking about, he's here you know." Danny could hear him now, make out the detail of his words. Statto spoke again, louder still. "Yes, he's here.

The weirdo, the looney man, the preacher, the great big lummox. He's here. He can hear you. He's perhaps stupid, but not deaf, surely?" the corner of the pub calmed to almost silence, everyone now aware of Statto's presence.

"Calm down Statto. We're only having a bit of a laugh. We deserve it after this evening, surely?" More laughter, but Statto remained unmoved.

"I'm glad you lot find it funny. At least it shows that there's some interest." Danny's muscles tightened as he saw Statto turn towards him. "You Danny, you only half listened to what I said at the football, and didn't even manage that for Richo's retelling tonight. Is it no good for you without the money? Is that what really interested you in the first place?" *Not you too Statto?*

"Me and money Statto? Get real mate. I was listening earlier, and I was just now. I think it's a great idea, it just wasn't expected. Where did it all come from?"

"Where did it come from? Where did it come from says Mr Happy. Well Danny, did you really think you were on your own these last years, that no one else gave a fuck? Did you? That everyone else had just lied down and rolled over, because Danny was the only person who'd lost something?" Danny heard the sound of silence. "Well you can wake up Danny boy, there are others who feel like you and I'm one of them. And the rest are just waiting for the right opportunity to come along, and then we'll join in too. But the fact is that if you do fuck all, then fuck all happens. It's a scientific theorem, some well-known professor will have his name next to it. Now, you might be so wrapped up in yourself that all you can do is lie down and suffer, but I'm not. I'm ready to do something." The others moved towards them from the bar, three looking shocked and Al sporting a small grin. "Tonight I had a chance and I took it. It's a start and now I've got something to work with. What I said earlier, I believe in, and I'll do everything I possibly can to make it happen, with or without you," Statto's voice quietened and slowed, as if a great weight had been taken from his large shoulders. "With, or without you." How do you follow that?

"Well on that note, it must be my round," Richo saved him again, breaking the silence. The others happily made some noise and turned to the bar to help him out. Statto's fixed gaze didn't waver. How could he have not known, not seen how his friend was feeling?

Richo passed by him, placing a drink into his hand, whispering as he passed.

"Talk to him Danny, he needs you." Talk to him? To say what exactly?

Damn it, he had to go over. Taking a swift sip of his beer he moved across towards Statto, braving the stare that dared him to come closer. Comforting someone the size of Statto was like a child comforting his father, but Richo was right. Statto had worked himself up and needed reassurance. Danny sat down next to him and they both took nervous sips of their beer.

"I tell you what Statto, you really saved me tonight," the words somehow flowed. "I was trapped, in a right mess. Too angry and just not seeing straight. Thanks for coming in and saving me." The silence from his friend was nearly as off putting as the eyes that were exploring him. He carried on anyway taking confidence, as he so often did, from an unhidden source. "And what you said afterwards was just poetry, beautiful. You really do have that knack of getting your message over in the best way."

"How would you know, you weren't even listening," the voice betrayed a hurt. "Not the first time at the ground, not even here for the replay."

"Come on Statto," now a soothing voice. "You know me. I may not have been looking but I heard it all. You're right, people will always come and watch the shirt, so long as they know that the people who are wearing it are trying," his effort to bring alive Statto's words didn't seem to be impressing his friend.

"Some back up would've helped, so we could all get

behind this thing and make it work," Danny was stunned. Statto's look was nothing but deadly serious. He'd lived every word that he'd said. Laughing it all off with Benjamin the next morning wasn't going to be an option.

"Look Statto, what you said was great. The idea's wonderful and makes lots of sense…" Why had he paused? Where were the words he needed to carry on?

"But. Makes a lot of sense but?" Statto's voice was accusing, he was starting to wake up. "Look Danny. We've got to do this. It's our chance. Not our only chance, but the best chance we've had in the last five years."

"Our chance for what Statto?" his question was honest and inviting, Statto's energy starting to take him over.

"Our chance to start over again. To break the grip that money has on our game and to play again. We can use this game Danny. Use it to remind people all over what they used to have. Show them what they're missing. Remind them of what they had before, of what they can have again," the Statto flow was back in place and Danny felt it submerging him.

"But Statto…"

"But again Danny, change it."

"No Statto. People tried when it all happened. People better than us, bigger than us, they all tried, but they couldn't hold it together. What can we do that they couldn't?" Silence again.

"Danny, we can't just complain. We can't just be sad or angry. To change things we have to do things, we need actions. I remember you, outside the ground that night. Telling Richo and Al that we were doing something, that we couldn't just give up. We need to organise and fight for what we want, because no-one'll give it to us. Yes, others tried, but the time was different. Most people believed they'd get something better in return. Now they see that isn't the case. Protest was a few emojis on an internet wall and funny pictures. The world's becoming practical again." Danny's mind turned, a ball on a roulette table.

"Okay, so we could do it. We could put the game at the Works ground. It holds around three hundred people, perhaps more if you count the ones who'd be in the clubhouse. That'd be great I admit, and good to see, but it won't bring back the game that we loved." Did he sound as resigned as he felt?

"Who knows? The first round of league games in 1888 there were just twelve teams taking part. The FA Cup final in 1872, Wanderers versus the Royal Engineers, they reckon there were about two thousand spectators. It all starts somewhere." Statto was now well and truly back, his eyes gleaming with mischief and intent.

"But how?" Danny was now fully focussed and in support "Look at us. How are we going to organise it all, who's going to lead us through?"

"How will we organise? Look around you Danny. Can't you see the best of the brains in the town? What more could we ask for? And who'll lead us, you will of course, like you always do." Like you always do?

"Me? Lead? You are joking aren't you? You know me Statto, always daydreaming. I never stand up and give orders, how the hell can I lead?" How could Statto have even suggested it?

"Your problem Danny is that you're too stupid to even see what's around you. You've been leading us since we first met, though I must admit that you were less of a miserable bastard then than you are now. Okay, you're sometimes a bit of a dreamer, but when it matters you're there, alert and leading. The factory this morning, tonight at football, you just click and lead. Natural as you like. You're our leader Danny, and you can lead us through this, I know it."

"And what about you Statto? These are all your ideas, this was all you talking. How do you fit in to your master plan?" There was that focus and calm again.

"You know me, people don't follow Statto, they just listen to him. I'm all words. But we both know where we want to go. We want the same thing in the end. If I have some ideas about how to go about it and if you're willing to lead us there, what could possibly go wrong?"

Danny stood, looking around the bar, everything now making sense. Most of the others looked on, their attention captured by his sudden movement.

"Listen," he was loud, determined and a full silence followed. "Statto's right. This is our chance to show everyone that we can do this. We can organise this game and give this town something to shout about. Not only that, but we're going to beat those Blue bastards while we do it," five minutes it had taken, for him to turn into Superman, not bad. Richo stepped forward.

"Ladies and Gentlemen, I respectfully ask you to raise your glasses. To Danny, to the Whites and to Boxing Day!"

"To Boxing Day!!"

9 ADVANTAGE BLUES

Another Saturday morning trip into town for Danny, but this time on foot and not alone. Was the blonde girl with him pretty? How could he tell, she was his sister.

"Well it all sounds great to me," the excitement in Annie's voice was clear. "Mum and Dad seem up for helping too. It should be fun." Fun? Danny would wait and see. It was certainly going to be interesting though. Almost a week had passed and the idea had been running round his head all week.

"You still get the feelings? When you walk past?" she knew him better than he knew himself as they approached Cherry Lane. He hoped his smile only showed happiness.

"How could I not. Football was everything for me." Except that he was never quite good enough at it. He hadn't inherited his Dad's skill for the game, but his love for the game was never in question. He'd had trials with local clubs, but was never going to make it. Too small, too slow, no skill, the list could go on forever. Had it ever bothered him? No, just being there at the games was all that had mattered to him. The sounds, the colours, the atmosphere. Had his Dad been disappointed? He'd certainly never said so. In any case, even if he had been a success there'd be nowhere for him to ply a trade as a lower league footballer. The teams no longer existed.

"So what are your plans then?" her soft voice woke him from his dreams.

"Plans? Well I thought we'd have a couple in the Bell and then it's anyone's guess. I suppose the only certainty is that it won't be the Sky Bar today," he chuckled at the memories from the week before. Good memories and warm weather, what more could you wish for on All Saints day?

"Not that you idiot, I didn't expect anything different. Plans for the game, for Boxing Day?" she was even nicer when she was annoyed.

"Well what more is there to do? Mum's going to be knitting scarves and baking cakes from now until Christmas Eve, when she'll then try her hand at making some of those wooden rattles. Dad'll be very supportive and give us a shout out on Radio Geriatric when he does his next sports round up. Sorted really," the shared laugh was warm and full of love.

"And apart from that, did you have anything else lined up? In case she doesn't manage to get the rattles out in time?"

"Well to be honest, not really, no. I'd sort of hoped that, well, after a few days cooling off everyone would've sort of forgotten about it. Or gone a bit cold on the idea," he didn't like the sound of any of the thousand words that her look gave him.

"But seriously, have you got a plan? It might seem like a small thing, but I'm sure it'll catch the imagination a bit. Say we get a couple of hundred people turn up. We should make sure that there's at least a show." She was right, as always. He just needed to figure out what needed doing, how it had to be done and who would do it. Simple.

"Don't worry little Sis, one thing's for certain. With the team that we've got, everything'll be right and ready come the twenty sixth. It can't be that difficult can it?"

The last five hundred yards were quick, full of the intrigue behind soup tins and yoghurt pots, the joy that Annie experienced every day learning how to manage a Co-Op supermarket.

Annie pushed through the door to the Bell and Danny followed.

"Eight weeks? Shit, we'll never do it in eight weeks," Al was just slightly more animated than normal. "How are we going to do it?" Danny stopped dead. What was going on?

Over in Statto's normally quiet corner was a bar table full of coloured papers. Geeta was leaning over the table and they were in deep discussion. As they saw him enter he received a crisp salute and a sympathetic looking smile. Was it him or Annie who'd deserved the sympathy?

Richo, Dev and Harish were in active discussion near the bar. Writing, nodding, shaking, crossing out. On and on.

Marlon was sat quietly near the window, sipping on a glass of sparkling water and looking on with an undisguised smile. What was he doing there?

"See Annie, I told you everything would be okay." Her smile was comforting.

"Look, I told you Marlon, you can't be in our team, so fuck off," Richo paused from his discussions and everyone stopped to listen. Statto looked up from his papers and lists and joined in.

"To be honest Marlon you'd look great in White, but seeing as you're a Blue bastard, you may as well fuck off."

"It's a free country and I'm just sat here quietly on a Saturday lunch time enjoying my drink and the spectacle. I ain't going nowhere," a wide smile accompanied his reply.

"Let him stay," said Geeta. "If we need any information we can torture him." She flashed him an equally wide smile back.

"I imagine that with him having to work with you all day he's used to that already," Statto's comment was greeted by laughs all round.

How could Danny have hoped that they'd forget about it? His chest tightened slightly, it was time to take on his role as leader.

"So then Marlon, starting later are you? Typical Blues, never prepared and leaving things to the last minute. I'm glad you're here. You can see what we're up to and then you can run back to your masters and tell them all the gory details. There's nothing better than an enemy that's rattled and scared." The nods of approval and signs of recognition around him tightened his chest a little bit more.

"Starting late?" Marlon's reply was immediate. "Not at all. In fact we're finished."

"Finished my arse," interrupted Al. "You load of freewheelers have no hope. As we see in the factory everyday a piss up in a brewery would be largely above your capabilities. Ha." Marlon just smiled and continued.

"Tuesday lunchtime we met in the canteen. Marsha was there with her clipboard," he paused, content, as if the clipboard had magic qualities that could alter the destiny of the situation all on their own. "Tuesday, Wednesday and Thursday we had trials at the Works ground. We had players from the Works, the Albion and Saint Peters on the first days and then all comers on Thursday. Over two hundred players in all. Her bloke's sorted out the homepage and the blog," it was easy to feel sorry for Marsha's bloke, "then Edith and the WI have organised a Christmas market and cake stall. Winston's been fishing for sponsors and that's the kits, the balls, the referee and the ground hire and stuff sorted." He scanned round their faces and chuckled. "So, as you say. It's best not to leave things too late. And there's nothing better than an enemy who's scared."

"Fuck off Marlon!" in unison. Marlon rose majestically from his seat and walked slowly towards the door, his white toothed smile sparkling. Reaching the door he turned for his parting shot.

"Anyone want to buy a raffle ticket?" he spluttered out, and then was gone.

"Eight weeks? Shit, we'll never do it in eight weeks," Al took over from where he'd left off.

The Blues had stolen a march and they'd be playing catch up. But they could still do it, Danny was sure. They just needed to stay calm. Once again he took the floor.

"Right then, first up the players. Any ideas?" Richo raised his hand, just like being back at school.

"Me and the boys've been going through a list of the people we know. We reckon with us included we've already got eight."

"Eight. With us included? What all of us?"

"Yep."

"Now hold on," it was Statto. "I don't mind standing in the middle of those small goals on a Monday evening, but if you want to win and think that I'm going in big goals on a cold Boxing Day morning, you've got another think coming. I'll be trainer or physio or something, but don't expect me to play." Richo's face twisted in thought.

"Well, we've got seven then."

"Seven? Have you got many names left to go through?"

"Well, sort of. A few," Richo was staring at the floor.

"That's great work Richo," it was out of his mouth before he'd realised. Not that he'd have wanted to stop it, even if he'd been quick enough. "We just need to add a few more names then. I know that winning isn't the important part, but I'd seriously like to beat the bastards. If they've really got a squad made up from the Works, the Albion and Saint Peters then it's going to be a tough job, but this town's got some good players. We just need to find them. I think we should do trials this week. We won't need three days, not like those tossers, let's say Tuesday night."

"The day of single combat."

"What's that Statto?"

"Tuesday Danny. It's named after the old Saxon god Tiw, the god of single combat. The fight to the death. A good choice of day." Danny's nod was vague, acknowledging the new knowledge that he'd just picked up.

"Single combat, great. So, any ideas how to get people there?"

"I could set up a Facebook page," Statto's announcement was greeted with silence.

"Facebook?" questioned Richo. "That died about three years ago. You'd get more coverage if you went down the Chapel on Sunday morning wearing a sandwich board." Laughter all round.

"But I've still got over three hundred friends and we often talk about football, the old days."

"Okay," it was time to shorten the conversation. "Do your page Statto and let's see what it brings. Any other ideas?"

"I'll send an announcement through the local union network," offered Al. "I can send it out Monday and should have numbers for Tuesday morning."

"Shit Statto, you're Facebook page's starting to look good again. With the state of the factories and the age of the employees round here you'll get more interest on Facebook than through the union," Richo again. An annoyed Geeta jumped in.

"Okay then Richo, you smart arse. Everyone else gives us ideas that pale into insignificance compared with the magnificent seven that you managed to put on your list. Have you got anything smarter than that up your sleeve, or are you all idead out?" her glare was piercing. Richo said nothing, Geeta continued. "Me and Dev'll get some stuff up round the Tech. There are a few good lads there. We'll also spread word around the community centre and my dad knows lots of people in the cricket team who go to the mosque too. Harish can cover the hospital," she fixed Richo with a stare. "Obviously not for the patients, but there are quite a few male nurses and doctors up there."

"And I'll do all the shops," it was Annie's turn. "I can get stuff to all the supermarkets tomorrow. Then I'm off on Monday so I can visit the town centre."

"Brilliant," he'd been right, how could they fail? It was all starting to fall in place. Seeing that it was now his turn for ideas he continued. "For the publicity we should also be thinking about some big posters. I don't think we should advertise in the papers, it'll cost money that we haven't got, but one thing this town doesn't lack is empty spaces for flyposting."

"My dad could get us some posters printed up. Nothing fancy, but the basic stuff. His boss'd let him get away with that," Richo looked pleased, at last offering something worthwhile. Danny saw Annie reward his oldest friend with a smile.

"Great, so Monday night no one plan to come drinking after 5-a-side. It's operation fly post," laughter all round. "My Dad also offered to try and plug the game on the radio. I know it's only local town radio, but it's better than nothing."

"Don't underestimate it Danny. There are lots of people round here who'd love to get out for a good cause, who rely on that radio for their information. If Big John could give the game a shout then that'd certainly start spreading the word." There were nods of agreement all round.

It carried on all afternoon. Every time a topic came up someone had an idea. Mary and her WI would be called on, pretty much as the Blues were also using them. They'd probably even be sitting in the same room, singing Jerusalem whilst twin white and blue scarves escaped from the clutches of the knitting needles.

Seven o'clock, where had the afternoon gone?

Football as they knew it may have died but the Eurovision Song Contest still captivated the nation. That night the event was coming live from the Royal Albert Hall, following Robbie Williams' success of the previous year. They all left feeling great, like they'd finally started something that would soon become real. Walking home it started raining for the first time in weeks. The song from Britain got three points and came last.

10 TRIALS AND TRIBULATIONS

The Elizabeth Park changing room was alive to the bouncing of a ball inside and the dripping of rain outside. The rain had finally started to slow about an hour earlier, the pitch would be fun. An old face, familiar simply because it was old and looked like all old faces, looked round the door and wished them well as the groundsman bid them good evening.

"What if no one turns up? We've only had a couple of days advertising. It's short notice at the best of time," Danny heard the worry in his own voice. "We'll have to try again next week perhaps, or the weekend. Do you think we'd get people turning up at the weekends to try out? They should come, when they hear about what we're doing. But next week'll be better. It must be the rain that's put them off. They must think we've cancelled or something. Either that, or all the good players around have already signed on for the Blues. The bastards, just looking to win aren't they."

"Shut up stupid, it's only a quarter to. Listen to yourself, you soft git." Thank god for Statto and his reason. Footsteps, but not a player surely?

"Surprise!" it was Annie. Dressed up in her Co-Op

uniform and holding a pile of fluorescent jackets.

"What are they for sis?"

"Yes, I'm fine thanks Danny. The day was a bit tricky, but I've managed to get out on time to come and help you out," she smiled her sweet sisterly smile as she put him in his place. "I got these off the guys who collect the trolleys, just in case you need them."

"Need them? We're not going digging up the bloody road or anything like that," he was starting to get annoyed and didn't care if it showed.

"Look Danny, you've got two possibilities tonight. Either you'll have a hundred people all turn up with white shirts on, or you'll have a hundred people all turn up with different coloured shirts on. Either way you'll need to split them into teams, so they can play against each other. I know it's not perfect, but at least with these you can have the yellows against the rest." Of course, how could he have been so stupid?

"Well, at the moment you're the yellows and me and Statto'll be the rest. Nobody's going to turn up. We've blown it already." More sounds cut him off, footsteps and Richo telling jokes. Through the door they came. Richo, Dev, Harish and two others that Danny vaguely recognised.

"Good evening Danny," Richo used his most theatrical voice. "May I introduce you to the two people we were working on at the weekend. Both with a lot of experience at senior league level and both prepared to die for that white shirt." The newcomers cheered. "The short one plays at the back and is commonly known as Rodders. The even shorter one's known as Donaldo and has been terrifying defences since he was a kid." Hellos were exchanged all round.

"Welcome to the trials lads," Danny put on his leaders voice, "but please bear in mind that these are trials. Being invited here by Richo guarantees nothing. This is a case of the best men winning, of the best squad being chosen to represent the town."

"From where I'm looking yoff, I don't see an awful lot of competition at the moment." Rodders' assessment was good and they all laughed some more, finally moving into the corner and starting to get changed.

"I'll wait for you outside, here are the bibs." Annie took the hint and was replaced by Red Al, his arms full of clipboards.

"Hi Danny, Statto, boys," Al was as deliberate and precise with his speech as ever. "I thought we might need these." Richo looked over from the back of the changing room.

"Need those? What for Al, are we doing some sort of customer survey? Or collecting signatures for another strike?"

"Not at all Richo," Al ignored the insults. "Say we get a hundred turn up." More laughter came from the back of the almost empty changing room. "What are you going to do, play fifty a-side? Of course not. You'll need to split them up. Watch more than one pitch at a time. And how's everyone supposed to remember who was good and who wasn't? Who deserves another chance and who should be put out to grass? You need lists you see. Lists, so that we can compare notes and put everyone where they should be." More laughter from Richo and his group. Danny just looked on silently, hiding more feelings of stupidity. What had he thought? That he could just turn up with a bag of balls, have a kick about and then pick his team? How clueless had he been? Annie and Al had certainly saved him tonight.

"Right then, Statto, Al, Richo. We'll get a clippy each and when people arrive get their name, contact details and preferred position. Then we'll get some games going and you take a good look. Note the best players and bit by bit we'll get them all on the same pitch. Do you understand?" The calmness was coming again, his body starting to take control. The changing room might be empty at that moment, but he knew that the people would come, that everything would be okay.

Clipboards were collected and the normal changing room banter started to fill the room. At last, some movement. Let's keep it going. He looked up to the door, seeing it was blocked by the massive frame of a person. A person who's approach had either been hidden by the laughter of the group or had been silent in its nature.

"Good evening," said Danny. "And you are?"

"Tone," came the reply, one syllable, seeming more than enough from the giant of a person.

"Tone? What, as in Tony, or Anthony?"

"Just Tone."

"Okay, and what position do you play?"

"I'm the best fucking goalkeeper you're ever going to see sunshine," a sentence at last, ending in a smile with an up curved lip. "And if anyone says different they can have some of this." Tone flexed his right biceps and gave it a loving kiss.

"Great," said Danny with a small grin. "Give your details to the lad in the corner, get yourself changed and you can start warming up." Further conversation was meaningless and he just wanted to see the boy play.

Tone entered the room and, the doorway now uncorked, others started to follow. He could imagine how Noah must have felt as all of the animals entered his Ark. Trying to match each pair he saw them all enter, the boys from the Tech, the union lads, the shelf stackers, trolley pushers, butchers, bakers and candlestick makers. Weren't there a couple of doctors there too? It'd be impossible not to find a team that wanted to play in the match, wanted to pull on that white shirt and take every muscle to its limits for the cause. How could they not win?

"Right then, get the games started," Danny's shout cleared the changing room. He had six teams in all, plus a few subs. He looked over every player, checking for the signs of something special, much like a horse trainer at the sales. In this group were the players who'd make the difference between glorious victory and bitter defeat.

"Try and stay on your feet lads, there's no point in people getting hurt. We know you can all slide in from five yards on a wet pitch. We're more interested in who can stay on their feet." He barked out his orders and his sergeants passed on the message to those too involved in the game to have heard.

"What do you think of your lot Statto?" He would count on Statto's opinion for shaking the teams up, but he'd have the final word.

"Richo's boys, Rodders and Donaldo look worth it. There's the little lad at right back who looks useful too, and the big lad in midfield for the yellows. The rest are middling. We might have a couple to try out, but there's nothing special." Danny nodded in quick agreement.

"Good, give them a few more minutes to settle in and then send the best seven or eight over to Richo's pitch. You keep the ones in the middle, there may be some who are just having a bad start, and send the rest over to Al."

Fifteen minutes was nothing to show your worth on a football pitch, but time was precious. He wanted a squad of sixteen for the match and a back-up squad for the first team to play against in training games, if their love of the Whites convinced them to stay around. He wandered over to Al.

"Anything special?"

"There's a few who obviously know how to play. One centre half on each team and the lad with a ponytail in the middle over there. They're obvious. A few others we could perhaps try out." He needed to pass more time with Al. He was great with a clipboard, but not the best at spotting football talent. He picked out the two centre halves straight away. They both knew what they were doing and the ponytail was running the show.

"How's our friend Tone getting on?" he had to ask.

"Well, we've only got two proper keepers turned up and he seems to know what he's doing. In any case, if you don't want him I'm not fucking telling him," Al chuckled as Danny again explained what to do next.

"Right lads, that was a good first twenty. Take a break and we'll tell you where to go next. Then we'll have another look." The players swarmed round Statto, Al and Richo, and he detected the first signs of disappointment in their body movements. At least it showed they cared. There was no fear about giving out the bad news later though, he was in his stride, the automatic pilot having taken over. He shivered recalling his dream the night before. A big guy charging around upfield like a loose horse on the battlefield at Crecy or Agincourt, with one red sock, one blue sock and an overhanging belly clearly visible beneath his old Whites top. Well, if he had turned up Danny had missed him and he'd already gone home.

The lesser players had already given up, now forming a barrier around the top pitch, watching and cheering any piece of action. The middle pitch was still furious, people not yet giving up on a last minute chance to be given the opportunity they craved. A lightness came over his shoulders and head, it would soon be time to decide.

"Statto, give them all a break for fifteen. We'll be back with the last details, one final session to help us make the final cut. Well done everybody, you've made me very happy and proud, each and every one of you." Where that came from he didn't know, but the murmurs of a cheer greeting it told him that he'd said the right thing.

Danny and Richo were huddled together on the route back to the changing rooms as the old jogger slowly came towards them. Danny gave him a quick glance in the half-light provided by the pitch side floodlights.

"Fuck me, Dick?" he sensed Richo staring at him, as if he'd gone mad.

"That's right, it's me. Danny isn't it? Big John's lad?"

Danny nodded and Richo followed his eyes. This was no old jogger.

"What are you doing here Dick?"

"Well, I was up at the hospital tonight with my daughter. She was seeing the midwife, and I saw the posters for the trials. She told me straight away, 'go on Dad, get home and get your boots and get down there', so here I am. Not too late I hope?" They now both knew who the old jogger was. Dick Sparrow, the Whites' record goal scorer, with two hundred and forty nine goals in his five hundred and sixteen games. Statto had said it so many times that even they could remember it. But Dick Sparrow was young, athletic, forever moving and causing defences problems.

"Not too late Dick, but are you sure?" Dick's smile was warm and knowing.

"You know what Danny, I do still get to look in the mirror from time to time and yes, I have changed a bit," he laughed out loud. "But I've still got it you know. I never had pace, or strength. I just knew where to be. And then I knew which part of my body to use to get the bloody thing in the back of the net. Two hundred and forty nine times as I recall," another good natured laugh. "Look, I've kept myself fit and in my head I'm as sharp as I've ever been. This game would mean more to me than you could ever imagine, to get that last goal. The one that takes me to two hundred and fifty. And against those Blue bastards too. All I want's the chance. Put me on the pitch and see how I compare. Just give me the opportunity to prove myself." Dick asked, but there was no pleading.

"We've got the last thirty minutes to play through, and then we decide. Everyone's tired already, so make the most of it," Danny winked and Dick nodded in acknowledgement.

The first shout came out from one of the tech lads.

"Dick, is it really you?" Dick just gave a little smile and slightly raised his right hand, in a way that would've embarrassed the King. Then it started. A slow, rhythmic clap in time with his steps. A hero that many had worshipped on the terraces on a Saturday afternoon was now amongst them. Not just amongst them, but wanting to join them, to help them defeat the enemy.

"Well you can stop with that clapping, have you seen the state of him? I've only given him a chance out of pity. Right, one last thirty minutes for you to show us what you can do. You've all been great, but unfortunately we only need sixteen for the final group, so give it your best." And with that they started.

The twenty two left on the pitch were of every shape and size imaginable. Competent and proud, despite not being the best. Proud they were White and desperate at this stage to make the final squad.

"What do you think Richo, were we right?"

"I think so Danny. The yellows have definitely got our first choice defence, look how tight they are." As he spoke Dick Sparrow started a diagonal run across the yellows centre backs. He checked mid-flight, the pony tail in midfield putting through a perfectly weighted ball on to his left side. With a shimmy he was past the last defender and through on goal. Tone charged out, spreading himself big, looking up just in time to see the ball float over his head and into the net. It had been less than three minutes.

"Well, then again, it might be a bit early to talk. Old pony tail's threatened all night, but never really shone. If he picks another one or two like that he might just make me drop you instead. Ha." Richo laughed again, while Danny smiled. The game continued to form, the yellows remaining solid and holding the possession and the threat, whilst Dick Sparrow and the pony tail combined on the counter three or four times, ripping holes at the back and forcing Tone to display his shot stopping abilities. Sighing, he knew it was going to be alright. They might not win, but they wouldn't be embarrassed. No one was going to hammer them, that was for sure. Just four days ago they didn't even have a plan, just ideas. Now they had a team.

"Right then, that's your lot." The last session was brought to a close some five minutes early. "Get back and get changed and then we'll let you know the news and what the plans are from now until the big day. I must admit I don't know how to thank you all, whether you've been picked or not. Just remember why you're all here, because you want to be a White."

"Whites! Whites! Whites! Whites!" came the chant. Even Dick Sparrow was there, pumping his fist into the air as Tone walked beside him, explaining the detail of each of his saves.

He'd chosen the right words again.

11 NO ROOM AT THE INN

The changing room was a kaleidoscope of colours, noise and steam as people showered and changed, all eager for the news.

"Well he can't honestly expect to be in the list," said Richo. "He knows he isn't going to make it." Danny looked intently at the list Richo mentioned, clear in front of him.

"I'm not sure." Was that a hint of doubt in his voice? "Statto said all along that he didn't want to play, but Al? He's the only one of the regular gang who isn't there. And he never even got the chance to play."

"Of course he didn't, he knew he wasn't up to it. That's why he turned up with his clipboards." Danny was still unsure. Hurting Al was the last thing he wanted to do, but there was no way that Al was going to make the team. Where was he?

People were already starting to form a group around the door, but still no sign of Al. Clippy in hand Danny moved amongst them, hoping to find his friend and speak with him alone.

"Danny?" yes, it was Al's voice. He turned and there was Al, yellow bibs in one hand and clipboards in the other, his eyes firmly fixed on Danny's chest. He looked as though he wanted to speak but Danny could see him becoming paler and paler. What's wrong with him? "Look, I'll see you later," finally Al's words came out. He dropped the bibs on the floor, pushing his way back into the muddle that was the changing room.

"Al?" Shit, what's wrong with him? Danny looked down to his clipboard. No, you fool. The list of players was facing outwards, and Al had seen the team clearly in large capital letters. So much for talking to him one on one. He'd have to find him later. The caretaker was waiting to lock up and it was time for Danny to let them know.

He listened as he cleared his head. All of the normal jokes you expect in a changing room, especially as people nervously wait to see if they've made the cut. He remembered it well from trials at school, area and county level. Even from some of the lower league teams. He especially remembered when his name hadn't been read out. Anyway, this time he was reading the list and he was ready.

"Right then, now's the time," his shout brought silence. A movement in the background attracted him, a door slowly closing. Was that Al's head leaving the room? Forget him for now and focus. "I've already said it before, but a thousand thanks to everyone. Some'll make it, some won't, but I hope that everyone can stay with us and help out when needed." Lots of nods, grunts of approval and even more nervous jokes and laughter. "The squad'll be sixteen people, and here they are." He breathed one last time and read the list with a calm clarity that he didn't know he had in him.

"Tone, Dev, Rodders, Cooge, Smiler, Myself, Harish, Griz, Ling, Richo, Donaldo, Billy, Weeble, Crock, Limm and last but not least, Dick Sparrow." Dick's name raised a small cheer and then the room burst into animated conversation. Disappointed looks were few and far between as everyone was keen to talk about the players who'd represent the Whites.

Ten minutes later and it was all over. He was last out of the changing room as the groundsman locked the door. The players had already gone, spread out across all of the pubs in town, leaving him alone as he came down from his last rushes of adrenalin. Well, not quite alone. At the end of the corridor someone was waiting for him.

"Don't you trust me with the bibs, or do you need them early tomorrow morning?" her smile was hiding something. "Did you see him?"

"Yes, we bumped into each other in the ladies changing room. I think I caught him a bit by surprise." Danny handed over the bibs and they walked towards the car park.

"How was he? I didn't even get a chance to talk with him. He saw the team sheet by mistake and just left." Danny felt her spare arm forcing itself between his arm and his body.

"Disappointed. You know his dreams of playing for the Whites were just as big as everyone else's. He just kept going on about his dad, saying how he never practiced enough as a kid," they both walked on in silence. Annie's car was alone in the car park.

"You want a lift to the pub?" He shook his head, a walk would do him good. "Don't worry, there's still plenty that needs doing. I'll find things to keep him busy, you just concentrate on the football. It'll take a while, but I'm sure he'll be okay."

Danny smiled at her and they silently embraced. His first big success and first big failure, both on the same night. He guessed that was how it went.

12 THE BATTLE OF LOVERS VIEW

Danny's stomach gave off that strange tingly feeling as he arrived at the meeting place. He'd actually organised something himself and would be putting his plans through their paces that evening. Well, more correctly he'd be putting his players through their paces, as they left the pitch and started working on stamina. Looking round most people seemed to be there, though the brooding Tone confirmed that there were still some stragglers.

"If they don't turn up in the next five minutes I'm gonna put 'em down for good." It was cold and Tone seemed to be in no mood for hanging around. Statto was doing his best to defend Ling and Limm, both of who had to work late. "Oh and you'd know, would you big man," Tone wasn't in a forgiving mood. "Funnily enough I work too, and everyone else here. If we can get our arses out in the cold at this hour, then surely the Chan brothers can too." There was laughter in the background, though not from everyone. "Look Danny, its brass monkeys here. Can we get on with it, before mine drop off?"

Danny looked at his team. He couldn't deny that since Bonfire Night everything had got colder and the training more difficult. Not because it was physically harder, he'd seen them getting stronger with each session, but because they just weren't used to it. How could you expect people to go from liking a game of footie to being top level sportsmen overnight?

"Well here they are then," Tone broke the good news. "One of them's puffing away on his vape and the other one's chewing on a fucking banana. Would you believe it? Come on you bastards, we've been waiting for at least half an hour." Half frozen cheers and stamped feet greeted his news.

Danny searched for the word, the feeling he got when the cigarette smoke blew away to reveal his team. Pride, that was it. He couldn't imagine which sort of God could've put together such a group. Perhaps it was Tiw, Statto's famous god of combat? They wouldn't let him down. The Blues may have chosen their players from the top local teams, but his players would die for the Whites.

"Right then, get stretched up, all of you." He stretched himself, overhearing their still excited conversations. Weeble and Crock were enthralled by Donaldo and Rodders' stories of Area teams and professional trials.

"Let me remember boys," Richo had a gleam in his eye. "Too short and too slow?" They all laughed together.

"They'd be adding in too fat these days. Ha ha." Rodders gave his belly a little slap, happy to get in before one of the others.

Pony Tail, Danny now knew, was also called Griz and could even trace his name back as far as being called Nigel. His only trials had been at Oxford, the University. There he'd studied medicine and fallen in love with a local girl, finally ending up at the hospital in town.

Cooge, Billy and Smiler were all young boys from the supermarkets, dug out by Annie. Younger and fitter than the rest. Doing ninety minutes wouldn't be a problem, but their skill and ability to mould into the team required work.

That just left the normal 5-a-side crew, plus Tone and Dick Sparrow.

"So are you up for the run tonight then Dick?"

"I'll probably be staying near the back Danny, trying not to get injured if there's a bunch sprint at the top." Imagining Dick sprinting against the rest made Danny smile. His speed was now in his head and over the half yard necessary to get in front of an opponent.

"Wise choice, we don't want you to risk that two hundred and fiftieth goal just so you can beat Billy here to the top."

So, he had the skill and the desire. What could he do to get the stamina necessary to give them any chance against the more regular players in the Blue team.

"So don't tell me yoff, a bloody long run up and down that hill? You've got the Grand Old Duke of York signed up again I imagine?" Rodders woke him, and he returned a surely apologetic looking smile.

Deciding on the training had been a challenge. 'Ask Dad,' Annie had said, 'he'll know what to do'. But how could he do that? What would Big John, his Dad, think if he admitted that he didn't have a clue, that he'd no idea how to prepare his team? No, he'd thought for himself. For the close game, lots of one touch on the 5-a-side field. For the team game, lots of attack versus defence, using the practice squad to make up the numbers. And for the stamina, running up and down Parson's Hill. Surely not named after a man of the cloth, how could such a man have imagined such a bastard of a hill, but a Parson of sorts, none the less. Starting at the edge of town it slowly meandered through the last of the houses, before taking a steep rise through some trees. Then there was an incline of up to ten degrees of winding slope for one and a half miles, ending up on Lovers View, both of the towns clearly visible from the overlooking summit. Yes, Parson had been a bastard.

"Right then lads, you've all guessed, but I'm afraid we need this. This is what's going to make the difference. When the game enters those last ten minutes and all of those Blue bastards are on their hands and knees, begging for mercy, we're going to just kick in to that extra gear and murder the bastards. Why? Because we were brave enough to put in those hard yards, that extra work. Because we understood that any car, every car, needs power under its bonnet. Because we saw that the only way to get us there was to get on up that hill."

"Run Forrest, run," a shouted reply to Danny's words as the motley band of players started the slow jog towards the edge of the houses, the long winding road all black and forbidding in front of them.

The group soon settled into a natural order. Danny found himself almost at the back, with just Tone and Dick Sparrow behind him.

"Can you imagine George Best and Frankie Worthington doing this sort of stuff?" Danny gave a grunt and a shake of the head, already unable to speak. Statto was beside him on his motorbike, carrying the water and valuables, and didn't appear to have the same problem speaking. Enjoying the opportunity to have a one sided conversation Statto continued to tell him the tales of managers old and new, and all they had brought to the game. Danny just looked straight ahead, the pressure in his lungs getting higher and higher.

In front of him a smaller group had broken away, in some sort of King of the Mountains spurt, only to have stopped at a clearing about four hundred yards from the top. In the air was now the clear sound of vomiting and laughter. Statto left him, speeding forwards.

Arriving at the clearance with a pounding heart and blurred vision Danny held his sides and looked towards the floor, breathing deeply. Around him the noises finally became ordered in his brain.

"Come on Ling, get it all out sunshine," Rodders howled out as the sound of heaving came again from the back of the clearing.

Looking up Danny could now take in the scene. Nothing spectacular, most people sitting around in small groups, while a clearly unwell Ling emptied the last of his stomach contents. Only Tone seemed irritated.

"Come on you lot, get a move on and leave him here. We're right near the top, we can pick him up on the way down. How are we expected to beat those Blue bastards if we can't even run up a hill?" Tone pleaded.

Breathing deeply and still unable to speak Danny raised his hand, pleading for peace and quiet. Not needing further encouragement the group became silent.

It rose straight away from that silence, a rhythmic beat accompanied by an almost inaudible whirr. The pace remained constant, but the sound got louder and louder. Distracted, Danny stepped out in to the road and looked down the hill. Gradually he started to make out the shapes of people moving towards him, closer and louder, the sound of synchronised footsteps building with every second. It looked like a ghostly legion of Roman soldiers, quick marching towards them. Focusing in the dim light of the road lamp that the group was passing, he started to make things out.

"Fuck, it's Ted Holmes, on a mountain bike." No Roman legionary, not even a Lone Ranger or a Tonto. Just Ted "the Trainer" Holmes. And the noise behind him could only be one thing, the Blues out on a training run of their own. "Of all the hills in all the towns, why did they choose this one?"

"Watch out lads, shit on the road. Ha ha ha," Ted's high voice screeched out in warning. "Step in this lot and it'll take you a while to clean it off. No now, seriously, there are some dodgy bastards lurking in the clearing. Just keep your eyes ahead and keep going, we're nearly at the top in record time. They might look all scraggy and harmless, but the damage could be irreparable." Ted was now level with them, peddling his bike as if he was on the flat, and the Blues were all looking to their right to see a dismal looking band of people, barely passable as sportsmen.

"Losers", "Wankers", "White Arseholes," the cries exploded, one after another. Tone surged to the roadside, finally being held back by Statto, whilst the others just sat down, looking bemused at the neatly lined Blue train powering its way to the top of the hill. Benjamin, Dave and Marlon were there, as was Arnie one of the other 5-a-siders.

"Last two hundred lads, come on then, put it in," and off they went. Accelerating round the last bend and disappearing into the night.

An incandescent Tone started pulling people to their feet.

"Come on you bastards, don't let them get away with that. Let's get up and after them. We can catch them up from here and sort them out at the top." There was nothing on offer except resigned looks. How would they ever be able to compete with a group like that? What was the point going to the top? Surely it'd be best to just turn round and get to the bottom before they were overtaken again? He could see it in their eyes, to a man thinking the same, but no one daring to say it. No, they'd been hurt, but they had to show that they were still in this game, that they hadn't given up. Seeing Ling back on his feet his body once again took over.

"Now listen to me," something in his tone seemed to calm them. "This is all about damage limitation now, and using the situation to our advantage as best we can. They've seen what we are, or at least what they think we are, and I don't think that toughing it out'll make a difference. Their biggest problem will be complacency, not taking us seriously. So that's the fire we have to feed. I want you all to straggle up there, fight with each other. Not literally Tone," he shot another glance, making sure he was understood. "Lounge around when you get there and moan and groan. We'll let them run down first and then we'll follow. Let's get this over, put it behind us and regroup. Then we can show the bastards what we can really do. Let them think that the game's won and we've lost nothing. Okay?" No cheers, but at least a handful of nods.

Slowly in twos and threes the group set off. Statto raced past, hoping to arrive first and take the brunt of the Blue laughter. Danny fell in next to Dick Sparrow and they started their jog to the top.

"Well done Danny. Not an easy one to get out of this," the words were comforting. "Your Dad would've hated running up this hill. It's for you to tell me if he's evil enough to have made others do it." With a smile they started the ascent together.

Twenty yards from the top and the sound of laughter, good.

Ten yards from the top and the sound of shouting, very good.

The top. Fucking Tone! To his left Tone was surrounded by a group of Whites, holding him back as he reared up like a wild horse to get out of their grip. Even from a few yards away Danny could see blood pouring from his nose. To his right the Blues surrounded Arnie. He too was trying to get past them, though with perhaps a little less enthusiasm than Tone. He was sporting a bruised eye, already puffing up. Danny had missed another battle.

"Come here and say that again Mr Schwarzanegger and I'll give you another one," Tone wasn't finished yet. Statto came over to fill him in.

"It was all going so well, then Arnie came over and started giving Dev and Harish a bit of extras. I guess it was just because he knew them from 5-a-side. A few quick punches and it was all over." Looking around again it was clear that thoughts of the invincible Blue legionaries charging past were far away. Good.

"Can't you control your thugs Danny, this is

outrageous. We should report him to the police, this was just common assault," it was Benjamin, with Holmes in tow. Statto came to his aid.

"Come off it, I saw it all. It was Arnie who threw the first punch. Best to forget it all and move on, games between boys. You've had your fun running up the hill and we've completed our intensive circuit training, so why don't you just calm your boys down, turn them round and get off home to bed."

"Intense circuit training, ha? So how did you decide whose turn it was to sit down, to smoke and to throw up? We saw you all, knackered just jogging up a small hill. I'm going to have these boys so well drilled they'll rub your snotty little White noses so far into the ground that you'll smell nothing but shit for the rest of your lives." Benjamin seemed more than happy for Holmes to do his talking.

"Oh you're not still upset about that thing on the telly are you?" Statto on form again. "Come on, get out of here before we let Tone loose to sort you all out."

"Threats outside of the workplace are getting too close." Looking at Benjamin's smile Danny could never tell if he was being serious or not. "You're lucky that I like you Statto, and that this game was all your idea, otherwise we could really fall out. Come on Ted, let's get the boys back down to the bottom and then let them go home. I guess they'll need a longer rest tonight to get over all that laughing they've done."

Final insults exchanged, the Blue legion was quickly organised and heading back down the hill.

"Take a rest boys. Griz, can you take a look at Tone, make sure that beautiful face isn't damaged for good?" There was little chance of them catching the Blues up on the downhill run, despite their weight advantage, but he didn't want to take any risks.

"I'm a gynaecologist Danny, but I'll take a look." Perfect.

Danny took the final steps to the top of the hill. His pulse quickened as below he saw the two towns, the fifteen miles between their centres seeming nothing from this height. The river that ran through the valley had brought two tribes together thousands of years ago, and to this day those tribes still existed, side by side.

"Beautiful, isn't it?" Statto had joined him. "The towns seem closer together every time I see them. You can hardly tell the difference between them in some places. And look, you can always spot Cherry Lane from up here." Unsold and unloved Cherry Lane was easy to pick out at night time. Just to the centre of town, amongst the lights from the terraced houses and late night stores, there was a black hole, brutal and barren. It always reminded Danny of the heart of the town, ripped out, leaving the rest of the buildings somehow lit up, but with nothing to course the lifeblood through its streets.

"Yes, it almost makes me cry Statto, just seeing the darkness, the emptiness of it all."

"I know, but don't worry. We're the energy now. We'll light it up again. They won't be able to hold us back." Danny smiled at his friend's never wavering belief. They could never be sure of the result, but they were sure that they would do the deeds.

"Hey up Danny, are we going back down or not, it's bloody freezing up here," the shout from below reminded him of where he was and what he'd been doing. "And I've only got one fag left, and I'm saving that for later."

A quick nod between them was all that was needed.

"Okay, okay. We're going. Take it easy going down, especially those of you who may be carrying a little bit more weight than the others," they laughed, he liked that. "And when we get back we'll have a quick half hour with the ball and then call it a night."

"Come on you Whites!" it was Weeble, the rest echoing his cry as they slowly started their descent.

13 FOUR CALLING BIRDS

The cafeteria at the Co-Op wasn't Danny's normal lunchtime place, but two meals for fifteen quid and an invite from Annie had sealed the deal. It was bright and clean and full of old people, the ones who seemed to spend all of their days spread out amongst the multitude of superstores around town. A raised hand caught his eye and he walked over to the table where Annie was waiting for him.

"I got you a ploughman's, hope you don't mind." They embraced and he sat down, intrigued by the excitement in her voice.

"So what's the news then, that can't wait until Saturday?" She looked like she was almost ready to explode and that made him smile.

"It's done, the big reconciliation. Last night at San Lorenzo." Could she see his confusion? He took a bite of cheddar.

"Ah, the big reconciliation?" she was clearly disappointed and had no apparent problems letting him know.

"Danny! All you care about is the bloody football. Don't forget this is all about the towns too, bringing them closer together. We thought that Dad and Winston would be a good place to start, seeing as how they haven't talked to each other for the last five years." Yes, she'd said something about that after the trials, he remembered now.

"The silly old gits. All those years of friendship thrown away like that."

"Well Dad did go and get Winston's team relegated and all that, just before they went out of business," her smile was back.

"But it wasn't Dad's...." her hand was raised.

"You sound just like him. Anyway, it's all fixed now, and with them both behind you things can only be easier." There she was right, the two doyens pushing together could only be good. Biting into a pickled onion he saw her sitting there, the girl in class who knew all of the answers but still waited to be asked.

"So I hope you're not just going to leave me hanging. I'll need all of the details." Well at least the details that you can give me in the next fifteen minutes, because there's more work to be done this afternoon. The genie was released from the bottle and the story tumbled out.

The four girls had arranged it all. Winston was already in San Lorenzo with Edith and Laetitia when Annie and his Mum had arrived.

"You should've seen the look on his face when he heard Dad and looked up." He would've liked to have seen that.

Sitting them down together had been the easy part, getting them talking was different.

"Edith got them talking about the Horseshoes on a Sunday morning and then Mum got them going on the White versus Blue matches in farmer Robin's old field." Her smile was now joy, and he didn't need a mirror to see his own. The stories they must have heard a thousand times. Between mouthfuls of tomato he even found himself taking the lead.

"I can hear Dad now, going on about 'those bloody

flies' again. And Billy Holmes wanting to be Manchester United and getting thrown in the river at the end. And Winston must have surely reminded him of the Diggle lad nearly taking his knackers off with his rugby boots. And that got them both laughing together did it?"

"Warming up perhaps, but they had plenty more tales to take them up to the laughter stage." It must have been just like the Ghost of Christmas Past. He could have stayed there all afternoon reliving the stories again himself had he not needed to be back at the factory in ten.

"So Dad's forgiven?" Annie's face took on a more serious look and her voice was slower.

"Winston understands that nobody could've stopped the Blues folding, and that childhood friendship's worth a lot. I'd forgotten how much he cares you know. For the people who followed the Blues, for the people who work in his factory. He fights for them you know?" Danny hoped he was still fighting for them now, if the rumours were true. He leaned forwards and took her hand.

"Thanks Annie. You're right you know, this can't just be about the football, it's about showing the bastards that we still care." She squeezed his hand tightly.

"And your old friends? Have you seen Al lately?" Danny frowned and took a last swig of his drink. Al had been doing the impossible and ignoring him at work. "Don't worry, I've seen him. I'm sure he'll come round, just leave him with me for now," he nodded his thanks, having nothing else to offer.

They said their goodbyes and he started back for the factory. The four ladies had done the unimaginable and managed to reconcile Big John and Winston. And with their combined might behind the match, anything was possible.

14 SNOWBALL

Another Monday morning in Marshalls car park, but this time early enough to park right next to the door. Danny now found sleeping difficult and waking up easy.

"If we get here any earlier he's going to have us switching the lights on Danny," Richo was always lively, even on such a cold and dark December morning. "I would've thought that after a weekend like that you'd have been happy to stay in bed a bit longer and get a bit more rest."

It had been a great weekend. Lots of good training time with the ball and the first full training match against the reserves. The Whites were starting to look like a football team, the memories of Parson's Hill a long way behind them. Richo continued.

"And I couldn't help but notice you're becoming a bit of a local celebrity too. When we were out yesterday morning they couldn't get enough of you," a large self-satisfied grin broke out across Danny's face. Being stopped in the street as a kid had been a regular occurrence, but it had always been his Dad, Big John, who they were interested in. Closing his eyes the sounds of Sunday came back.

'Good luck Danny, give them one from me.'

'If you need anything just let me know, any way I can help.'

'Make sure you give those Blue bastards a good kicking from me Danny boy.'

Three, four, five times he'd been stopped walking into town, and the encouragements had continued as he'd toured the shopping centre afterwards. People of every age group and gender, all starting to take an interest in the game to come.

'We heard your Dad on the radio, we're all behind you!'

Yes, his Dad, of course. Somehow the shadow had to stay. But it was clear that ever since his Dad and Winston had met up the ball that they'd set rolling was getting bigger and bigger. A snowball.

Better quality posters had been put up in places where they couldn't be torn down and small reports were appearing on the local radio and in the local press. They'd found a sponsor for the balls, another for the referees, another for the medical tent. How he hoped they didn't need the medical tent. Yes, the snowball was getting bigger as people started to take an interest and the day approached.

Walking out onto the almost empty floor they had their choice of place while the others slowly arrived. There was the normal mixture of excited talk about weekends and resigned silence at another week's work. Danny just couldn't wait to get the day over, waiting for the match to be one day nearer. Don't wish your life away they said. In this case he was willing to ignore them.

"Right then you lot," Benjamin announced the start of the meeting. More news about contracts that they'd bid for and offers that they'd provided. Dave followed in prescribed order, but Danny was by then far away. Dreaming of glory on the football field as he dispossessed Roy of the Rovers and the Whites put another nail in

Melchester's coffin. The sound of hand claps woke him from his dream, people moving to take their places telling him that the meeting was over as another Monday began.

She had a nice arse Geeta. He should know, he'd seen it enough times, stuck out from under his machine as she methodically worked to try and solve another problem. He'd once confused her for Marlon, but that was just the once. Yes, she had a nice arse.

"Any news Geets, the boss is on his way round to see us?" Danny talked quietly under his breath, his eyes following Benjamin around the workshop. He could already imagine himself receiving another bollocking in front of everyone. They'd barely had time to get started up before the red lights started turning and the alarms announced that line 3 was down again.

"I think I've got it, but I really need Marlon for this one. And he's stuck on line 7." Two lines down at once was never fun. He looked up then breathed deeply as Benjamin came to a halt in front of him.

"Well, well, well Danny. What a surprise to see your line down again. I'm sure you do it deliberately, just to have some time off and put me out of business. It seems that being a loser sticks eh? A loser in life and soon to be a loser in football. Anyway, Dave'll surely sort yet another mess out on your behalf when he's finished on 7. What you can do is make sure that you and the rest of the Fab Four are in my office at lunchtime. Twelve sharp and don't be late. Unlike yourselves we're busy men, we have a company to run you know." With a turn he was off and away.

"No shouting? No insults?" Richo came out from the corner he'd been hiding in.

"A few insults Richo my friend, old habits and all that. But no shouting, as you observed. I think he might be starting to like me," they both laughed out loud, causing Geeta to bang her head as she tried to look to where the laughter came from.

"So what's the story, what's come over him?"

"Well I think it's a bit early for Christmas spirit, so it must be that he's getting wrapped up in this match too. He wants to see us, all of us, in his office at twelve. You tell Al and I'll let Statto know," Richo moved away leaving Danny on his own. Yes, he was right. The game was starting to affect everyone who touched it. A Benjamin who didn't shout when his machines were stopped wasn't a normal Benjamin. Hearing the whir of the machine he looked up and Geeta was there giving him a big thumbs up. He bowed in appreciation as another lot of high quality printed clothing parts started to roll off the line, heading towards the top end 'Made in the UK' fashion market.

They all arrived at twelve sharp and entered Benjamin's office, where Dave and Marsha were already settled at the large table. Unlike Winston's office, stuffily perched high up in the factory looking inwards over the workshop, his son had chosen a large open space, with views out over the surrounding countryside. Danny was sure that Lovers View was up there to the left, peering down over the town and the valley. Everything was neat and tidy, with proudly framed certificates on the wall. The Queen's prize for innovation, the chamber of commerce prize for excellence. Would there ever be any King's prizes to replace them? A photo caught Danny's eye, a young Benjamin with the Blues team. Dressed up in the full kit and proudly holding the FA Vase, won at Wembley in front of over twenty thousand Blues supporters. Full kit wanker.

"Right then, now that the famous five are here we can get started." Geeta turning up had surprised him. Then again, she was one of them and had as much right as the others to be there. Al was still brooding, standing apart from the rest of them.

"Don't tell us Ben, you've decided that the public

humiliation would be too much and so you'd prefer to call it off and just give us the thousand quid?" Statto opened the sparring.

"No, we most certainly don't want to call it off. We did have a few problems a couple of weeks back with broken ribs. The guys just laughed so much when they came across you useless bastards crawling up that hill, but they all seem to be recovered now."

"Except perhaps Arnie, but his was a broken nose wasn't it?" Benjamin replied with one of his smiles, the sparring was over. Surprisingly it was Dave who took the floor.

"We may have scored too early."

"We may have what Dave?"

"Scored too early. You know, been too quick out of the blocks," Danny exchanged a confused look with Statto. Dave wasn't finished. "Ticket sales are through the roof boys. Oh, and girl. Erm girls." We aren't even selling tickets, what's he on about?

"If I may perhaps explain?" Marsha coolly took over. "The fact is that we've been doing a bit of research, you know, talking to some of our key stakeholder groups and customer segments." The confused looks had got no better. "From what we can figure out there should be at least five hundred people coming to watch the game from the Blue side, give or take the standard error linked to our research techniques."

"I've no reason to doubt the error on your research techniques, and to be honest no desire to know what torturous methods you've been using, but what does it really mean?" Statto was clearly following the route, but not understanding the destination.

"It means you thickos," Benjamin had held off as long as he could, "that the Works ground on South Road isn't big enough. It can comfortably hold three hundred and at an absolute push five hundred is okay. Now we already have five hundred coming to cheer the Blues to victory, which is the absolute limit. Even assuming that you lot can bring a friend and a family member each, of which the friend part may be difficult for some of you, then there'll be too many people. Heaven forbid that you actually manage to get some of the poor sods off the street to come, then we just can't handle it. As things stand, the ground and facilities just aren't big enough." Silence. Not through fear of looking stupid but from the bombshell that Benjamin had just dropped. Danny could see satisfaction on the face of Statto and confusion on the face of Richo. His heart fluttered, the ground wasn't big enough.

The silence continued, ideas surely whizzing around heads. Harrod Road had been sold years before and Cherry Lane was closed. There were no stadiums larger than the Works ground in either town.

"But how big a ground will we need? If you think you're already at five hundred, plus let's say the same again from the Whites, we need somewhere that can hold a thousand. Imagining that we still have a few weeks to go, there'll only be more who decide to come along between now and Christmas. Then we'll have the last minute tag alongs, just like at Midnight Mass, the ones who come along with a friend. How big do we need? Two thousand?" Statto was still trying to size the problem.

"One thousand, two thousand, it doesn't really matter. There's nothing that big within twenty five miles of here." Benjamin had already done the maths.

"Well there's the rugby ground, the Bears. They're playing away over Christmas, at the Tigers on the twenty seventh. I only know because my Dad goes to watch them now and again," a blushing Dave was treated to varied surprised looks. It was thirty miles away, but a plan at least.

"Before anyone asks, I've already contacted them," Marsha's comment was no surprise. "The ground's free that day. Normally they wouldn't want to hire it out, especially as it's already cutting up a lot this year, but because they know Winston they'd be willing to let us have it."

"So we just have to get everybody there then. I imagine that most'll go in cars and there should be trains and buses on Boxing Day too. The ground isn't far from the station, so people could walk down. Sorted." Richo's grin melted under Marsha's stare. She hadn't finished her sentence.

"As I was saying, they would be willing to let us rent the pitch and facilities for the day, for twenty thousand pounds."

"Twenty fucking grand, just to rent a pitch for the day?" Al's reply exploded. At least he was still interested. Danny didn't want to let their only idea die so quickly.

"Can we make it work, can we get twenty thousand in time? We've got sponsors, for the balls and the officials and everything. Surely we can up the stakes a bit and cover the ground?" Had he sounded desperate? Twenty thousand was a lot.

"When I told Dad he just laughed. If Winston isn't prepared to ask around, then it must be a bad one," Benjamin's no go was the final nail.

"So what then?" The ten minutes since Danny had been elated at the news that the match was too popular for the Works ground seemed an age ago. This new problem was outside their areas of expertise and he knew it. How could they possibly raise twenty thousand pounds in such a short time, and even if they did would the people still be willing to go and watch the match if it was so far away?

"There might be another option," Geeta's quiet voice cut through the silence. Danny joined the others in slowly turning towards the back of the room. There was an excitement about her that he'd never seen before.

"So, the quiet grease monkey at the back's got something that we've all missed. I suppose there's a cricket pitch somewhere that we can convert, only known to the Asian community is there?" Al stepped forward protectively, but Benjamin raised his hand resignedly "But do go on and let us know what we've been missing."

"It's nothing certain, but I could have exactly what we're looking for. I've got some last minute investigations to finish, but I'm sure that by tomorrow lunchtime we should be able to visit and see."

"Visit and see what Geeta? Your last sentence was all a bit Secret Squirrel for me. A lot of words that didn't really tell me anything." Benjamin's voice got louder as he spoke.

"Okay, okay. We'll fix the meeting now, and I'll let you know if I have to cancel. Meet me tomorrow at twelve thirty, outside the ground."

"But outside which ground Geeta, outside which ground?" Benjamin's agitation was higher still.

"Why outside THE ground," she said with a laugh. "Outside Cherry Lane. There's a small door at the back of the main stand. Meet me there at twelve thirty tomorrow."

15 THE SECRET GARDEN

Cherry Lane, and again a spring in Danny's step. Could he remember the last time he and Richo had walked to the ground in daylight?

"Any idea what Geeta's got planned?" That was the question everyone had been asking for the last twenty four hours, and he had no more of a clue than the others.

In front of them the stadium, functional and workmanlike. No superstores or hotel complexes here, just a handful of windows hiding offices behind and a small opening that had doubled up as ticket office and club shop. His smile got even broader as he remembered the hours spent queueing for tickets for Arsenal and Leicester in the Cup, their big days away when the whole town was alive with talk of the Whites.

"Older and shabbier, but still home eh? And there are the old gates with that padlock keeping us out. Look at it? I swear that someone must be coming here and polishing it every day," Danny was excited.

To the corner on the right he saw the small door that Geeta had talked about. Huddled together next to it were Statto and Red Al, Marsha, Benjamin and Dave. Danny and Richo walked over to join them.

"How come you're always late Danny, always the last? Do you do it deliberately just to piss me off?"

"Sorry Benjamin, I didn't realise it upset you so much. If I'd known I'd do it even more." It wasn't banter, he'd never be able to talk with Benjamin like he did Statto and Richo and the others. But the conversation was easier, different to how it would've been several weeks before.

"So now we just need our Indian princess, the guardian of secrets and mysteries. I wish we could get this goose chase out of the way and then start the serious work of trying to raise some money." Did Benjamin really believe that they could raise the money? No, they were stuck. It was Geeta's secret, or nothing.

A slow creaking noise coming from the small door prevented Benjamin from continuing. They all looked to the source of the noise, the opening door slowly revealing Geeta at the end of a long, dark corridor. She smiled nervously.

"About bloody time, we've been waiting for ages. Come on let's get this pantomime over with and then we can sort out the real business." Calm down Benjamin. "What are we doing here and where are we going?" Geeta returned his impatience with one of her most radiant smiles.

"I do apologise Benjamin, but I had a few people who needed some last minute convincing. What you're going to see will amaze you, but there are risks associated with it. Risks that others have taken and risks that we'll have to take. Come on, let's go and meet Dilip and Reg." Before anyone else could speak she turned and entered the dark corridor. In silence they followed.

The echo of steps was the only sound as they walked along the poorly illuminated walkway. On either side of the corridor Danny could just about make out the shapes of doors, solid and windowless. The journey was quick, only about twenty paces, and then he was blinded as light poured out of a door opened in front of him. Squinting he took the last steps, following the others into a small room. Gradually the sight before him became clearer, revealing it as the resting place of a table and two chairs, an apparently dead ostrich and two old gentlemen. The source of the bright light was a brilliant sunlight, streaming in through a double window. Geeta carried on from where she'd left off.

"This everyone is Dilip, and this is Reg. A long time ago they used to be the groundsmen here." Danny looked over the two men. Dilip small and seated, a Whites ski hat on his head and a mug of milky tea in his hand. Reg stood tall and proud next to a door on the other side of the room. His overalls were open at the top, revealing a plain white shirt and a Whites tie. Both looked nervously at the newcomers to their world.

"Alright, alright. Nice to meet you and all that, my name's Benjamin, now what the bloody hell are we doing here. I'd appreciate it if we could get a move on quickly so that I can stop holding my breath and get back outside." Dilip had been on the verge of speaking but was clearly shocked by Benjamin's outburst. Geeta moved beside him and spoke softly.

"Thank you Benjamin. You're not on your own, so perhaps we can let Dilip say what he needs to say, in his own time?" Benjamin wilted under the looks from the others and crossed his arms. Dilip slowly stood, his eyes passing around the assembled visitors. Finally he started to speak in a firm assured voice that seemed to Danny to take even himself by surprise.

"As Geeta knows from my daughter's wedding I'm not really one for speeches," his nervous laugh betrayed his deliberate icebreaker, "so I will try and make this as short as possible. Until five years ago now we had spent over fifty years between us preparing the pitch inside this stadium, so that the Whites could go out every Saturday and entertain us all." A muffled derisory snort could easily be traced back to Benjamin. Dilip carried on, looking determined not to be put off. "We must be honest and say, to appease our snorting colleague in front of us, that the level of the entertainment did vary from week to week and from year to year. But we always prided ourselves on the fact that it was more due to the quality of the players than to the quality of the pitch." Dilip joined in with the giggles from the Whites in the room, seemingly pleased that his second joke had hit home. "And then, as you all know it ended." Danny gulped, the finality of Dilip's phrase catching him unprepared. Looking round he saw that even Benjamin was now drawn in, waiting to hear what could possibly have followed. "Or rather it should have ended. Initially we were left with keys in case visitors needed showing round, but it was impossible to let our beautiful pitch go to ruin. And so we became knights, like Ivanhoe and Lancelot, and coming here became our quest. No further words can describe what we have to show you and so I will not try. I will simply ask you to follow Reg and see for yourselves."

Reg opened the door that had been hidden behind him in silence and within a handful of steps had a further, larger door open too. The others quickly followed.

"Fuck me, it's magnificent." Bunched in at the back of the group Danny was still in the corridor when he heard Al's voice. The other voices followed, joining together in excitement and wonder. Urgently he pushed himself through the last few steps.

Instinctively his right hand felt for something solid, something to stop him falling. Landing on Marsha's shoulder he breathed in deep gulps and tried to focus. Richo and Statto were hugging each other in front of the most glorious green background he had ever seen, a football pitch in perfect condition, an oasis in the desert. His nose tingled with the smell of recently cut grass and lime coming from the brilliant white lines showing the limits that should not be passed. At each end were goalposts, nets pulled taught behind them showing where the ball should be placed. A giant Subbuteo set before him, crying out to be played with.

"I've seen it Geeta, but I don't believe it. Dilip, Reg, you're the most amazing people I've ever met. I can't thank you enough for the pleasure this gives me," Statto was walking around, shaking hands, slapping backs, his large face the new owner of an ear to ear smile.

The initial shock subsided, they grouped together, everyone eager to have a say.

"It's true that the rest of the stadium needs a bit of work, but we should be able to find space for at least a few thousand if we need to," Dave was just as excited as the rest.

"Exactly, we've still got over three weeks until the game. And I'm sure that if we ask nicely Dilip and Reg can help us out too?" The two groundsmen returned Statto's pleading smile. His next comment never arrived though, Benjamin stepping out quickly into the middle of the group, his shaking head and raised hands silencing everyone.

"Hold on, hold on you lot. These two may have been taken over by the madness of their quest and the lure of a place at the Round Table," Danny like the others turned to stare. "But think about it for a minute. This ground belongs to the Council. We can't just put our heads in the sand, like your bloody Ostrich used to when you were playing your normal shitty football, and ignore it. The pitch might be great and the stands passable, but you can't just break and enter into someone else's property and have a kick about, cheered on by a thousand or so of your mates. We'll never get away with it." How could they have got carried away? Glances were exchanged rapidly as they searched for answers.

"So what are they going to do? Arrest us all? We wouldn't be breaking and entering, we'd be letting ourselves in with a key. And we'd be in our hundreds.

How would they stop that, the power and will of the people?"

"Sometimes Statto, for an admittedly big, but intelligent bloke, you say some stupid things. Using a key doesn't alter the fact that you're going into a place that you've no legal right to be in, so of course we'd still be breaking the law. And it's hardly going to come as a surprise to the police if it's put up on posters all over the town three weeks before the big day."

There followed more silence, as a clearly flustered Statto brooded and everyone else stood there with the reality that the perfect beauty just next to them may still be too far away to touch.

"Alan, do something useful for once. You're used to pushing me as far as you can without breaking the law. What would you and your renegade friends propose as a way of getting around this?" Benjamin asking Al for advice? Basking in his moment of attention Al put on a reflective face.

"Gentlemen, we have a choice in front of us. Oh, and you ladies too. We've a decision to take which is difficult but crucial. It simply needs to be taken and stuck with." Calm and considered, his years of Union training coming through. "As far as I can see the option that we discovered today won't allow us to play the match without breaking some aspects of the law."

"Great." Not what they wanted to hear.

"What we have to decide though, is do we prefer to find twenty thousand pounds in order to play the game miles away? Or are we willing to accept some legal transgressions, hopefully minor ones that would never be punished within the festive context of the event that we want to put on, in order to play the game at Cherry Lane?" Benjamin's answer was immediate.

"Well it's easy enough for you lot to want to break the law, but I'm a respectable factory manager here. Imagine the harm it could do to me and the business if we just decide to do that. And not to mention the sponsors. I'm sure they'd love to see their signs on the nine o'clock news as we're all carried off to the local nick."

"Choices aren't easy Benjamin, you know that. If you don't want to be involved you're free to walk out. If we need to give our sponsors the same choice then we will. But we have to believe, with everything that we've done and been through to get here, that at some point the Ghost of Christmas Present is going to look after us, to spread some magic from his horn of happiness on our heads." Danny hated agreeing with Benjamin, but he had to speak.

"But the police'll know, how could we ever keep it a secret?" More murmurs from around him. Al raised a hand.

"This is still the digital age Danny. We warn people now and Bam, we give them the new location just before kick off. Anyone planning to be at the Works ground for twelve o'clock isn't going to be too put out if they find out at nine that they've got to go to Cherry Lane instead. It's all a question of surprise. By the time they're all in the ground the fuzz won't know what's going on and it'll be too late to do anything. On Boxing Day they'll all be at the shopping centre trying to stop the old ladies fighting over coats in the sales, so there'll be no one around anyway. So all we need to do is say nothing. We leave a few lads at the Works ground just in case, but we start spreading the word now that there'll be some last minute announcements. And for the non-internet savvy we'll open all of the channels up."

"Open the channels up. What channels?"

"Dave, dear Dave. We also have The Red Line. I'll give you no details, but just imagine that there are networks of communication, designed for the older discerning gentleman, er and lady, that've been used for spreading industrial unrest across the region for years. Just leave that with me." Danny quickly passed round the faces.

No real smiles of joy, but not the despair of a few moments before. He even felt a surge of excitement himself at the thought of what they'd do.

"Right then, we'll put it to the vote. Those in favour? Those against?"

Unanimous. Problem solved.

16 PRACTICE MAKES PERFECT

"Sakes Weeble, what'd you do that for?" the words were spat out, along with a mouthful of the rubber beads that covered the artificial pitch. Trying to get up a sharp pain spiked through his ankle. Damn! With only a couple of weeks to go the last thing Danny needed was people being injured, especially himself.

"Sorry Danny, I didn't mean it. You know what it's like on this surface, especially when it's wet," Weeble was as honest as the day was long, and certainly had no need to hurt anyone. But that was practice, needing to be intense enough to get match fit, but not so intense that people got hurt.

"Griz, take my place with the yellows. Ling's holding for the moment, so try and get forward with some runs. And all of you, try not to hurt anyone," the orders were shouted out as he limped off the pitch, every step giving him more pain in his left ankle. The sessions he'd planned carefully. Whites attack vs Whites defence. The midfield split across the teams so he could try out combinations and strategies. The Whites subs were spread around as their positions dictated and the remaining spaces were taken up by the best of the players who'd missed out at the trials. Fitness and strategy was nothing without that sharpness that came from playing proper, competitive games. Finally reaching the edge of the pitch he stood next to Statto, turning to face the play.

"You going to be alright Gaffer?"

"I'll be alright, don't you worry. And don't call me Gaffer." Being called Gaffer had been fun at the start, but was now starting to annoy him. The more it seemed to annoy him, the more Statto used it.

"He was just too slow. The surface didn't help, but he was just slow. It's going to be a big pick, that back four." Like the whole team, Statto. No choices will be easy.

"I know, but it's got to be picked. They'll all still have the chance to come on and be a hero though." Fine drops of rain were clearly visible, drifting past the floodlights. He'd always seen the game being played on a bright, crisp Winter's morning. Cold was never nice, but could always be run off. A wet surface was murder, with mistimed tackles and poor passes. And who could forget the feeling of running around with wet pants after that first sliding tackle? His focus went back to the play.

"Will we be any good Statto?" His friend looked around the pitch, at his notes, up at the floodlights and back around the pitch. Then he fixed Danny with an almost crazed stare.

"Winning isn't everything Danny. We'll not be embarrassed, but we've got to be realistic. Their boys are regular players and know each other well. True, we've got ourselves some good lads, but they're not the same class." That sounded like a no then.

"Yes, but we've still got time. We'll be better when the match comes, we're fighters. We're getting better with each session."

"I know Danny, but let's just be realistic." Pain in his ankle was forgotten as his head throbbed and he balled his hands into fists. Statto almost seemed to give up once the game was arranged, as if just playing it was enough to meet his needs. For Danny it was more than that. He still had the Blues and Benjamin to beat.

"Right then, take a break lads, that's good. Ten minutes for a breather and then we'll do the wing play. Yellows, you break down the wings and get those crosses in. Sixty seconds or timed out. Colours, you just have to stop them."

Orders shouted he hobbled to the centre line and sat down on the bench. The pain wasn't so intense now, it was just a small knock. A good day's rest would probably be enough. Looking again at Statto the anger came back, 'Won't be embarrassed' my arse, we'll win this.

"Are you okay Danny? I can take a look if you want," Griz offered as he walked past, trying to bring his breathing back to normal.

"It's all okay, just a little knock. I'll come and see you at work if it gets any worse." Griz, like most of the others, had struggled with the fitness work. Now they were playing more they were all feeling better. All of them were one step further down the road, one rung higher on the ladder than they'd been before. One step in front of the other, that was what he'd done. He was sure they could win, that they would win. Feeling the weight of another person sit on the bench beside him he turned, ready to tell Statto where to stuff his negative vibes.

"Oh, it's you."

"It is indeed, don't mind me coming along do you? Thought I'd come on down and see if it was worth putting a few quid on you. Ha ha ha." John's laugh boomed out over the pitch and Richo looked over, giving a quick wave. Danny was stunned into silence. "Have you got nothing else to say? I can go if you want?"

"No, no. It's okay, stay. I'm just a bit surprised to see you, that's all. You've never really bothered with us before. Stay and have a look. You might even have some advice for us. Some tips? Give the lads a bit of a speech or something." Something in his Dad's eyes was worrying him. Was it sympathy? John spoke again, somewhat subdued.

"Now then, the old John might've done as you asked, as a favour. Either that or he might've told you that it wasn't worth it because your team was a shower of shit. Or he might've even laughed at you and shook his head in despair. But, the new John wouldn't dare. He wouldn't go and talk to your team if you paid him. Let's just say that he's happy to be here and that he's happy to see what you're doing, but tonight he's just like everyone else's Dad, dropping in to see how his boy's getting on." See how his boy's getting on? His Dad had never spoken like that before. Recovering from his surprise he replied.

"And so when did he appear then, this new John. I bet Mum's glad he's arrived," he dared the joke and a little smile.

"Glad he arrived's an understatement. It was thanks to your Mum that the old and new one bumped into each other. Ha ha. No, I think he finally found himself when he realised what wonderful children he had. When he realised the great things they were capable of doing, of what they were capable of achieving. And that they were doing it by themselves and for the good of others. Taking on this team, this game. It hasn't been easy for you, I know. I could see it when you came round and told us all the stories. Then I was walking down town on Monday and old Mrs Wilkes stopped me in the street, and she said 'Hello John, you tell your Danny from me that we're all behind him for the game. And thank him from us, because at the moment this town needs something to give it a bit of excitement.' Can you believe that? Someone stopped me in the street and they didn't want to talk about me. And then it all sunk in, and I got it," John wiped a bit of quick out of his eye and carried on, looking straight ahead at the team in front of him as they tried to work a chance down the left wing. "So I don't think I really need to talk to the team, or to anyone else about the details of the game. You're the only person they want to hear from." Silence. A long silence while they both watched the session, while they both thought about the words that John had said. "Not playing tonight?"

"Got a bit of a knock on the ankle. Weeble, the daft bastard, diving in on a night like this. It should be alright though, I'll give it a rest tomorrow and then be back after that. Fresh as a daisy."

"You'll need to be to beat that lot. Have you been watching them?" John's voice was taking on a new energy.

"Watching them, what do you mean?"

"Have you had any of Red Al's boys hiding in the bushes, taking a peep at them? Formation, strategy, stuff like that?" Hiding in the bushes, what's he talking about?

"That's all a bit cloak and dagger isn't it. As long as we stick to our game plan, we can let them worry about us."

"All very honourable son, all very honourable, but knowing your opponents is key, they all did it. Detailed dossiers and everything. You see that bloke down there, with the red windcheater? Sitting on his bike like he's birdwatching, or more probably owl watching at this time of night? That's Dave from the factory. He's been taking notes and videos all night." What, him over there? Yes, there was someone there yesterday too, far enough away to go unnoticed, but close enough to video and observe.

"The cheating bastards eh? It's a good job it's Dave though. He doesn't know much about football, but if he's been videoing us every night then someone else could be taking a look. I'll see if Al can get some of his lads up to see them tomorrow, or perhaps Statto even. If we're behind the curve again, then I should probably send the big guns in." How could he have been so naive yet again. To not have thought about scouting the opponents, to understand his enemy. Had he done anything right?

"No need, there was a big gun there earlier tonight, and last night. Oh, and last weekend when they played a friendly against the Works. If you buy him a couple of pints after the game tonight, he'll probably tell you all about it," their eyes met and they both smiled.

"Looks like you've got a date Dad, though don't blame me if you roll in late and Mum gives you a hard time."

"Ha ha ha. If only. I'm on the radio again tomorrow morning, plugging the game as usual. I tell you what, I reckon it's going to be a tight fit down that Works ground for the match. Especially if all of the Wilkes' are going! Ha ha ha."

"Hiya John, sorry to interrupt you two, but we're nearly finished with the corners Danny. It's gone really well. We've got thirty minutes left, do you want a mini game? We can do Yellows against colours like before, or some more set plays?" No, they needed to do something different, what could they do?

"No Statto, let the dogs out. Let's have the Whites against the rest. All-out attack, let them get the feel of knocking a few goals in."

Statto left to pass on the instructions, leaving them alone again.

"Come on, try a bit of weight on that ankle. Talk me through what you've got and what you've not." Strolling together towards the half way line the two men carried on talking, finally stopping to take in the end of the session. How well could they perform together when things were easy? It was always then that teams lost their style and shape.

In the end they managed it easily. He'd given them a plan, an image, which they tried to recreate every time they played. It may not have been the best, but it was theirs and he was sure that if they all stuck to it they'd be able to beat the Blues when the big match came.

Looking on, Danny and John talked through the rest of the team, the players, their stories, their strengths and weaknesses and everything that Danny hoped they'd do when the time came. John just listened, no 'ifs' and 'buts', no reprimands. The thirty minutes just flew by before Statto blew the whistle and off they went, the players running past them on their way to the warmth of the showers.

"Well then Statto, they look like they can score when they're up against the chickens, but can they defend? Is it going to be a '63 game or what?"

"A sixty three game?" John didn't have a chance to reply, Statto was in like a shot.

"Boxing Day 1963 Danny. Way before our time, all of us, but it'll live in the memory for ever. In the first division there were ten games played and sixty six goals scored. That's over six goals per game. Fulham versus Ipswich finished 10 – 1. Ten one! They were the days. They played each other again on the twenty eighth and Ipswich won 4 – 2. They must've still been enjoying a drink or two over Christmas in those days. And it wasn't so long ago that those foreign managers were moaning that the lack of a winter break hurt their teams in Europe. Bollocks to them, the selfish bastards. Why should three quarters of the country be deprived of what they were used to, just so that Liverpool and Chelsea could go an extra round in the Champions League. The Winter break never hurt them during the years when they won the Cup, only the years when they didn't. So yes John, I reckon it'll be a '63 game. There'll be a goal or two, of that I'm sure."

"Ooh I hope so. If I'm going to get up early and traipse out to the Works ground to watch you lot I want at least a couple. And you needn't worry about your lot drinking too much. Mary's already organised a girlfriends, wives and mums meeting and there won't be any alcohol on the Christmas menu for you lot, just pasta and bananas. Ha ha ha."

Father and son headed to the car park, Danny's ankle feeling better with each step.

"Right then, I'll see you down the Bell in a few minutes. You're buying and I'm spilling the beans on what those nasty Blues have been up to these last few weeks."

His eyes followed as John walked to his car and drove off. As the car finally pulled out he smiled to himself.

"Come on then Statto, let's get them sorted out."
There was no reply, Statto had long gone.

17 THE WEELWRIGHTS ARMS

Nine quick steps took no time at all and Danny had crossed his flat from bathroom to kitchen. He slapped his face. The adverts had promised a refreshing wake up after his shave, but it hadn't arrived yet. Did he really have to go out that night? No training, just the works Christmas party. Take a night off and have a few drinks he'd said, for better or for worse.

Distraction, that's what he needed. The radio clicked on and the sound of Christmas filled the room. His Mum must've tuned into the local radio one day and he'd never had a reason to change it back. All buses delayed due to roadworks or swimming pools closed for cleaning, essential news for their local listeners. And Christmas music. Annie and Geeta would no doubt be hearing the same and dancing along, a glass of wine in hand, as they got ready to go out.

Looking in the mirror above his fire place to straighten his hair, he saw the card. On it an old stamp that still bore the head of the Queen, no doubt bought with many others to avoid a long gone price rise. A postmark from Chester, a place he'd never visited and didn't believe he ever would. The name, George Raymond, and address written with neat, precise handwriting, just as it had been for each of the last five years. He'd bought the flat off Mr Raymond's son, at least a year after his death, so the intended recipient he sort of knew. The sender? He'd no idea, but he'd named him or her Bob to make things simpler.

The Christmas sound track had now taken on more of a swing feel, as some crooner of yesteryear took his turn at the microphone. He snorted out an unexpected laugh as the image of the girls was replaced by one of Red Al. Still distant after the trials, but years of friendship didn't disappear that quickly. He could almost hear him singing along, dressed in jacket and tie with matching handkerchief in his top pocket. There would surely be a plan to enchant Brunhilde with a devilish smile and a witty story, the poor girl.

He took the card in his hand, poised to open it and read the secrets within. Perhaps there'd be an address, so he could write to Bob and tell him the sad news about his friend George. But no, how could he? He could imagine Bob now, writing the name on the envelope, a smile warming his face as he thought back to the childhood that he and George had spent together. The smile getting larger as he wrote his wishes in the card, memories flooding back of Christmases they'd shared with their families. His face, now absolutely beaming as he signed off 'your dearest old friend Bob', perhaps a little snigger as he placed his pen down and recalled the best times they ever spent together, the thoughts that Christmas and time and distance can make so special. Did it make any difference to Bob if his card was unread? He'd certainly survived five years without one being returned.

Another change of music, now it was Wham! and Last Christmas. The vision was now of Richo and Statto at the end of the night. Richo transformed from charming man to a state of disarray, Statto looking exactly the same as he had at the beginning of the evening.

The room became darker and quiet as Danny switched

off the radio and the main lights. Lucky old Bob. As he placed the Christmas card in his pocket it hit him. Bob didn't need anyone to read his cards. His pleasure came simply from writing them. Wishing everyone Season's Greetings via the internet and donating money to charity would give Bob no pleasure at all. Walking out into the dark night Danny laughed to think that the only card he'd received in the last five years had been for someone else.

The town was alive, groups of people arm in arm, singing, talking, dancing even. The sights and sounds of the time of year as they all went to visit friends or colleagues. No, not yet for him, he wasn't ready. Time to take some time out and have a drink on his own.

"Just past Hazel Lane eh? Right, I'll take a left here and go to the Wheelwright's," he said to no one in particular, making up his mind. No one he knew ever went there.

The turning took him down a couple of back lanes, next to an old water way that could have at one time been a canal. Once an estate pub there were no houses left to claim it. He wondered if any wagons had ever passed this way, or if the name had been chosen by hazard a couple of centuries before. He was certain though that nobody inside would have the necessary skills to change a broken spoke on a race bike, let alone repair a large metal rimmed, wooden wheel. Passing through the door he entered an interior just slightly warmer than the outside. The pub was almost empty that evening, just two other customers, both resembling characters from Dickens novels and huddled around a small fire in the corner. Next to them the dartboard, the only entertainment the place had to offer.

He took a pint of Shippos. A bench backed up to the window invited him over and he took a sip of the light brown beer, savouring the taste of the olden times. The froth on his glass dried and faded as he watched.

BOXING DAY

"Well I would give you a penny for your thoughts, but one there'd be nothing worthwhile in them and two you'd waste the bloody penny." How did he get in without me seeing?

"Benjamin. What the fuck are you doing here? Aren't you supposed to be at the Christmas party?"

"Me and you too. I just needed to get out a bit, to go where I could have some time on my own. And then I find the emptiest pub in the town and you're here."

"Well, now you've seen me you can piss off and leave me alone."

"You impolite bastard. Aren't you even going to let me sit down and finish my pint? The opposing managers always used to have a drink with each other after the game in the old days. If you do it now at least you won't ruin your Christmas even more after you lose the match." Danny grudgingly nodded towards the seat opposite.

"Sit down then, and keep a look out the window for anyone else coming into the pub. It's embarrassing enough being here talking with you, let alone someone seeing me do it." They both smiled, there had been at least respect, if not friendship, in Danny's voice.

"A little bird told me you were injured. Not bad I hope?" Benjamin smiled.

"A little bird. Now that wouldn't be a greater rain coated tit called Dave would it, sat on his bike every night with his binoculars. We're going to call the police tomorrow night. I'm sure he can see into the nurses' flats from where he sits, the pervert."

"Well at least we try and hide him. Your Dad just rolls up in his big car, bold as brass. Arnie told him where to go the other night and he gave him a right mouthful back," Danny joined in with the smile spreading across Benjamin's face. "So what does he say anyway, your Dad?"

"That we're doomed and you're going to absolutely batter us. To not even bother turning up, just let you parade around the ground to your adoring fans. And

Dave?"

"That you're useless and we'll beat you by three or four. That you've got no shape, no game plan and no hope. That your first team's only spent about thirty minutes playing together in the last week and a half. Then again, he never did know much about football. I just needed to get rid of him, he was getting right on my nerves with all his cliché speak," again they both smiled.

"It frightens me sometimes." Shit, where did that come from? 'It frightens me'? They'd shared a few sentences and a smile or two and now he was telling Benjamin that he was frightened.

"I know," Benjamin's response was immediate and natural. "One minute it was just a game of football and the next, boom."

"Boom?"

"Yes, boom. My mum's knitting scarves and baking cakes. People in the street are telling me that we've got to stuff the White shite. Hundreds of people are watching and waiting to see if we can pull this off."

"Yes, and you might be used to all of this, the responsibility and all that from the factory, but I've never had it like this before in my life. So many people relying on me, counting on me to make this game happen. I don't know if they expect us to win or not, but they certainly expect us to put on a show."

"You're right, but forget the factory. This is completely different. Work is work, but beating you lot is life or death. No one can imagine losing to your lot on Boxing Day. I see it in their eyes as they talk, the expectation's something else. And sometimes I just don't know if I can do it, if we'll actually make it happen." Sipping their beer together they spent the next minutes in silence. How had they got to this? The scraping chair announced another round.

"You know," Benjamin hesitated, looking squarely at the table. "You know I always wanted to be you." What?

Danny's eyes seemed to double in size, surely now taking over his entire face.

"You wanted to be me? Why on earth would you want that?"

"Why? Big John's son? The Dad who wowed the crowds every week, who stopped and talked to half the town every day, who everyone looked up to. And our families would spend time together and you'd go home with him and I'd be left with Winston." Could he drown in his own saliva? Benjamin's storm died down and he quietly sipped his pint. There was no sign of embarrassment or regret at all, no sign of distress. Had Danny even needed to be there, or would any set of ears have been suitable for the small outburst? Well if Benjamin could do it.

"Well at least you managed to follow in your Dad's footsteps, to make him proud." The top of his new pint gave him focus. He'd been right, anyone or no one could hear the words, it was speaking them that mattered. "You wanting to be me really makes me laugh, because I always fucking hated being me. Always shamed by the fact I could never be John Junior, Little John or whatever else they'd have called me. Statto once told me about the history behind surnames. How each village knew that to survive it needed a Butcher, a Poulter, a Carter, a Fletcher and all the rest. How kids were forced into doing the same job as their Dads, to learn their trade and make sure that the Bakers always provided the daily bread. It always made me think. If my Dad had been John Footballer and I'd been Danny Footballer, and if my village had depended on me for survival, then they'd have been pretty fucked," Danny's facial muscles set into an almost crazed smile. "But that wasn't the case. The whole village didn't expect me to be as good as my Dad, so they were saved from my incompetence. But he did. He never said so out loud, but I could see it in his face, at every opportunity he created for me to show them what I could do, at every door he opened for me. The disappointment and the pity. The sadness that I'd never be able to do what he'd done. So if you really wanted to be me, you'd have been welcome. You've shown your Dad what you can do and I'm sure that Winston's very proud. I've never managed to get out of that shadow, to feel the warmth of the sunshine that you feel." There, he'd had his turn too. Benjamin broke the silence much quicker than Danny had expected or hoped.

"But you're wrong, you've got it all wrong. This is your village and you're giving them the game that they need to survive. Danny Footballer's doing what's expected of him. I overheard our Mums last night and they're raising us to an almost God like status. John would never have had the brains or the courage, Winston would've still been working out the details and hope to play it next year. We just put our heads down and did it," they both drank to that. "We don't have to be good by being the same. We can always be better by being different, being new. Our world isn't their world. We'll never get back to their days, so it's normal that we'll be seen in different ways. Let's face it, in both towns combined there are three butchers, no bakers and two cobblers. Ostlers, fletchers and the rest went away years ago. Forget the past and focus on now, that's what matters for us, and as things are at the moment we're doing a pretty good job." Danny looked up at Benjamin for the first time in minutes, seeing a belief in his eyes, a sincerity he hadn't necessarily detected in his words.

"You're right. In just over a couple of weeks we're going to give these towns a spectacle like they haven't seen in a long time." The refreshing wake up had arrived.

They talked more, all about the game. The challenges and the hardships of organising their teams. The work behind the scenes that would make it all a day to remember for the hundreds of people they expected to attend. The funny events from training and the people to watch out for. It wasn't a conversation between friends, Danny never believed that they'd be friends, but it was a conversation between people who had a common passion and a degree of respect. They laughed together and they sympathised over problems and challenges, two people facing the same test, which would be resolved on the same day. Benjamin looked at his watch.

"Quarter to ten. It's time for me to put in an appearance. They'll be expecting a few words of comfort, even if they do all look on me as Ebenezer Scrooge," at this they both laughed.

"Yes, it should be safe to go. I think Red Al's carol singing should be all finished by now. Just watch out, in case he's got Jingle Bells lined up as an encore. I'll follow you in a few minutes. I wouldn't want to turn up with you in any case, you know how quickly rumours start up, especially after the Christmas do." They looked each other in the eyes and Benjamin held out his hand.

"What happens in the Wheelwright's stays in the Wheelwright's, eh Danny?"

"Yep," they shook on it and Benjamin got up and left.

Danny sat back down and finished his drink, if possible feeling two stone lighter than he had in a long time. The two Dickensian characters by the fire had long gone, three replacements seated at the bar in eerie silence. Crossing the room he put his hand in his pocket and carefully took out the card, giving it one last look. Don't worry Bob, your secret's safe with me. Keep on writing your cards every year and savour all of the memories that they give you. Good old George must have been a great bloke to give you such good memories. The envelope floated down into the fire and a multi coloured flame licked up before quickly turning into smoke.

It was cold out and he fastened his coat for the ten minute walk over to the Bell and the end of the party.

"Good King Wenceslas looked out, on the feast of Stephen......"

18 GETTING THE BAND BACK TOGETHER

Danny shuddered as he sat on the stone bench, every muscle in his body reacting to the game of football he'd finished just a couple of hours earlier. The match against the Spartans had been their first against a proper opposition, though thoughts of it were a long way away as he waited for the others to arrive. He looked towards the bus station, picking them out straight away. Who could miss Annie's light step and Al's rigid march?

He winced as he stood up and a quick embrace and a too formal handshake followed. Not forgiven there yet.

"So how's it gone so far then?" *Let's get this over with and have a rest.*

"Brilliant. We got them both just as planned. Though it didn't help much with Al telling them both to eff off and threatening to hit them." *What?* His look received an icy return.

"You have to be careful Annie. Now that there's a bit of celebrity about the game everyone's looking for a piece of the action." *A piece of the action?* His eyes pleaded and Annie obliged.

"Fat Frank was apparently not fat enough. It's true that if we'd known that in advance we'd have found him a bit quicker. Looking for a fat bloke in a mobile phone shop in this town isn't the easiest of tasks after all."

"It's true, he looks like Richo now. Spends his Saturday afternoons out on his bike instead of eating burgers. He can still get the band back together though. He just needs a replacement euphonium and to find a new drum for one of his girls." That was good, Al was starting to lighten up a bit.

"And then Bill Swithins wasn't tall enough to be Ollie the Ostrich, even without his costume." It gets better. He should've missed the match and spent the whole afternoon with them.

"And he's a Blue bastard, can you believe it? All those years he dressed up as our mascot and he supported the Blues."

"Which is why you told him to eff off twice," Al's smile suggested that he'd taken some pride in his work. "He was so sweet though. He told us that he'd seen a panda costume in a charity shop and asked if the WI ladies would be able to alter it for him. His face was a picture when we told him we still had the original. So we've got one band to belt out some tunes and one mascot to entertain the kids. That just leaves the atmosphere to find." People said that their heart sank and Danny now understood why.

"Indeed, you've saved the best 'til last. And many thanks for inviting me along for the ride." On hearing his last words Al almost jumped to attention.

"Not that I know why you were invited. We've done quite well on our own to be honest, so I don't understand why we need you for this one." Perhaps he hadn't lightened up after all.

"Come on Al, we agreed that it would be better for us if Danny came along. And as it's that time of day, I think I'm about ready for a drink." Annie was the leader and they followed.

The White Hart was on the other side of town, an estate pub hidden between the old terraced houses where the workers at the local factories used to live. The houses were now full of young people with the means to buy their first home, but the pub had kept just enough of the older type of client to avoid closing like so many others had. The White Hart, the badge of King Richard II, and the fifth most popular pub name in England. The grand reputation of the name bore no resemblance at all to the pub as they approached early that evening. It was neither light and airy as the White promised, nor proud and majestic like a Hart. They all took a quick look from side to side, and when no ambush came they entered.

Instantly taken aback by a noise that wasn't evident from the outside, Danny's eyes quickly scanned the room. Every colour, size, age and gender of person seemed to be equally represented, as if the pub had been designed by some equality department somewhere. They crossed the floor to the bar, treading softly on a mixture of old wooden boards, thin carpet and spilt beer, accompanied by numerous pairs of eyes that had already picked them out as outsiders.

"So what are you three after, directions or drinks?" a young barman with an out of fashion beard greeted them with a smile.

"Drinks'll be fine thanks, we know where we are," Al's response was short and to the point, with no sign of the fear that Danny was starting to feel. There was no longer a television in the bar, with no sport to watch any more there was no need. An old fashioned jukebox was playing old music just loud enough to make it easy for the three to talk together without fear of being overheard.

"I can't see him anywhere, can you? I thought he might perhaps have a table in the corner or something." Al made it sound like they were looking for some sort of gangster.

"Nobody knows exactly what he was in to, or still is probably, but they all said that this was his HQ. People would come here, for orders or merchandise or other things, and then leave. What he was doing nobody knew, but doing something he definitely was," Annie was more excited than anything else. Was Danny the only one who was scared?

"That's right, and then every Saturday afternoon they'd all follow him to the ground for the game. He'd organise it all, from the welcome party for the away supporters to the singing and chanting inside. If anyone got out of line he'd have them sorted out, and if anyone didn't get out of line they risked the same. I ran with them for a while when I was younger, not that they'd remember me. There were tens of kids like me who'd come and go, but the core of the group were his boys. He was like a feudal lord in a way." Perhaps his badge was a White Hart too, or an ostrich? Al was straining his neck, looking again round the bar, trying to find the man they were looking for.

"He'll see you in a couple of minutes." What the? Danny turned quickly to see the still smiling barman behind them. "The Fist, he'll be free in a couple of minutes, then you can see him. Don't worry, he knows most of what goes on in this town." The three of them exchanged confused glances between sips of their drinks. Danny wasn't feeling any better than before.

A door that Danny had failed to see in the corner opened. People came walking into the bar in ones and twos, each one leaving the pub directly, with only quick glances and nods as communication to those who stayed. Five, six, seven people in all. Al talked quickly.

"The young lad at the back, he works for the local butcher. He was involved with the union lads for a while." He had more to add, but no time, as the man guarding the door beckoned them over with a nod of his head.

Striding quickly across the floor they passed through

the door that had been left open for them. Danny looked uncertainly at Annie as the door closed behind them. Al took another swig of his pint.

The sound of concrete under his feet announced their entry into a long, narrow back room, surely an old skittle alley. At the end of the room, sitting on the plate behind a large table, was the man they'd come to see. Early fifties Danny guessed and dressed in just a fashionable tee shirt, despite the cold outside. This displayed perfectly his tattooed arms, the rippling muscles keeping the skin tight and the pattern clear. The tattoos hadn't stopped on the arms however, spreading up his neck with stars and moons, like ivy growing over a country house. Above that a round face, saved some of its ridicule by a goatee beard and bushy sideburns, leading finally to a full head of hair. Below the table a pair of stonewashed jeans and some brightly polished Adidas Samba training shoes. It was almost like coming across a member of an ancient tribe lost deep in the Amazon forest. The face was bright and intelligent, two dark blue eyes shining in the middle. Danny sensed those same eyes burning into them, moving from one to the other, finally settling on him.

"So, Big John was too busy to come along himself was he?" the grin was unsettling. The voice deep and clear, almost as if he were an actor in a period drama.

"We're not here on his behalf, I just happen to be his son." Don't show him fear. "We want to talk with you about the match, we're trying to…" His interruption left no doubt that he had no interest in the story.

"I think you'll find that my playing days are behind me, though if the rumours are true about the crock of shit that you've got lined up to represent the Whites, I may be able to come out of retirement. Just for the last five minutes perhaps?" He liked grinning, like he was amused but a smile would be too much.

"They're playing quite well actually. They should give a

very good account of themselves," Al cut in and The Fist fixed him with a stare that would've melted lesser people.

"Alan isn't it? Yes, I remember you. You had a few months where you wanted to be in my gang," he sang the last words like Gary Glitter would have done years before. "Well in the end you weren't what we were looking for. You had far too much sense to get mixed up with my boys. And as for the Whites, I'm surprised that you hadn't heard that they lost 2 – 1 this afternoon to the Spartans, so I think the Blues will probably rip them to pieces." Another grin. Al seemed to be completely knocked off his track. Not only had The Fist remembered him, but he also seemed to know everything. Annie tried to take some control.

"Look Mr, er Mr Fist," he laughed. "Winning the game isn't what's important. It's playing the game, showing this town that we still have something to hold us all together. That's what we're trying to do. And to do that we want to get as many of the old crowd together as we can."

"So you'd like me to polish up my bovver boots, get my scarf out and waste my Boxing Day watching a few local kids run around would you?" still the grin. "Because at the moment that just isn't happening. A cold morning up the Works ground's the last thing I need for my arthritis, I can assure you. So thank you very much for coming, but if you don't mind I have further business to see to before it gets too late." Looking down at his table he started shifting pieces of paper around, clearly back about his business. From the corner of his eye Danny sensed Red Al changing gear. Please Al, not now.

"What, some more drugs to sell? Or more people to beat up? Is that what you've to see to? We know what you're like, you and your gang of lowlife. We came here in good faith to give you a chance to prove that you still care. To prove that the Whites still mean something to you and to this town. I know it won't be the same as before, but we have to start somewhere. I thought you were a fighter, but you're just a nothing, a nobody. Sitting in your dark little room organising your dirty deeds." Danny's heartbeat had doubled in the seconds it'd taken Al to explode. In front of him The Fist was maintaining his grin, but was clearly rattled by what he'd heard.

"You Alan should shut your mouth, turn around and leave now. You know so little of what I and my associates do in this town and it does you an injustice to talk, such, utter, bollocks!" his accents on the last words were brutal.

"No, we won't leave. Not yet." Danny stared at Al, wondering from where his courage came. "You say you work for this town and that you care for this town, but we see nothing. You have your little group of friends locked in here all afternoon, who leave the pub as soon as they're out of the room. You have your gang of hoodlums who've followed you for years, causing trouble whenever they could…"

"Whenever I let them Alan, not whenever they could. There is a difference," his fist slammed onto the table and they all stood motionless. Finally The Fist sighed and leaned back in his chair, a reluctant story teller who'd decided to tell a story that he knew he shouldn't. "The world that we live in Alan is full of people who were all born good. This world has, in some cases, changed these people. Small things, big things, all come and go, but in some cases they leave marks. Now these people need leaders, someone to tell them what to do, where to go. In this town Alan, it is I who give them this leadership. Politicians, our Mayor being a prime example, believe that they can talk to them, can appeal to them, but they're very mistaken. They'll never have the influence that I have. So what I can do is control them, to reduce the damage that they cause," he fixed Al with an almost sympathetic stare. "I knew as soon as you tried to get close to us Alan, that you didn't need controlling. You were good still, not like the rest. That's why you soon went away and found other friends." The three were silent, taken aback by the honesty with which The Fist had spoken. "And as for my friends this afternoon, we're working together on a very important project. At this festive season of the year it is more than usually desirable that we should make some slight provision for the poor and destitute, who suffer greatly at the present time. We choose this time, because it is a time, of all others, when Want is keenly felt, and Abundance rejoices. My friends were representatives from the local shopkeepers. We will certainly be trying to distribute a bit of Christmas cheer and help some people out." Sitting back he closed his eyes, almost as if telling his story had exhausted him. "So if there's nothing more for you to add, then please do leave me to get on with my business."

It was now or never. Without him realising his fear had disappeared, and Danny had one throw of the dice left.

"Listen, we appreciate the story you've told us, and even if half of it's true then you really do deserve the gratitude of the whole town. But we've more to tell as well. There's one secret left that might persuade you yet to come and join us," confidence was now flowing through him. "All of us have memories of you and your boys at Cherry Lane. When they were in fine voice, and fine humour, they created the atmosphere that the Lane was famous for." The Fist nodded in agreement and acknowledgement. "Well the secret's this. The game won't be played at the Works ground, because it's too small. There are hundreds of people coming to the game. Hundreds of people who remember the rivalry, who remember the importance and life that football used to give to this town. To fit all of those people in there's only one place around here capable. Cherry Lane. We're going to play the game at Cherry Lane." Breathing out deeply, like an athlete coming down after completing an event, he was finished. His target sat in front of him animated, off balance for the first time.

"Impossible! Cherry Lane has been in a state of decline

for the last five years. You'll never play a game of football there." Thrown by his lack of knowledge The Fist had lost his cool.

"It appears that you don't quite know everything going on in this town. We know because we saw it, we walked on it. It's magnificent, better than it's ever been. And there's a place there where you always used to stand that'll be empty," seeing The Fist so helpless was good. Nodding like a dog, in awe at the news he was hearing. As if to twist the knife Annie joined in, her voice gentle and comforting.

"So all we now need to complete the deal, win, draw or lose, is you and your boys. Imagine it, Cherry Lane bouncing again to Frank's beat and to your songs," The Fist was now completely still, like a statue praying, eyes closed and in deep thought. How long could he stay like this? Rocking forward he opened his eyes.

"I never dreamed these last years that I'd hear such a story, that the Lane would be an arena for sport again, and it makes me very happy to hear it. Listen, I'll come along, and I'll bring my boys." Excitement tingled all over Danny, the final piece falling into the puzzle. "But, there'll be a price," he paused. "I want a banner. Not a small one, a big one, big enough to cover the entire end, like the ones they used to have in Italy and Germany. I want the badge, in the middle, and I want the motto underneath. And I want it so big that they can see it from the International Space Station. You get me the banner, and I'll give you song and dance and laughter, and the Cherry Lane roar like you've never heard it before."

"Fuck off. Where are we going to get one of them from with a couple of weeks' notice, by asking Father Christmas?" Al's earlier calm seemed to have quickly turned to anger. "Why can't you just come along and join in like the rest?"

"Leave it Al," Danny stared at The Fist as he spoke. "Don't worry, we'll get you your banner. You just make sure you've got enough people to wave it up and down, otherwise you're going to look a right old idiot. We'll be back soon," he turned to the others. "Come on, we've spent enough time here already." He grabbed their arms, dragging them out with him.

"What was all that about Danny? Where are you going to get a bloody great banner?"

"Have faith Al, have faith. Just don't talk to me about it now. We'll sort it out, don't you worry." He was right though, where were they going to get a bloody great banner from?

19 ELF AND SAFETY

"Here early again, are you looking for a promotion?" Danny turned slowly towards the familiar voice.

"You know me Geeta, anything to be in the boss's good books." They shared a warm smile, the warmth needed on the cold December morning. There was still lots to be done, but everything was now clearer and easier. The things that he used to do only out of instinct, whenever there was an emergency, he could now do as and when he wanted. Today was going to be the perfect time to demonstrate it. It was time to act.

"Are the others here yet?" her look was surprised, almost as if the urgency of his question had caught her unprepared.

"Al and Statto yes, Richo came with you?"

"In the small meeting room in five minutes, quickly before the shift starts, tell the others." Could they really do this?

He was the last to arrive. The looks on the faces showed that Al had already shared the good news and that it hadn't been well received. Statto turned towards him.

"A fucking big flag, visible from the space centre. Has all of this pressure sent you crazy Danny?" Take that stupid smile off your face Al, we can do this. Now then, here we go.

"Come on Statto, where's your adventurous side gone? We've got the best brains in the town here. It's only a flag after all."

"Only a flag? What are we going to do, get Griz to nick all the sheets from the hospital, paint them and get the WI to sew them together?" Nice and positive Al. It was time to sort things out, once and for all.

"Look Al, you either want to be part of this or you don't. I'm sorry you didn't make the team, but there were lots of others who missed out too," Danny took no pleasure from the look of distress on Al's face. "The fact is that we're very close to the end now, but we still have some hills to climb. You can either stop moping around and start having some fun again or you can fuck off." Was that clear enough? In front of him Al was motionless and the others stared at him, surprised looks on their faces. He'd soon see if Al was going to be fun again. "Right then, that's actually not a bad idea Al. At least the part about getting the WI to sew smaller pieces together. Now come on give me some more." One by one he looked at them.

It was Geeta who broke the silence. He'd known that it would be, it had to be.

"Well, in fact I think I know how to do it." Statto looked surprised, Danny had never doubted. "I think there's a way to make the machines print differently. To take a big picture, split it up and print it out in pieces," Statto snorted, the others remained silent.

"Geeta, with all respect, the machines can't even print and cut out the same picture and keep running as they should." Danny raised a hand, silencing Statto and inviting Geeta to continue.

"Trust me, please Statto. I'm sure it'll work." Two minutes left, he had to finish it now.

"So what do we need?"

"I've got everything I'd need ready. Statto needs to

solve one problem for me in the control room and then we need a whole lot of material, plus access to a line for a couple of hours."

"Oh yeah, we'll just ask Winston if we can borrow a machine for a day shall we?" Not you as well Statto?

"Leave the material to me. My uncle's got some stuff that I'm sure he'll let us have," Richo ticked the first box.

"And leave the machines to me," Al's smile was ear to ear. "Mind you, we may have to work a night shift."

"Great, whatever we need. Statto, have a chat with Geeta and take a look at her problem and we'll talk later. Come on, another day beckons."

The echoes of the alarm had long since died away. Somehow the time passed slower when Geeta's arse was replaced by Marlon's balding head, searching in vain for the cause of the latest stop. How on earth could the finest German machinery be so often bamboozled by a piece of cloth? The top of Marlon's head transformed into a wide grin and he crawled from under the machine, in his hand the culprit of the third stop that morning.

"Okay Danny, it's alright now. I've saved your little arse one more time, so don't forget it when you're buying your Christmas presents." How could someone as nice as Marlon have ever got on the same side as Benjamin and the others?

"I just like keeping you fit for the match Marlon, you know that. You'll probably spend most of that on your hands and knees too, so get used to it." As they both smiled he picked up his radio, ready to instruct Statto to start her up again. It was twenty minutes until lunch break, nearly another half day gone already. He was counting down the days to Christmas now like a nine year old waiting for a new bike. It felt good.

Geeta was walking quickly towards him, looking troubled. Stopping in front of him she leaned forward, speaking quietly.

"Looks like there's some sort of problem. Dave says to get to Benjamin's office now." Now? This didn't sound good.

When he arrived Dave was huddled into the small space occupied by Benjamin's assistant, straining to hear what was coming from the closed office door.

"What's going on Dave?"

"Shhh, I'm trying to listen." Two seconds later Dave shook his head as he gave up.

"We're stuffed. It's all gone pear shaped. They just rolled in like the mob and they've been going at it for over an hour now. The game's off, we're finished," as he spoke Dave's head shook slowly from side to side.

"Slow down Dave, who rolled in?" How was Dave ever made production manager?

"The Council Danny, the Council and the police. We've been rumbled. There are a couple of suits and a uniform. They haven't stopped reading the riot act since they arrived. Fortunately Marsha was in there already, so she should've taken some good notes, but from what I can make out they're on to us and the game's off big time." The bastards. His hands balled into fists as he stared at the closed door.

Eventually the door swung open, releasing a loud female voice as it did. Danny and Dave took an immediate interest in the calendar on the wall.

"So you should just consider yourselves lucky. If your stupid plans had gone ahead you would have been in more trouble than you'd ever imagined. At least this way you should avoid prison." The owner of the voice humphed and started to leave the office, her accomplices behind her.

Slowly Benjamin followed, looking around him in silence. Things weren't good. Whatever had been said had taken the face normally modelled on confidence and turned it to one void of hope. Using his hands Benjamin silently invited the two of them into his office, to be greeted by the sight of Marsha carefully studying the notes she'd taken.

"So then, where to start?" his mouth finally freed from the forces that had held it, Benjamin opened the conversation.

"We're fucked. I heard most of what they said, the games off," Dave's outburst did little to help Benjamin, who had nothing to offer but a sigh. Marsha took over for him.

"I'd have to agree that on first hearing things don't sound too good, but nothing's over yet," Marsha's slight optimism had no effect on Benjamin's face.

"Well let's start with the bastard who grassed us up. It's got to be Holmes, the smarmy git. Who else could it be?" Danny felt a relief in blaming someone, even if he didn't yet know what he was blaming them for.

"Or we could start with that pillock Red Al, and his great idea to just say nothing and turn up on the day. That worked a treat didn't it?" Benjamin was going tit for tat.

"We all voted Benjamin. Al explained the risks and we all decided to go ahead anyway." Only a woman could get them back on track, and Marsha was conveniently placed.

"Or we could just start with the facts, and see where that takes us? Right, good. So we were in the presence of Walton, clearly the leader and seemingly employed with the sole aim of disrupting our match. She gave us some civil service titles, but was surprisingly hard and determined," Marsha would easily have recognised that. "With her was Patel, the only one who's been voted in, but he was quiet. He looks after Sports and other things. The uniform was Witham, deputy chief constable. Also very silent, but provided supporting nods and grunts." And Benjamin, still emotionless and quiet?

"So that's who, now for the what, yes?"

"It's coming Danny, hold on. You're right that they were here based on 'evidence received', and they assured us it was all for our own good. To help us avoid some dreadful consequences such as serious fines and potential imprisonment." Was that a flicker of movement from Benjamin? "Anyway, our problems are pretty straightforward and all revolve around one central subject, so here goes." Danny and Dave sat down as she double checked her notes. Marsha then cleared her throat and started.

"Everything revolves around access to the stadium, and as importantly the actual ground that it's built on. It's Council property and with no authorisation we'd all be breaking and entering and therefore breaking the law and risking a fine and possible imprisonment."

"But we'd be using a key, the groundsmen have got a key." Oh dear Dave, not again.

"The Council would of course love to be able to help us out, but there are lots of considerations and time's short. This was all going straightforward until Patel did talk at one time about 'true owners', at which point Walton shut him up with an icy glare that I would have been proud of," she laughed to herself. "But that could mean anything and nothing."

"So it's just a case of getting them to change their minds then? Then we're ready to go?" Danny's mind was whirring through a hundred scenarios. What was the problem there?

"Just a case yes, but they obviously came here to let us know, quite clearly that they didn't want to do that. IF we could manage to persuade them otherwise there would then be small things like insurance and permits. And that gives us this," the thud of a large file dropping onto the table woke anyone not paying attention. "The stadium itself is nowhere near suitable to stage a match, with no fewer than twenty four points that would need fixing in order for the necessary permissions to be obtained." What little hope there'd been in Benjamin's face just disappeared.

"It's true that if all of those pages were stuck together

it would be a list longer than my arm." Danny feebly tried to brighten the tone, but Marsha came back quickly and positively.

"To be fair there are a few of the points where we might need specialist help, but on the whole we should be able to do most of them with some good old fashioned hard work. It's just a case of manpower and time."

"So not too bad then?"

"There's other stuff like security and stewards, but nothing that's impossible," the hope in her voice finally seemed to be waking Benjamin from his trance. His hand slapped down on his desk as he leaned forward.

"Right then, listen up. The whole thing stinks. That was no normal meeting we had, there's an agenda hiding somewhere behind it, and we need to get to the bottom of it. Walton and all of her resistance is there for a reason and we need to understand it. Marsha, start having a closer look at the list of work and see what we'd need in order to get it done." Needing no extra encouragement she got up and left, taking Dave with her.

Danny and Benjamin's eyes met, memories of their evening together in the Wheelwright's coming back. A quiet knock on the door broke their unease.

"Laetitia, what do you want?" Danny was shocked to hear the name and turned eagerly to see the face. Had she been crying?

"I'm so sorry Benjamin, I really am. It was Ted who told her all about the game. As soon as she knew she was like a raging bull in the office. Mayor Banks didn't stand a chance, or at least he didn't have any energy for a fight."

"Ted the turncoat? Can't you control your boyfriend?" Benjamin's tone was calm as he questioned his sister.

"Ex-boyfriend, but that story can wait. Listen, I've got some information that could be useful. We haven't got much time." Sitting down again they prepared for more stories, and Laetitia obliged.

"It's a bit of an old tale in fact," she started, "that first came to light a few years ago, when the Council started to look at redeveloping the ground. I've been researching the story since I first heard about it, mostly in my spare time of course, because it's quite interesting and could also bring clarity to the Council when it comes to the status of the ground. Now, I don't want to bore you with history, but quite a lot of this is very old stuff, so here we go. After the invasion by William the Conqueror the land around here was given to one of his Lords, a William De Lisle-Hubert. The De Lisle-Huberts continued to be the major land owners around here right until the early 19th Century, even though they changed their name to Herbert in order to make it less French sounding during the Napoleonic wars. Bad business decisions during the industrial revolution reduced the family fortunes though, and in 1869 the last part of Herbert land was finally sold off to one of the local self-made men of the time." Danny could see an admiration in Benjamin's face that he shared. Laetitia had been very careful to share her eye contact between the two, giving nothing away. "Now to football. Playing the game was banned on several occasions through the years. The ruling De Lisle-Hubert in 1640 was particularly upset when a new ban was sent down 'to prevent the playing of football on the King's Land and the Land of his Lords'. More out of frustration than real power he decided to give a piece of land to the people, to make it common land. He hoped that this would give people the right to play their matches as and when they wanted, without fear of breaking the law." At this point she gave them both a hard stare. "Through the ages the land has been moved between various authorities' control, but always on the understanding that it remained the property of the people, and that they had the right to play football upon it."

"And that land's the land around Cherry Lane?" Danny already knew the answer, but asked anyway.

"Exactly. In the late 1800s when the council of the

time were deciding how to manage this piece of land that was getting more and more in the way of the town expansion, they firstly made it into local grassland and finally turned it into a proper stadium."

"So you're saying that Cherry Lane's free to use for football whenever we want? That we can play there on Boxing Day?"

"Not so quick Danny. The ground belongs to the people, but the stadium's still Council property," his initial optimism faded. "That makes questions like access and liability even more complicated. In addition there are also new rules about common land, with ownership often now reverting to descendants of the original owner. Or in the absence of them, directly to the local authorities."

"So now it does belong to the council, and they can finally sell it and develop?" Benjamin almost sounded interested in buying.

"So it now means that local Councils have to go through a set process to ensure that there are no living descendants before ownership reverts. Now all of this so far my colleagues from the Council are aware of, to some degree or other. But what nobody except me knows is that I think I've found a descendant of the Herberts." Looking at the shock on Benjamin's face Danny could only imagine how he must look himself.

"Which means?"

"Which means that we could put serious pressure on them to change their decision, with the support of the Herbert. From there anything's possible, we still have a chance."

20 THE NIGHT SHIFT

"Richo, where the fuck are you?"

"I'm over here Al, don't worry I'll have some light on soon" The mild click of a light switch settled some of Danny's nerves and prevented Al from needing to answer. They were all there, the four musketeers and Milady, out of breath through the excitement of what they were doing. It would be wrong to say that they'd broken into the factory. Breaking in meant climbing over fences and forcing old locks. They'd simply driven into the car park and walked through the door, kindly opened for them by Kevin the security guard. Red Al had called in a few favours and a few crumpled notes had been exchanged, but that was how things worked in the security industry.

Danny looked around him as bags were dropped and computers placed. He smiled as Al carefully placed a pack of sandwiches on an empty desk. It was good to see his old friend back to normal.

"Right then, this is as bright as the light's going to get. We can't risk putting the main lights on. Someone's bound to see them out here, so we'll just have the emergency circuit on. You've all got torches?" Heads nodded all round. "Right then, over to you Geeta." Geeta replaced him in the middle, an exchange that he was happy to make. With a deep breath she started.

"Okay, so you all know the plan?" Did Danny have anything to do?

"And what a very good plan it turned out to be," Statto looked impressed and seemed pleased to praise her.

"It'll probably be a long night, but just focus on your jobs and everything'll be fine. Any questions?" There were none. Like mice they scurried off, kit in hands, leaving Danny alone.

He scratched his head and looked around. The factory, so familiar in the day, was a place that he hardly recognised in the darkness of the security lighting. What were they doing? It was no surprise to see that they were working on Line 3, his line and the one they knew best. Geeta was tapping away on her laptop next to the control panel. The extra light from the screen lit up her face, giving her a ghostly look that suited her. How long had she been waiting to try out her ideas? They'd never know.

"Bastard."

A reflection from the floor placed Richo somewhere next to the printing unit. Like a scuba diver he was passing under the machine, guided by his miner's lamp, and evidently having problems carrying out his task. No matter how much he swore there was surely a smile on his lips.

Up in the control room a macabre shadow danced across the window. Knowing that it was Statto's face that formed it made it no less frightening. What was frightening was Al, fighting his way through the material that would finally be used to make the flag. He supposed that now was as good a time as any.

"Need any help?" a shake of the head, no words in answer to his question. "Just tell me what to do and I'll do it," not even a shake of the head. Danny waited.

"I wanted to play in this game more than anything else in the world you know," finally Al spoke, searching an answer from Danny's eyes with a vacant stare. It would have to be honesty.

"Al, there were at least fifty others who came to the trials with that same dream, and hundreds more who would've done if they'd known about it. My only thoughts were to get the best eleven out on that pitch. I just want to…"

"Win. I know that. At least now I do," Al took some steps towards him. "Look Danny, I'm sorry. Sorry for being such a great big pillock. I'm just glad that after all of it you still don't mind me tagging along," Al's large hand reached towards him. Before Danny knew what happened he'd taken his friend in a large embrace.

"You soft git Al. You and tagging along have been the last ten years. You manage to do more to help us out when you don't want to than most people do when they do want to. So shut up, forget everything and tell me what I need to do." They hugged again and moments later were two old friends, sorting through uncle Mick's material, separating the good from the bad.

How long they spent sorting the material he didn't remember. The bottle uncorked they exchanged stories of the good old times with ease. Finally Geeta came round, the stern look on her face suggesting that now was the time. No, it wasn't stern, it was concentrated, proud, excited. Anything but stern.

"Right then, it's time. Time to see if this thing can really print lots of small bits of jigsaw puzzle. We'll start her up slow and then jog her through a few cycles to make sure that everything's in place first." She connected the manual controller and line 3 whirred into life. In the silence of the empty night it sounded as loud as a low flying airplane coming into land, surprising them all. Al hurried out of the workshop, returning quickly with a wide smile.

"Don't worry, you can hardly hear a thing outside. And he's a sleep anyway."

Reassured, Geeta hit the button once and the

mechanism moved forward a carefree cycle. Twice more she pressed and twice more a painless movement forward. Crack! She ducked as push number four rewarded them with a loud bang. The violence of the sound in the silence of the night was extreme. Almost diving under the machine she was gone. For long seconds nothing, just the sound of movement, a rat beneath the floorboards. Silence and finally she emerged, a grim look on her face.

"Well?" Al looked petrified.

"Dave's glasses, the ones he lost this morning," she broke into a wide grin, clearly unable to keep up the pretence. The breath that Danny had been holding surged out of his lungs. Whatever stress he'd been feeling had now all gone.

Back in position she started jogging the machine through its cycles again. Ten, no problem. Twenty and everything was going fine. Now to automatic mode on slow speed. One, two minutes and still no problem. Right then, full speed, her smile getting broader and broader the faster it went, before finally bringing it again to a halt.

"Well then, that's the easy bit done. With the new pieces it still turns. The question remains though, will it keep turning?" It would be difficult to be worse than before. "Al, could you get some material, ten pieces should do. Statto, it's your turn." Al carefully loaded several pieces of material and all eyes went on Statto as he opened up his computer in business like fashion.

The start was instant, nothing gradual this time. Al's material was carried along the seemingly flatbed surface, first printed and then cut. It was impossible to see the results on the machine bed and together they moved to the end of the machine, slow steps followed by faster ones. They had arrived, the moment of truth.

"Amazing. Just like a giant puzzle. Just not cut right at the moment. It looks like The Fist will get his banner after all," the smile on Geeta's face was a picture. Taking quick steps, Danny breathed shallow breaths as he placed the pieces of his own puzzle in place. He nodded quickly, they were going to do it.

A sharp noise jolted Danny from his contemplation. Another pair of Dave's glasses? No, there was a bright light and a sound. Steady, footsteps. Not a divine intervention surely. Squinting as his eyes adjusted to the glare of the fully lit workshop, he focussed in the direction of the footsteps. The rough shape of a body, the head still obliterated by the bright lights. Finally focussing he saw Winston approaching. Winston? It couldn't be, not at this time in the morning? Looking around him he quickly saw the realisation sinking into the faces of his accomplices. Before any of them could talk the footsteps stopped and Winston's clear voice rang out in the near empty workshop.

"Well, well, well. What have we got here? I know that we have a few orders that need finishing before Christmas, and I know that Dave likes you all to put in a good shift, but I didn't know that he'd put on a night shift." Good natured at least. Danny's whirring brain was stopped by a female voice to his side.

"It was all my idea, blame me for everything. The material's all ours, we haven't taken anything from the warehouse, honest. I really, really am sorry because you've always been very good to me, to all of us," Winston raised his hand and Geeta obeyed. Danny felt his temperature rising, angry that he'd let Geeta take the rap. Angry too that he had nothing else to add. In silence he joined her, looking down at the floor, staring at the pieces of the giant puzzle that just a few minutes earlier they'd hoped would make their name. Now they looked like shrouds, waiting to wrap around their discarded bodies, once Winston had fired them all.

"Calm down Geeta, please. I don't often come to the factory at this time of day I can assure you, but tonight I had some documents that needed collecting." Danny saw

Winston look in his direction as he tapped the file under his arm. "I don't expect that you often need to come at this time of night either, so I'm assuming that you had a good reason to be here too?" he smiled at them, looking more like an elderly school master than an angry owner of their workplace. "Or at least I did until I saw the badge on that pile of material on the floor. Where on earth did you get a Whites banner as big as that from, and why on earth are you cutting it into pieces?" Geeta had offered to take the rap, and now she deserved to take a bit of any glory that might be flying around that night. Danny looked over to Geeta, his eyes inviting her and she obliged, telling her story from the very beginning.

As she finished Winston took the two pieces in his hand and dropped them to the floor. Again he spoke in his kind, reassuring voice.

"And so you're telling me that, once you've changed the cutting rules, this machine of mine will be able to print you out a whole flag, perfect for sewing together?" her nod seemed to confirm and Winston sat down, indicating the machine with an outstretched hand. Danny walked behind her, close enough that he could whisper unheard by the others.

"Well then Geeta, you've been waiting for long enough, and now it's here. It's your time, to show what you can do." He quickly squeezed her hand.

A few more taps on Geeta's keyboard and Al was again loading material as the machine whirred back into life. Five minutes it took, no longer, and at the end a perfectly printed, perfectly cut flag lay in pieces on the floor. Geeta wasn't finished with being the boss, and Danny didn't mind one little bit.

"Right then lads, get it packed up and I'll drop it off with Mary and the girls tomorrow morning. If everything goes to plan we can take it down to the White Hart tomorrow night. Richo, you can take the new connectors out and…."

"No, leave them. We'll see how they go tomorrow." The volume and speed of Winston's intervention surprised them all. "If you really believe that they can help out, we can do nothing worse than give them a try out between now and Christmas. Well done, all of you. Well done." He started to walk down the workshop, towards the stairs and his office. Danny joined the others as they set about tidying up, silent and bewildered, doing everything they could to give Winston no excuse to change his mind. The sound of footsteps stopped. "Oh, and Geeta, I think that Benjamin might like a word with you in the morning."

Out in the car park it was all animated chatter as they placed the material in the back of the van. Danny could hear them, excited that their plan had worked, excited that they'd been caught red handed, excited that they'd got away with everything. The Fist would have his banner after all. Driving out of the car park Danny stared in front.

The first challenge had been successfully negotiated, now he just had to make sure that there would be a game for the flag to get waved at.

21 THE THREE WISE MEN

The Copper Kettle coffee shop was just next to the Town Hall. Danny flopped into one of its leather effect sofas and squeezed his eyelids shut. The smell of the coffee from his cup wafted about in front of him. What chance did caffeine have against the adrenaline running around his veins? The three hours of sleep that he'd squeezed in after the night shift had helped him to focus again, to focus on his life that was currently flashing by like a train through a country station. The evening spent with John, Winston, Benjamin and Laetitia, preparing for the meeting that would take place later that morning. The night spent with the rest of the gang, making The Fist's flag. All the time making sure that neither group was aware of the problems that the other was experiencing. Diddley dum, diddley dum.

Laetitia had been great. Filling them in on the Herbert story and promising them that her discovery could be revealed, if it was absolutely necessary. She had more detail about the apparent hold Walton had on Mayor Banks and also about the other concerns over the state of the ground. It was also her who had arranged the meeting for that morning, their one chance for the old men to try and assert some influence over the Mayor. Yes, she'd been great.

"Danny," his eyes opened a fraction, revealing Winston taking the seat opposite him. Neatly dressed and showing no signs of fatigue from his own night time excursions, he quickly took a document from his folder, leaving Danny to carry on with his thoughts.

"Morning Winston. I would give you a penny for those thoughts, but you've got enough already. Ha ha ha." Who else could it be? Rolling forward Danny saw his Dad arriving, with Benjamin following closely behind.

"Good morning BIG John," Winston's emphasis on the 'BIG' was perfectly weighted to have effect without being sarcastic. "I hope you had a fruitful night. You can add Private Investigator to your list of accomplishments now can you?" The newcomers sat down.

"Indeed, indeed. So is that your blackmail dossier then?" his Dad's eyes were firmly focussed on Winston's folder.

"Oh I wouldn't say that. I couldn't possibly think of this morning's meeting as anything other than a discussion. Blackmail's a term reserved for extortion of money and favours, while we'll simply be asking for the community to be allowed to use what rightfully belongs to it." They all knew the potential importance of the contents of the folder, so carefully collected the previous night during Winston's visit to the factory. Was he at a tennis match? Danny's head was just moving from side to side as the wise old men spoke with each other. Was his emptiness due to tiredness or anger? Neither, it was relief. It was time for others to play their roles.

"And Walton? Do you have anything?" John's eyes sparkled as Winston finished the question.

"Oh Indeed I have. It wasn't even tough in the end. One look at the Council website and I was half way there." John leaned forward, his eyes darting from side to side. "It's Duckface," a mouthful of tea exploded from

Winston's face.

"Duckface?"

"Yes, exactly. You remember, old Kylie Donovan, the one with the pouty lips. Duckface we used to call her at school. The pout's died down a bit, luckily for her, but the rest of the face hasn't changed at all. Well, apart from filling out a bit." Did even Winston know what he was talking about?

"Kylie Donovan's putting pressure on Banks? Is that what you're trying to tell me?" John fixed Winston with a stare.

"Come on Winston, wake up a bit. We've got kick off in a few minutes. Walton, the one who's leading the dance, she's Duckface. Or she was at any rate. It looks like she went away and got married, changed her name, got divorced and came back. She obviously kept her new name, for fear of people realising that she was Duckface, but I spotted her straight away. It's her causing all the trouble." At last, at least it now looked like Winston understood.

"So now we know who she is, but do we have any idea as to why she's wanting to get in our way? She's been away for so long, I can't believe she's got any local grudges."

"Other than the fact that we all used to call her Duckface. It could be Duckface's revenge. Ha ha ha." Winston sighed, Danny started to feel frustration.

"Come on Dad, we haven't got long. So who could she be working with?" Taking a sip of his coffee John leaned back, definitely looking pleased with himself.

"Well we had the same question, so we dug a bit deeper. Annie had a play with some of that facial recognition stuff and found this photo somewhere in that old Facebook thingy," a newly printed photo was pulled out of John's pocket. Not a remarkable photo, just two middle aged people in a loving embrace, with carefree smiles for the camera. The woman was clearly Kylie Donovan, and the man they knew well. It was unmistakeably Holmes, Billy Holmes and Kylie Donovan, arm in arm and posing for the camera. "It was taken three months ago as far as we can tell."

"But isn't Billy still married to Mel?"

"He is indeed. And that could be information that's useful to know." More ammunition for the old men, but could they use it?

"If you're right I think we've more cards to play than Holmes has, when it comes to Banks. We'll soon find out anyway. Let's keep all of this quiet though, until we're sure that we absolutely need it," Winston was taking the lead and John nodded in agreement. Benjamin reminded them all that he was there.

"Anyway, it's almost time. You're sure there's nothing else that we can do?" Shaken heads all round. "So we just need to find Laetitia's mystery man then." Yes, the mystery man. She'd surprised them, kept it right until the end. Someone to help them with the legal talk she said, seeing as she wasn't invited to the meeting. Some Open University student who she was mentoring and who'd been helping her to find the last Herbert. One more piece of intrigue and mystery to add to the rest on this morning of the unknown.

"Come on Winston, off we go. We've got Mister X to find and brief before we go in."

Walking out of the café Danny started to feel it. He'd felt it many times before as he'd looked at his Dad, a feeling that he knew was jealousy. As a kid it had nearly destroyed him. On this day it just made him feel stronger. He was getting used now to fighting for this game, but now it was time for the oldies to take over. He'd sit there powerless, jealous that Big John and Winston were in there fighting for them. Jealous but proud, and ready for the next steps, whatever they may be.

It was mild outside again, the changeable weather that was forecast to continue over the next days. Anything could happen. Danny looked around but there was no one there who looked like they were Laetitia's legal friend. Winston spoke quietly, as if to himself.

"Looks like they're late. Open University she said and she claims to have never met him in person. But he should know us? I can't honestly think we'll need him, not with everything we've got lined up." The four of them stood around waiting. A voice from behind startled them, despite its quietness and even measure.

"Well, well, well, if it isn't the grand old gentlemen of the twin towns," Danny turned quickly with the rest. What's he doing here? There was no mistaking him, the neatly groomed beard and bushy sideboards struggling to find a hiding place on the round face. The smart black trousers and almost neatly pressed shirt were well topped off by a raincoat, all standing atop a well-polished pair of Adidas training shoes. John was first to speak.

"Well my word, Marley, what are you doing around here? I thought you only came out on Christmas Eve. Ha ha ha."

"I see your humour hasn't changed much these last years John. Though that trick that you did getting those Blue bastards relegated really did make me laugh."

"There's no need for that Marley. That team was my life. I've only just started talking to him again, so don't get me going," the three older men looked at each other and laughed, With no idea what was going on Danny did the obvious and joined in.

"Do you three know each other?" Was it possible?

"Know each other? We're old friends from childhood, drifted apart as young men. One became a top footballer, one became a respected business man and football club owner. And I became The Fist." The special look that he gave Danny made no attempt to conceal the pleasure that this revelation was giving him.

"So what brings you here today? It's a bit out of the way for your normal work isn't it?"

"You still don't get it Winston? I'm here because of your daughter." Danny was beginning to feel ill. Not only did The Fist know his Dad, but he was also studying law part time and was going to be a key player in the day's meeting. The news seemed to be sinking in with the others too.

"So you're.."

"The story's long Winston and we don't have time. You know that looking after mum like I did took away a bit of my childhood, especially the bit where I was supposed to learn. Well I took it up again recently and Laetitia has been a great help to me. And then we started to exchange recently on some local topics where she needed help. It was the least I could do to be that help, especially as the subject is also something close to my heart."

"So what've you got planned for today then?"

"Me? Nothing special at all. I'm hoping that you've got enough stories on these bastards to keep them quiet, and I'll just make sure that the correct procedures and regulations are followed. There are a few points that I may need to emphasise, but I really am relying on you two to do all of the talking," there was no emotion in his voice as he spoke, matter of factly. Winston and John were going to have to win the war.

"And the big secret, the last of the Herberts?"

"If, and only if, it's needed then I've been trusted with the information. But that's a big if. So then, we've got five minutes for you to tell me everything you know," and with that the Three Wise Men huddled around exchanging information, leaving Danny and Benjamin alone.

"Didn't get to say much did we," Benjamin's statement was expressionless.

"It wouldn't have helped much anyway. This is a game for the oldies. Are you staying?" Benjamin shook his head.

"No. Dad says I've got to go back and see Geeta. Wouldn't explain why, he just said that the Line had been running all morning without any stops, and I should perhaps ask her why." The sly old dog. Winston was missing no opportunities. "You stay though, let me know as soon as there's any news." Avoiding any last good byes Benjamin left.

Forgotten by now Danny looked on as the old guard entered the Council Offices. Melchiot, Kasper and the other one, the Three Wise Men. Everything was now in their hands and all he could do was go back to the café and wait.

His old seat was waiting for him, a Danny sized hole in the middle. Drained of his adrenaline, and with nothing to do but wait, the heavy eye lids were soon closing in rhythm to the café music. Four calling birds, three French hens. A subconscious smile formed, he knew little about global warming or the capital of Slovenia, but Christmas poultry was easy to his lips. That was tradition for you. At the disturbance of every new customer he jolted forward and scanned the exit towards the Town Hall. Nothing again.

Jolted again he stopped, still and shocked. How long had it been, an hour, longer? His stomach dropped, nothing but disappointment remaining. No, it couldn't be. It wasn't supposed to happen like this. Where was the surprise, the tension, the dreaded wait to hear the news? In front of him were the Wise Men, brazen in their laughter and smiles. Were there any surprises left to be revealed? It was the perfect Christmas present, found in a cupboard in July. Danny forced a weak smile as he pulled himself to his feet and went to join the party.

"Ha ha ha, Danny boy you should've seen it. A master class in negotiation." And bribery no doubt. John's enthusiasm raised his smile up to level five.

"So it's sorted?" he didn't need to ask. The others didn't need to answer.

"He was surprised at the start. Mayor Banks was

expecting some younger opposition." Like him and Benjamin no doubt. Winston was ready to carry on.

"Surprised at the start and he never recovered."

"Duckface tried to steady the ship and blind us with procedure, but our legal representative was having none of that," The Fist gave a polite nod of acknowledgement.

"I thought that the Billy Holmes connection had done it, but finally she came back with her last gambit, she went all in." Winston the poker player? It wouldn't be a surprise. "She put everything on that old fairy tale, on the last Herbert." Danny's interest grew and he jumped in.

"So you told them who it was? You know the name?" Fever pitch. One surprise present was left to be opened.

"Signed, sealed and delivered. All of the proof that was needed, all of the documents official and stamped."

"Ha ha, come on Winston, tell him. The last Herbert's only bloody Marley, hiding his royal heritage all along." Danny's head almost spun round completely as he shot a look at The Fist, who even managed to look menacing with a large degree of discomfort on his face.

"You?"

"Yes Daniel, me. It's a very long story that I'd prefer to keep to myself, so don't think that you need to tell it on the mountains." The Fist, Lord of the Manor and all that. One last rush of adrenaline hit him.

"So that's it then. We've won. The game's on?" The look on Winston's face gave comfort. Danny's eyes were then pulled towards his hands, as he noticed now not one, but two large folders.

"We've won and we can use the ground. IF," Winston paused for dramatic effect and raised the new folder in the air, "IF we can fix all of the things noted in this file and obtain all of the necessary permits. Before Monday morning." Who needed an easy life anyway? "So still a bit of work to do, I think." The work would be done, but now was time for winding down.

"Well it must be your round Lord Herbert. I'll have a

pint please. Ha ha. Who'd have thought it."

"My name's Marley and it always has been John. It was my mother's name. I never knew my father, and I certainly never missed him."

"Yes, come on John. You can get them in. It must be a good twenty years since you bought us both a drink, thirty even. And I think we're going to need one. Mayor Banks was right, we may have won that first battle, but there's still a long, long way to go. The organisation we can manage, or we can at least do our best, but what we need now is people. Without them we'll do nothing." Danny was again relegated to being a spectator as the older versions continued. "Well, you seem to have the radio sorted, can you do anything about the television, the local news. Didn't you knock around with that presenter when you were younger?"

"I seem to remember I did, but I'm not actually thinking that a story like that'll actually help us. Ha ha ha. But on the other hand, isn't Colin Grant, the producer, one of your Dib dib dib friends Winston? Couldn't we tap him for a few minutes of airplay?"

By the time Danny's gaze found him Winston was already sat there, telephone to ear, just waiting for someone at the other end to answer.

22 CALLING ALL HANDS

Another day at Marshalls, his step springier than ever, fuelled by the Council backing down and the match being a day closer. The laughter of others always brought a smile to his face and today was no exception, the ripples hitting him even as he got changed. Trust Richo, right in the middle of the group with Marlon at his side.

"Come here Danny, have you seen it yet? We do look the dog's don't we?" Richo's excitement was evident and everyone parted to let him through. In Richo's hand was a newspaper. He called it a newspaper, though that was more because it was a combination of paper and print than the fact that it contained news. Yet another disposable item in a disposable age. Looking at the offered page he felt his body temperature rise by a good two degrees in a matter of seconds. His Dad in print he was used to, but his Mum on page three?

"They took it in the car park yesterday afternoon. Look at Richo, all playboy. Me, I'm just attitude man," the pride in Marlon's voice was undisguisable. And yet, there she was, beneath the Kitcheneresque headline 'Your Towns Need You'. Richo and Marlon in White and Blue shirts, face to face, their grins barely hidden beneath the confrontational pose that the photographer had been looking for. On either side, dressed in hat and scarf, were Mary and Edith. It looked like some bizarre Blue and White minstrel show, but it certainly did its job. Nobody could pass it by without laughing and being drawn to the story below, telling all about the match the next week and the need for as many people as possible at Cherry Lane that Saturday. Bring your gloves and buckets, your barrows and brushes. No one was too small or too old to help, all would be welcome. There were certainly no punches being pulled in that story.

He could just hope that it all worked. Big John on the radio all day, Mary on page three of the newspaper, and every known social network being networked as much as possible. Yes, they needed people.

The morning passed with nothing special happening, except for those seconds continuing to tick down. Statto made one of his rare trips out from the control room.

"So Danny, a good result yesterday then?"

"Indeed, it looks like Laetitia's special guest tipped the balance. Mind you, it must've been close to tipping with the other two sat on it already, either tipping or breaking," Danny giggled at his joke, but Statto was thinking of other things.

"Not just that though, we finished all our orders an hour before the end of the day. The big white bearded guy came a week early. And it looks like it was just us. Geeta and Marlon were pretty busy everywhere else." Trust Statto to have been thinking about the factory on a day where they needed presents from elsewhere.

"Must be something to do with those changes we made the other night. Anyway, I'm taking my afternoon. Christmas shopping," he detected the sympathy in Statto's frown. "So you're in charge. Now everything's running fine just don't let me down."

"As if I would."

Shopping for Danny was always done in proper shops. Paying a bit extra to put money into the tills of people whose name he knew, even if that often meant reading it off a name badge, was a price worth paying. His three presents didn't hold him back for long, all being bought in time for a late lunch at the café near the bus station. Lost in a bowl of pasta and dreaming of a wonderful Maradonna type run through the Blues defence for an injury time winner, the slight vibration coming from his inside pocket woke him up. Smartphones had never grabbed him, just a way of getting bad news quicker and more often. His small mobile could still do calls though, the incoming ones more often than not bringing him trouble. What did his Dad want?

"Good afternoon, British Gas, how can I help you?" Their trade mark answer, a response long out of fashion as the notion of any energy company being British was long gone. The lack of an accepted coded reply warned him that the call was serious.

"What, so you mean they want to do an interview on the telly, tonight?" More excited words from John.

"Yes, great news. Just between the national news and the weather? And on a Friday with the sports round up. Yes, especially with the Super League Winter break, they'll have nothing else to talk about. How on earth did you manage that?" John was eager to tell his tale. No, not blackmail at all, old contacts and a few favours, plus a genuine reporter's interest in community life.

"But why me?" Danny's hand went straight to the table, to stop him falling off his chair. Him, on the television, for everyone to see?

"And live, live? Are you sure it's a good idea Dad. Think about it eh, me and Benjamin. It'd surely make more sense if it was you and Winston. You know, the old adversaries, Blue versus White, like it was." Yes, they needed that angle. Seeing Big John on the screen would get them streaming down to help out, guaranteed. Danny could sit at home with a cup of tea and watch. If the television companies insisted on helping them out he wouldn't say no, he just didn't want to be a part of it.

"What do you mean they don't want you? Show it as it is, the youngsters doing something to help. They must be mad. What? But you said the youngsters, why would they want Mum and Edith too?" Things were going from bad to worse. Why say they want youngsters and then say that the two old dears would be on as well. An embarrassing interview was one thing, but front row seats in a freak show was something else.

"Yes, yes. Okay. I'll be there for five. Yes, I'll put a shirt on, something smart, but I'm not wearing a tie. Yes, I know. Thanks for letting me know. See you later." Eyes closed, breathe slowly, everything will be okay. Video killed the radio star and television killed the football star. But now he needed it to save him. Just the regional news, what would it be, five minutes, if that? With Benjamin he wouldn't get a word in anyway. Perhaps he'd get his hair cut on the way home, and take a look to see if there were any nice shirts in the new shop near the war memorial.

Five o'clock sharp, new shirt washed and ironed, old hair cut and gelled. The mirror at home and the glass doors as he entered the studio both confirmed that he brushed up quite well. His name was on the list and he was quickly shown into a room where Mary and Edith were already waiting. The picture in the morning's paper must have captured the imagination as they were both there with their scarves and rosettes on show. Two large hugs and a quick brush down later he took a seat, just as Benjamin entered the room.

"Danny, you pillock, why'd you have to do that?"

"Well it's nice to see you too, what exactly did I do?" Shit, how could they both have the same shirt?

"We're the Blues and you're the Whites. Was it too difficult to figure out? Put on a white shirt, put on a red, green, yellow or pink shirt, but not a bloody blue one, for crying out loud." The two mothers burst into laughter.

"Look at the pair of you. You've been like that since you've known each other. Always turning up in the same place, wanting to do the same thing."

"Yes, and always falling out because you didn't want to do it together." More laughter and a bigger, more embarrassing hug from his Mum.

"Don't worry my little boy, I'll go and see if they've got anything for you in the fancy dress department." Even more laughter as Mary and Edith left the room, presumably in search of a polar bear suit, or at worst a doctor's smock. Silence followed as the two of them considered the situation. Benjamin finally broke the deadlock.

"Any idea what you're going to say?"

"Not really, depends what they ask I suppose. We just need to say that the game's going to be great and they need to be down the ground at nine tomorrow. And for them to bring some tools if they've got some, because they might need them."

"Yes, all very practical that. But I imagine they want to ask us about the game too. How it got organised and everything, some of the history behind it."

"What, like how you used to whip our arses at five a side every week and one day I got arsey?" they both laughed.

"No, you always got arsey. We'd have to say that you got really arsey and that Statto saved you from losing your dignity. And a few quid too." Mary and Edith interrupted any answer he may have had, closely followed by John and Winston.

"Well here they are, the stars of the day. Ha ha. And look at them, like Siamese twins in their matching shirts. Ha ha ha."

"Well, we've just been looking for a new shirt for Danny and we can't find one anywhere. He'll have to borrow yours John."

"Mine, it's twice as big as him, he'll drown in it. Ha ha."

"Two minutes to make up," a new head appeared around the door.

"Come on, get it off and get it swapped. It's the style these days, baggy shirts." John huffed and puffed a little bit more but the exchange was soon done.

"Make sure you don't breathe out too much John," Winston sniggered as John finished doing up Danny's new shirt.

"Come on then, follow me for makeup. You'll be on in twenty minutes." Twenty minutes, plenty of time.

Make up, brightly lit with a couple of artists hard at work. No glamour, just quick and expert application. The news lady and the weather man liberated their seats and the boys were in. Ten seconds and his fifteen minutes of hair preparation was corrected and then it was straight into another room. Mary and Edith looked like an old time music hall act, somehow transported into this century to remind people of the good old days. Benjamin had the look of a film star, if only a minor one at that. Danny had no mirror but could only imagine that he looked a bit of a dick in his Dad's oversize shirt. The door opened and roving reporter Kate Goodman breezed in, beautiful and business like.

"Hi guys," big smile, no feeling, "and wow, ladies, you're looking just great. Go girls go. Listen, we'll have three minutes, which might seem short, but believe me, out there it's a lifetime. We'll be in the studio, on the famous red sofa and my questions will be quick and straightforward. Just try and keep your answers quick too and everything will be great. Now we've got Mary and Danny in the white corner and Edith and Benjamin in the blue, is that right? Great, well good luck and see you in two," and with that she was gone. He barely had time to look around before they were taken into the main studio.

Look at those lights, so hot and oh so bright. Had he ever been that blinded and that hot?

"Right then, on three we're live. Watch for the red light, two, three, go!"

In the studio there was no introduction music, just silence and an intense heat.

"Well here we are, just before Christmas and as we all know, that's a time for reflection and for tradition. Well this year a group of young people in the area had a pretty novel idea and have been working hard ever since to make it reality. Danny, tell us how it all started?"

It was strange to think it possible in such a hot environment, to freeze, but Danny could say nothing. It wasn't a case of his brain not passing information to his mouth, nor of his muscles not being able to convert the information to noise. He just didn't have a clue what to say. It was just a couple of seconds, but felt like hours. Finally he was saved.

"Well you know how it is for the youngsters around here, especially now that there's no football for them. They just thought that the towns deserved something special at Christmas, something to bring everyone out, to bring them together." Thanks Mum.

"Oh, so it's not just a story about a game of football then Mary?"

"Of course not, it's much more than that. Christmas was always a time for the communities to come together and play sport, right from the middle ages when people from the two villages that were here used to try and get an old pig's bladder from one church to the other."

"Wow, it really used to be like that?" Kate's feigned surprised added to the excitement.

"Exactly. But the sport was just a reason for people to enjoy themselves. After the match there was always the feasting and the celebration. That was what mattered."

"Really interesting. And these days, for what, five years

now, there hasn't been any local game on Boxing Day, is that right Benjamin?"

"Yes Kate, that's right. There've been no Boxing Day games in the area for five years now, and in fact, because we played in different leagues for quite a while, it's been twelve years since the two teams last played each other on Boxing Day." Smooth as a cucumber, the bastard must've been practicing all afternoon. They were coming to the last part of the interview and Kate Goodman was looking round for a reliable face for her last question. She passed over Danny, not even a hint of hesitation as she made the briefest of eye contacts.

"And so, Edith, tell us. What can we do now in order to help out? In order to make sure that this year tradition is restored?"

"Well it's simple really. All that we've talked about is what might be, because in fact we still need to do some work on the stadium. We need as many people as possible to come to the ground tomorrow, Cherry Lane at nine o'clock. And then, once we have the go ahead for the ground they can all come back and join us for the game."

"Yes, come and join us for the game on Boxing Day, but more than anything let us have a few hours of your time tomorrow."

"Well thank you ladies. You heard them everybody, they need your help. Cherry Lane tomorrow, from nine o'clock for anyone who can spare even a little bit of time to help restore this ancient tradition. Right then, now we'll go over to Damian for the weather," her smile froze as the lights dimmed and then went out.

"Thanks everyone, all the best," and she was gone. The cameramen and assistants wound down and left, the lights went off and with them went the heat. Danny touched his face, making sure that it had been the make-up melting and not his flesh. Reassured he stood slowly and joined the others, following them back to the room where their adventure had started. Kate gave John a farewell kiss and Winston a warm hug, just as another man entered the room.

"Well then, that's your lot. I really hope it helps you out. I can't make it tomorrow, but if all goes well I hope to be at the game, to see those Blues win again," the man shared a smile with Winston. "I may even see if I can get some cameras down there for the match."

"Thanks Colin, I would say that I owe you one, but I reckon that about makes it all square?" Colin smiled at Winston.

"Yes, that makes it all square. I was glad to be of assistance," with that he gave a mock bow and left.

"Well then you lot, well done. Brilliant. Mary and Edith, you were radiant. I can already see a lot of people being put off from going because they'll be in the shadow of your beauty and elegance. Ha ha ha. Benjamin, you were a natural. I know they don't really recruit people to work in these industries anymore, but if they did you should definitely get an application in. I'm sure your Dad'll survive without you. Ha ha. Oh, and Danny, you looked good. In fact that shirt really suits you. Come on then, let's go to the pub and celebrate. I imagine the phones'll be ringing tonight with offers and we'll need an early start in the morning."

He didn't even ask to change back his shirt. 'You looked good'. 'The shirt really suits you'. What a prat he must have looked, all tongue tied and quiet. Well, at least the others did a good job. How good they'd just have to wait a few more hours to see. Perhaps a little celebration apple juice would go down well after all.

As they left the building he quickly checked his phone. No messages.

23 O COME ALL YE FAITHFUL

Careful now, don't slip on that frost. Going faster would be dangerous, but Danny was late, and the sun breaking through the clouds was surely an omen. He was now into the Lane and breathless. Not from the run, but the sight before him. He was taking slow steps now, adjusting to the sights and sounds in front of him.

A long line of vans and trucks reached back almost to the main road. What could possibly be inside so many vehicles? Next to them was a long line of people waiting to go into the ground. Families, groups, men and women on their own, old and young, all in good humour despite the wait. And boy had they brought their buckets and brooms as requested. Behind it all, the main gates, open and inviting. No sneaking in a back entrance today. There was the padlock, hanging limp, no further function to perform. The same one he'd seen through teary eyes five years before, open at last. Ernie was busy setting up his tea stall at the side, no doubt kicking himself for not having got up earlier.

"Hey up Danny, if you've got nothing useful to say, better say nothing eh. Ha haha," a youth leaned out of a van window, Arkwrights Painters marked on the side. A

BOXING DAY

chorus now came from the van. "You Blues! You Blues! Beat the White shite, you Blues!" How could he not smile at that? A friendly faced driver got out.

"Take no notice Danny, we can pick them for their painting skills, but not the rubbish they support. The boss heard you might need some painting done. We've got a few spare pots left over from a job at the Town Hall in the back, and we'll even throw the monkeys in for a couple of hours if you need." Danny stepped forward and gave the man a big hug, a manly hug that was returned with interest. Where'd that come from?

"Thanks so much. I guess you just have to hold on a few minutes more and we should be able to get you in. Leave it with me," he forced himself on towards the gates, 'You Blues!' echoing again behind him and warm greetings coming from every side.

"At last the great star of silent television arrives. Were you out with Harold Lloyd last night? They're all in the old manager's office, you should remember where it is, I'm going to start letting people through in a few minutes." Marlon was on gate duty, keeping the hordes at bay. Soon they'd be open again, maybe only for a week or so, but open they'd be.

The manager's office, all bustle and noise. Marsha and Red Al were in conference in the corner, two long lists in their hands. He'd normally have cursed himself now for not thinking of this before, but why would he need to do that, with the two best organisers in the district on his side? Richo was drawing up some lists on an old white board in the corner, whilst Annie and Geeta wrote out coloured cards on a desk in the middle of the room. Laetitia, yes even she was there, was looking intently at a computer screen, while Dave connected it up to a printer. Benjamin looked over and smiled. It was the friendliest smile he'd ever given him, and Danny found himself smiling back.

"At last, Charlie Chaplin arrives," a mixture of laughs

and hellos from all around.

"Well then, what are you all waiting for? Don't tell me you needed me to be here before you could start. Poor old Marlon can't keep them out any longer and Ernie's already sold out of tea. Let's get this show on the road eh." The new confident Danny was now the only one he knew.

"Danny, you'll find things'll go a lot smoother if you just let us finish off the first set of job cards. More haste less speed, didn't your parents ever teach you that?" It was good having Red Al back on side. Al passed slowly again through his pile of cards, finally taking on his speaking in public stance. "Right everyone, I'll hand out the cards depending on who comes in and tell them to come to the office when they've finished. Hopefully most will stay and take another. Richo, you make sure you note down any problems and cross off the list everything that's been done." Not wanting to be out organised Marsha took over.

"For the speciality jobs we'll really need trained people and tools. I'll try and get as many of these out as early as possible, but you lot be ready. If we don't get the help we need then you're as close as we've got to trained people. And tools," giggling, she followed Al outside.

Attracted by the computer, and its owner, he crossed to Benjamin and the others.

"And what are you lot up to?"

"Well there's manual work, which you White shite are perfectly made for, you know fetch and carry and all that, and then there's the paperwork that we'll need at the end of the day. You'd best leave that to the brains. We should have everything set up in about half an hour, and then it's just a case of updating. So don't you worry, we'll be getting our hands dirty too," another Benjamin smile. It was becoming too often for comfort. Was he the only person without a job?

"Where's Statto?" he asked, to no one in particular.

"Went out about fifteen minutes ago, to check up on the tools. He'll be out there somewhere." Right then let's find him.

Out towards the pitch, down the corridors and through the doors he remembered. And then he was there on the edge, the playing surface having been fenced off by Reg and Dilip. Closing his eyes he raised his head upwards and breathed in deeply, his eyes opening again like a toy doll as he started the search for his friend.

Right then, where are you Statto? Not in the Main Stand behind him, Main because it was full of seats and was covered from the weather. Not opposite in the Barkley Stand either. Named after good old Jimmy Barkley, Chairman of the club in the 1960s. Seated above with standing below, the roof giving some cover from the rain that often came down over the hills. To his right, the Tip End was empty. Behind it was Blue, hence the name. An away end with no seating and no cover, guaranteeing fun when the rain fell. How could he have been anywhere else? Which Victory the Victory End had been named after no one remembered, probably Trafalgar, but it was there that Danny had stood through thick and thin, under its old roof. Two years spent in the Championship hadn't convinced the owners to convert Cherry Lane in to an all seater, yet it could still hold seventeen thousand people. He started his walk towards the lone man seated in the middle of the Victory.

The ground was rapidly filling up, people taking their places in the stands, their coloured work cards held tightly. Mayor Banks had also been good. There were Council workmen inspecting the roofing and repairing where needed. Walking past the Arkwright gang sprucing up the crush barriers at the bottom of the stand he politely smiled as another chorus of 'You Blues!' rang out. Slowly he climbed the steps, finally sitting down next to his friend, both of them looking down at the scene before them.

"They came Danny, they heard us and came. Well, they didn't hear much of you, but you know what I mean," there was joy in Statto's face. "I never doubted they'd come, that the game would go ahead. But never in my wildest dreams did I imagine that it'd be here, at the Lane."

"How many years did you stand here Statto, in this place?"

"Ten, eleven, twelve. I can't remember. Dad used to take me in the Barkley, with my uncles. Then I found this piece of magic here and never needed anywhere else."

"You know that Friday you're in the dugout."

"Yes. It'll be a privilege too. But if we're getting hammered I'm going to come here and shout 'What a load of rubbish, shift your arse Danny' along with the rest. I can, can't I?"

"Of course. You pay your money, you get your chance to criticise, just like everyone else." He stood and pulled Statto up towards him. Another manly hug, old friends renewing their vows.

"Get off that bloody grass you little hooligans," the shout caused him to turn. A large group of younger lads were running over the pitch, with Reg in slow motion pursuit. Behind them was a round faced, bearded man, muscular tattooed arms bulging out of his tee shirt.

"Come on lads, keep off the grass," he barked, his instructions immediately followed. "Good morning Daniel, morning Jason." Does The Fist know everyone's first name? "You can leave the Victory to me and the boys now. I understand there might be a few spaces free on Friday, but don't worry I've found a few new lads, never been before, who'll keep them warm for you," he looked Danny in the eye and smiled sympathetically. "Don't worry, I've told them that if all goes well they might be able to see some proper players one day too," and with that he roared a rugged laugh. "Right then you lot, the Victory is ours! We're looking for loose pieces of concrete. Pull the weeds out and give it a really good going over. Any pieces you put in the bucket, and you mark it with some coloured chalk," his raised hand showed them what chalk looked like. "Then you look for another piece and the boys doing the repairing will be around soon after. Right then, go." And off they went, like a mischief of rats as Danny and Statto started their walk back to the office.

In the Tip End a similar group, led by Benjamin and Dave, were doing the same work, preparing their territory for the big game. In the Barkley workmen were already repairing the broken steps as above them damaged seats were being removed and good ones wiped clean. From up high someone waved down at them. Danny couldn't see who it was, he probably didn't know them anyway, but he waved back, thanking the group from the bottom of his heart. Approaching the tunnel they bumped into Laetitia as she was walking out.

"I'll go in and get us a job ticket, if there's anything that Al or Marsha will trust us with." Thanks Statto, leaving us together.

"Before you say anything I know I screwed up last night. They chose the wrong man. Fortunately your film star brother managed to save the day." Could it always be this easy to speak with her?

"Well I thought you looked nice anyway, though your shirt did look a bit baggy," he returned her broad smile with interest. Perhaps he'd tell her the story in his words one day.

"Tish, we couldn't have done this without you." Had he just called her Tish? "Don't worry about Holmes and what he's done, whatever he's up to he's going to lose." After a day of manly hugs, this hug just came naturally. It was soon over, but it had happened.

"Thanks Danny. I know how much this game means to everyone." Slightly dreamy, perhaps surprised by the hug? "Anyway, I better go. Dilip's found a room full of new seats, so I need to see how many broken ones we've got, and figure out the best way to fit them all together. See you later," a flick of the hair and another smile and she was gone. Almost skipping down the tunnel he entered the manager's office.

It was chaos, two branches of the Women's Institute having turned up at the same time.

"Calm down ladies, there's room enough for all of you in the kitchen."

"David, you wait until I get you home later," the rest of the ladies roared. "If you want a cup of tea you make one yourself, we're here to work." Mumbles of agreement. Marsha came to Dave's rescue.

"Well actually ladies we do need a bit of help in the two end stands. We need to check all the crush barriers for rough edges. I've got lots of files here, so you just need to check and file. Those lovely boys from Arkwrights should be close behind, all ready to freshen up the paint. Edith, you can take the blue team down to the Tip End and give Benjamin a hand. Mary, get your girls down to the Victory End, but be careful, The Fist's there."

"Ooh good, we can certainly teach them a thing or two. Come on girls." The room shuddered as a hundred handbags were dropped simultaneously and the two groups of ladies left for the stands. An agitated Statto could now be heard.

"You want us to clean the shithouses? You are joking aren't you? Yes, I know that someone's got to do it. Yes, okay, okay. Don't worry, we won't let you down." Statto came towards him, shrugging. "We're on latrine duty mate. Big Bud's already done the Main Stand, but he had to go off to an emergency, some blockage at the shopping centre apparently. Not the best for the Saturday before Christmas. Anyway, we just need to make sure they all flush and give any that don't a bit of a squirt with the high pressure nozzle. Anything that doesn't clear out we need to note and Bud'll be back later."

"Sounds simple, where's the gear?"

"He left it round the back of the Tip, we can start there."

'Someone's got to do it' was ringing in his head as Danny's jaw dropped, leaving him looking like a goldfish. Yes, he'd seen the people checking the terraces and checking the seats, but that had clearly been the tip of the iceberg. There were families sweeping and washing floors, youngsters oiling turnstiles, doors being repaired and rehung, tea bars being shined and paint being peeled off where it had surrendered and renewed where a matching colour could be found. Signposts were being written out and fastened to walls, doors and anything else that didn't move fast enough. Geeta and Marlon were supervising whilst Big John and Winston handed out brushes, mops and buckets to the people still trickling into the ground. Even Mayor Banks was there, smiling for photos as he fixed the shutters on the ticket office door, carefully getting both the old club badge and the Council crest on his baseball cap in the picture.

Bodysuits, goggles and gloves, breathing masks and boots. Plus the all-important power sprays, all filled with water and fully charged batteries. Ghostbusters came the shout.

"After you Statto, I'll give you first shot." Statto entered the cubicle, inserted the end of his hose and pressed the button. The gentle sound of a smooth run of water as the cleaned pipe flushed down.

"One nil to me. Choose your pan." Danny entered trap two, inserted and pressed. At first silence and then a rushing crescendo as the water turned back on itself and sprayed all over him.

"Shit!"

"No, don't think so. Looks more like brick dust to me." Not giving up Danny gave it another squirt. Same result. "Just mark the door Danny, Bud'll sort it out when he gets back." It felt good.

The morning came to an end with people drifting off, hopefully with plans to come back after grabbing something to eat.

"What time are the lads due here?"

"I told them to get here for two. I don't want them to be a distraction, so best not have them too early." Danny's heart skipped at the prospect of the afternoon's training session. Time for the players get a feel for the pitch and sense the atmosphere. The Whites would take the Victory End, obviously. "Hey Benjamin, have you finished with the changing rooms yet?"

"The seating and floors are all done. Dave was just checking the lockers a while back. There's still a problem with the showers and the baths, but we should be able to fix that before Friday."

"Okay. Just make sure you keep Arnie in check, I don't want him going home crying again."

"Don't you worry, he's all ready to look after himself. Oh, and by the way we've got a new trainer. All of a sudden Tracksuit Ted became Timid Ted and decided he didn't want to play with us anymore," they shared a knowing look.

"Right then you lot, lunch is over," Marsha was still in fine voice, and was cracking the whip hard. Cards were still being written and Richo was busy cleaning his whiteboard. The problem pile was small and hopefully manageable and Laetitia was busy updating the paperwork in preparation for the final inspection. Could they have had a better team? He doubted it.

Slowly the players arrived, each one looking eagerly around at their surroundings.

"It was all a bit of a dream before, to play for the Whites," Harish was first to speak. "And then we said we'd play here, and now we are here. In this changing room, getting changed where my heroes used to get changed...." He had no words left, just his eyes betraying his awe as he looked around the room.

"This was always my space," Dick sat down. "Close to the toilets," he laughed out loud, joined nervously by some of the others. "We've got nothing to worry about today anyway. There's only a couple of hundred people out there, and they're more interested in weeds and broken stones than us taking a jog. Enjoy today, the touch of that turf, and then get ready for the next time you run out there. Now that will be something to be scared of."

His instructions given Danny joined the others walking out of the room, his studs clicking on the newly cleaned concrete floor despite his best efforts. His breathing got deeper and more difficult as the pace of their walk got quicker, the blue sky and green pitch tempting them forward. His heart beat quickened even more as the group broke into a trot, passing the welcoming waves of Dilip and Reg onto the pitch that had been lovingly cared for in secret for so long. Firm under foot with a full covering of grass. Not too long and not too wet, could there be a better surface to do battle on? There were whistles and shouts from the Victory End, but nothing could distract him from the beauty of the pitch and the perfection of its surface. As he stretched he found his chest loosening and his breathing eased. This was what dreams were made of. More silently than he'd imagined they went through the planned routines, the backdrop completed by the Blues and the security volunteers also going through their preparations.

It was done. They'd touched the turf and trained on the pitch, already a dream realised for most of the team. Soon they'd have their final challenge.

"All done Geeta?"

"Yep, just the problem jobs left now."

"Bud's just finished the last one, I think we're done." Danny could sense the relief in the whole group. Outside, in the dying sun Winston and John manned the main gates, like the Fezziwigs thanking everyone for their effort, wishing them a Merry Christmas and hoping to see them again on Boxing Day. Then the dark cloud arrived.

Three vans pulled up in front of the ground. An army of inspectors, each with a clipboard and a list of checks to be made, piled out. In front, unsmiling and waiting for someone to attack was Walton.

"Come on then, we haven't got much light left, so get round with your lists and be back here soon. You," her look fell on no one in particular, "you'll be getting nothing without the correct paperwork." The printer sprang into life, as if in defiance of her presence. They could do nothing now but wait. One by one the inspectors returned, their information entered into a laptop computer. From where he was stood Danny saw a map of the ground, the different sections turning either green, red or yellow as the information was entered. Green like holly, he liked that colour. Long after the last person had returned the discussions continued, Walton almost barking, Laetitia explaining and the rest looking on.

"Okay. It seems that you've been working very hard," there was no sign of gratitude or appreciation. "There are two areas of the ground that need to be cordoned off and are still unsafe." Yes, there'd been two red areas. "That done, you should comply with the necessary regulations to accept a crowd of thirteen thousand, six hundred and twenty nine spectators. Further inspectors will visit on Monday or Tuesday to check the sanitation and compliance for the preparation of food. Other than that I've nothing else to add." Could a person really explode? It was a relief to actually see her leave, her anger staying behind for a good few seconds after the door had closed.

Why's no one saying anything? Please somebody, say something.

"We've only gone and fucking done it!" Red Al howled with delight, giving Geeta a big, unexpected hug. She resisted for a second or two and then joined in. Laetitia ran straight towards Danny and took him in her arms. Marsha and Benjamin were next and then everyone yet unattached also joined in, hugging the nearest person and whooping with delight. They'd only gone and done it. Over Laetitia's shoulder he saw Reg and Dilip leaving the room, contented smiles on their faces. Your quest's over gentlemen, and now it's our turn to repay you.

The wild hugging fever rapidly died away, leaving a room full of people brushing themselves down as reality hit. Danny had more to do though, and he ran out of the office towards the main gates, catching the last of the helpers as they left to go home. Had he ever done a speech before?

"My Lords, Ladies, Gentlemen and hangers on from the Tip End." Cheers and jeers and whistles. "I, no We," he looked around him, "really don't know how to thank you, and all of the others who've already been and gone, for the efforts you've put in today. What I can tell you is that WE have been rewarded. The game can go ahead." Feeling his hand raised in the air in a victory salute, he looked to see that Statto was the guilty party.

Against all of the odds, they'd done it.

24 BRASS BANDS AND REINDEER

On his own at last, the lunchtime finish on Christmas Eve had given Danny the chance to walk into town one final time. Statto'd warned him earlier. 'Mum says it's mayhem. Hats, scarves and rosettes on sale everywhere, people talking of nothing else. Benjamin said it was even worse on the Blue side, but then again he's a lying bastard.' Well they did it for the people in the first place, what could be better? He smiled. A breeze was starting to blow, the day mild, cloudy but not yet raining. Anyone taking bets would certainly be leaning more towards Greg Lake than Bing Crosby, but nothing in life was certain. Just one last evening in the Bell to negotiate and then the waiting would almost be over.

Nearing the centre of town the decorations on the shop fronts became more extravagant, and the clank of shaken collecting tins became louder. The colours and sounds of childhood excitement. Well he was still a kid wasn't he? The sound of a brass band floated over. Jingle Bells, of course. He walked over to the band in front of the shopping centre. How many times had they already played it today, and how many times this year? On the back row a small girl was stood next to an old man. Did she realise that in order to beat his lifetime record she'd have to play it at least another thousand times? All that mattered was that people continued to come and play their songs for the people year after year, one generation following the other. An Away in a Manger and a Hark the Herald Angels later he put his tenner in the tin and moved on, sorry only that the plastic note wouldn't help with the rattling accompaniment for the next carols.

Further on and the clip clop of hooves and smell of horse shit confirmed he'd arrived in the Town Hall square. Pride of place was a carefully restored horse drawn fire engine from the local Works. The shouts and laughter of local children, old and young, rang out as they were pulled around the square by horses discreetly disguised as reindeer. It was all a long way away from the birth of Christ, and further still from the pagan festivals of the Winter solstice that had inspired people to celebrate at this time of year for centuries. But what harm could it do? Anything that encouraged people to spend more time with each other, and to do more to help others, shouldn't be criticised. The joy was clear in the faces of those queuing for their turn, highlighted by the glow of the lights, first put up for Diwali and then kept in place for Christmas.

"I would give you a penny for your thoughts, but I'd be too worried that you'd give it away before you told me," he turned and looked at her and they hugged. He'd arranged to meet here so they could spend time together before going to the Bell. "I heard the band playing In The Bleak Midwinter and thought of you."

"Why?"

"Because it's got Bleak in the title, and you've been a bit Bleak for quite a while now," she laughed, hugging him again.

"Of all the sisters in all the world, why on earth did I end up with you? Do you want a ride?" he indicated the Reindeer. "I'll pay?"

"No thanks, I had a go earlier. Trevor was kind

enough to explain everything to me and give me a spin."

"Trevor?"

"A new fireman, down from Newcastle. He's got a lovely accent. Plus a wife and two kids," they laughed together.

"So you've not given up on Richo just yet then." A scowl in return.

"I'm just waiting for all of the attention to die down after his photo session in the Advertiser. I'll get him yet brother, you wait and see."

"Well, if you still want him after all this time you certainly deserve him." Locking arms they walked over to the other side of the square, taking some tea and soup from one of the five stalls in the Christmas Market that were still open.

Could he remember feeling this relaxed? Sharing a bench they went through memories of Christmases past. Each strange relative or friend bringing laughter, and each tender family moment warm feelings of contentment. They listed the presents that had been received and then hidden away, never to be seen again. They were particularly sad when recalling the deaths of loved ones that Christmas had been unable to protect or wait for their passing. No, their Christmas had always been one of family and togetherness, with no mention of snowmen, roasting chestnuts or mistletoe and wine. Last of all they talked about their friends, and how they'd all changed in the last few weeks.

The wind picked up, the lights in the tree above their heads starting to move from side to side. The Band's playing of Rudolph the Red Nosed Reindeer was drifting all around them, just audible above the clip clops of horses' hooves and the chinking of the decorations in the tree. It was the end of the day and parents were starting to take their children home. They'd soon be getting ready for bed as the parents poured their first drinks, all excited for the arrival of Christmas Day.

"Come on then big brother, it must be time to go and see what the rest of them are getting up to in the pub. I'll even let you treat me to a drink if you insist. Now let me guess where we'll be going?"

The bell that hung on the sign above the door had been temporarily joined by two smaller, but shinier ones, and all three swayed together in the slowly building wind. Danny strained to see through the window, just about making out the skeleton of an artificial Christmas tree, the meagre branches barely visible under the faint lights and desperately holding onto their last decorations. Boom, boom, boom. The beat of music was just audible above the muffled sound of the voices hiding on the other side of the door. Where better to spend Christmas Eve? The team together and united.

"Slade."

"Wizard."

"No, Slade. If Al's in there it'll be Slade. He's the only one that puts money in the jukebox nowadays, and he always puts on Slade." There was only one way to find out. Danny pushed through the door, Annie following behind. The pub was a lot emptier than he'd imagined, the sounds on the outside having been distorted by the wind. Red Al stood against the bar singing a gusty trio with Bing Crosby and David Bowie. Pa rum pum pum pum. He raised his glass as he saw them, a full pint of bitter showing that he wasn't planning on showing any sympathy to the players.

"Evening Danny, Annie." Bing and David better make the most of him now, while he can still sing in tune. Geeta was already there with Gesine, Al's German fancy. Annie was quickly swallowed by them, at least saving Danny the price of a drink. Other players were scattered around, soft drinks in hand. He was relieved to see that they were taking it seriously. Dick Sparrow walked quickly over.

"Hi Danny. I'm sorry but I've got to get back home. Nothing personal, just that the latest arrival's a bit ill, and

I've got the rest of the family coming round tomorrow, so lots to do. I wanted to show my face so that I could wish you a Merry Christmas, but also to thank you again. I mean all of you, obviously, but I sometimes don't think you understand what this game means to this town, after five years of nothing. And what it means to an old man to be able to pull on that White shirt one more time and show his grandchildren what he used to do." Lost for words Danny leaned forward, avoided the hug and warmly shook hands.

"Dick, you don't know what it means for the rest of the team to have someone with us who made so many of our childhood memories. The thanks is all for you. Now you get off and enjoy those daughters and granddaughters of yours. Take it nice and easy and we'll all see you Friday morning. Merry Christmas Dick." A shared smile and Dick was gone, quickly wishing everyone season's greetings and then disappearing into the dark. Pa rum pumpum pum.

Mixing with the others, talk was of nothing but the match. Training in front a few people at the ground the Saturday before had woken all of their hopes and fears. How had his Dad and Dick Sparrow managed to live with that expectation week in week out? Walking out in front of a bigger crowd on the day would be something new for them all.

"Right then you load of girls, supping on your orange juices. I'm surprised the bar steward couldn't find you glasses that looked like your mothers' tits to drink it out of." Who else could it be? Tone had arrived, bringing along the last members of the team. "Four pints of your finest Christmas Ale please sir, and be sharp about it. My missus is already complaining that I'm wasting away, so I'll be celebrating the virgin birth with a few hops for company." Don't bite, it's all show. He'd told them to have a drink or two. Let's just hope it stopped at two. Pa rum pum pumpum.

"No Griz tonight Danny, got a bit of an emergency up

at the hospital. He's sure she's not a virgin, but the odds are it'll be out tomorrow and not tonight." Everyone who heard laughed as Richo passed on the news. There'd be many others working that night too. Not just the barman, laughing and joking as he took money on one of his busiest nights of the year. But those driving buses, working in hospitals or sitting waiting for emergency calls would all be having a very different Christmas Eve.

'It's Christmas time, and there's no need to be afraid.' Al was now duetting with Paul Young while Bing and David took a break. Sacrifice and giving at Christmas, but no saints here. Just some people doing their best to be better. 'And tonight thank God it's them, instead of you,' Bono would be upset at being drowned out.

Danny's vision sharpened, necessary now that the noise of tens of conversations crossed each other all at once and Red Al and Cliff Richard went through the full Christmas repertoire. "Ohhhhh, Little Town oof Beeeethlehem." He picked out Tone across the bar. No talk of presents and family from him, just a determined stare. Fear? Excitement? They all had the same mixture of emotions to enjoy. Gesine was slowly getting closer to Al, clearly impressed by his festive repertoire. She'd have to wait though, as Al was now back with Bing, but without David. Was it time for Danny to have a pint at last?

"Are you sure the gaffer will let you have that? I hear he's getting quite touchy and strict, now that it's nearly showtime," Statto and Richo had managed to find what passed as a quiet corner.

"Fuck off Statto," the three of them laughed as Statto wiped froth off his lips.

"I haven't had a pint that lasted me all night on Christmas Eve since I was sixteen. This is killing me. The things I do for you two eh," Richo was on small sips, no froth there.

"The things WE do for us THREE Richo, the things that we do for us three." Statto's emphasis of the words

WE and THREE was clear.

"Well, we've been a team for a long time now. The three stooges eh."

"Or the three wise monkeys."

"Certainly not the three wise men though," more laughter and another sip of beer. There was a strange look about Richo, like he was actually planning on saying something. He didn't disappoint.

"You know what though lads, I really do owe you one. What's happening at the moment's the bollocks. The game's a couple of days away I know, but that won't be the end of it, I tell you. One day I'll be able to look back on all this and tell my kids I was a part of it, and that'll all be thanks to you. You know, they say that to get involved in things like this you just need one idiot capable of having a good idea, and another idiot capable of making people believe it can work. Luckily for us we've got you two pillocks," another nervous sip of his beer. Perhaps he was planning a two pint night after all? "But look where it's got us. We've got a team of players willing to die for the Whites. Do you think that when they came along to the trials they thought they'd spend the next few weeks training almost every day, playing matches and all that?"

"And running up bloody big hills."

"Exactly. But no one's complained, no one's dropped out. Everybody's just dug in and got on with it. And then we've had all of the problems with the ground, sponsors, money and everything else. Do you realise what we did last Saturday? We turned an old football ground from a wreck to a stadium in a day. How do you explain that? People giving up their Saturdays, their time, bringing their tools. We've been in the papers, on the telly and everything. And I've been part of it all because of you two," Richo raised his glass and they joined him in a salute.

"Don't you go welling up on us now Richo, I can't stand tears on a party night. We still needed you to follow us too."

"Yes, and that's what qualifies you to be 'hear no evil', you daft bugger." Their friendship resealed.

Laughter from near the bar. Through the bodies Al and Gesine were following the advice of Mel and Kim and Rocking Around the Christmas Tree. It was a good distraction for the team, and even better news for Al. Annie and Geeta had made a second couple.

"How do you do it Richo?" it was Statto who asked.

"What?"

"What? Wake up every morning knowing that a creature as beautiful as Annie fancies you and do nothing about it?" Where had that observation come from?

"Do you think she fancies me? Even if she does, she's my best friend's sister Statto. Come on, there are rules you know," Danny and Statto placed their pints on the table in unison.

"The rules when you were fourteen change with the years Richo. Think about it, plonker. Not tonight though, obviously. We need you fit for Friday." More laughter from the three of them. Was there a better way to spend an evening together?

What's going on here? The singers on the jukebox all having a rest? Not Al unfortunately. He'd undoubtedly caused the pause in the singing and was now coming towards them. He came to a halt a few feet in front, arriving as the whole pub seemed to become silent. Hands raised, the last whispers died. Looks like it's going to be a speech.

"One and all, we are all very fortunate to be here today. To be in the company of the Whites team that will, two days from now, go forth onto the field of battle." Waving his hand in front of him towards the players a slight ripple of applause came from the gathered drinkers. "They were all selected for this task and are ready to do what is necessary to overcome the adversity before them. At the end of the day they'll surely be proud of the effort that they've put in." A fixed artificial smile prevented

Danny's face from moving. "What we should never forget though's that these warriors aren't fighting for themselves, they're fighting for us all. For this town and all of the people who live here. It's the White shirt that motivates them and it's the White shirt that represents us all." Cheers from the players and a few muffled 'you Whites' could be heard, as Al's voice rose in crescendo. "So I ask you all to now raise your glasses and drink, to the team, to the Whites, to our town and to victory!" he raised his glass at arm's length, showering Weeble with beer, but fortunately missing Tone by a few inches. "To Victory!" 'To Victory' came the reply. Seeing him winding up for another go the barman turned the music up and everyone was saved by Shakin' Stevens announcing a Merry Christmas for Everyone.

With the noise notched up another level Danny leaned back, his eyes again taking over. Al had nailed it. They'd soon be going into battle for the town, for their town. In just thirty eight hours now the whistle would be blowing to start that game of football. They'd done it. The bar was already starting to thin out and Elton John's invitation to Step Into Christmas was too tempting to turn down. He moved quickly, waving and shouting Merry Christmas as he went out into the cold silence that was outside.

The door closed behind him, there was now no turning back.

25 THE KING'S CHRISTMAS MESSAGE

'Has he been yet?' he heard the whispered question from days gone by, Annie excited in the next room. Waiting for the signal to get up and open long awaited presents. The memories were good.

Stretching in his bed Danny wondered what had made him sleep so badly. It certainly wasn't too much drink the night before, and he didn't remember having any flashbacks. No, it must be good old fashioned excitement, but not for presents, for the next day's match. His eyes closed again revealing Red Al singing, new friends, old friends. That was worth a smile. Parum pum pum pum.

His foot was now on the cold floor, making the short walk from small bedroom to small kitchen, stopping in front of his small window. No tears for the Virgin birth and no surprise Winter Wonderland, just a pale sky that looked like it would be happy to have a day off and stay just as it was. To either side the streets were empty, children playing with footballs or new bikes being a thing of the past. The churchgoers would already be singing of Angels from the Realms of Glory, whilst everyone else would be busily opening presents, preparing to visit friends and family for dinner or looking all over for some hangover cures. That was Christmas Day.

Tea, toast and the small living room, the tour of the flat was complete. His small Christmas tree and a copy of the Radio Times Christmas Special were his only concessions to the season, with the exception of a small nativity set in the corner of the room. He looked down on the assembled figures, Mary and Joseph intently looking at the manger in front of them, one shepherd kneeling with his sheep, one Angel Harking, one donkey and a cow. Perfect. There was Annie's voice again, pleading that it was her turn to place the baby Jesus in his manger as their grandparents looked on. No fights any more, now that it was his. He carefully placed the baby inside the manger, to be suitably adored on his birthday. The three Kings would arrive later, on Epiphany, a good reminder for him to take his tree down and avoid all of the bad luck. Did he believe? He'd been brought up in a country with a spire in every village and songs sung at school every morning. Harish, Dev and Geeta proved that everyone could get to know and love the most improbable of stories.

Religious duties complete he switched the radio on, greeted by Christmas music as expected. Unconsciously he started singing along, each song being at least forty years old. How was it possible to discover new music all year long and then go back half a century every Christmas? At least that way he knew all of the words. Parum pumpum pum.

They worried him, the deep blue eyes looking back at him. There was mystery in them, confusion. Underlying confidence? Worry, expectation? He brushed up well anyway and was likely to pass a maternal inspection and certain to pass a paternal one. He turned from the mirror, placed the three neatly packed presents in a carrier bag and was soon closing the door behind him.

Big John and Mary knew how to Deck the Halls. Garlands of flashing lights around window frames and doors and a snow effect tree, complete with tinsel, in the front garden. Where was the singing Santa hiding? Danny knocked and entered, bumping straight into Annie and nearly spilling her day's first glass of wine.

"Hello big brother. Merry Christmas," he gladly accepted the big kiss. Hearing the noise Mary rushed in and joined in the sequence of seasons greeting plus seasonal kiss. A mild ruffling of hair reminded him that he'd once been her little boy.

The smell of pine needles greeted his entry into the cosy living room. Finding seven differences in this room on Christmas Day was even tougher than in the Bell on a Saturday. John was firmly installed on the sofa, beer in hand. Not planning to help too much with dinner then? The corner was filled by a large tree, its branches barely visible behind the mountain of lights, bells, tinsel, bows and other assorted decorations. He added his presents to the small piles hiding beneath it. Plain carpet, patterned curtains held back with large bowed ties and a small coffee table covered in magazines and all sorts of remote controls. Along the side and in front of the pastel wallpaper a long sideboard. At one end a small cluster of cards and at the other bowls of clementines and nuts. Did Bob send a card here too? Through in the dining room the table was piled with cutlery, crockery and glassware, all ready to be placed when the time arrived.

"Annie says you had a good night last night?" if John had looked up from his glass Danny had missed it.

"We did indeed. Very quiet though, with the game tomorrow. You must remember from the 90s how it was?"

"Ha ha I do indeed. When you've got the whole of the town looking out for you to do well, you have to be on your best. Ha ha ha!" No pressure there then.

His body suddenly jolted as a mixture of perfume and Christmas kitchen was accompanied by the chatter of the ladies. The second glasses of wine were already in service and Annie smiled as she handed him a glass of orange juice. The smell of the turkey was wonderful and intense. Deciding that the baby Jesus might have eaten turkey had been an excellent choice. Stuffing mixed with the honey from the carrots and parsnips, butter used for the potatoes with a background of Christmas pudding. The fresh baked mince pies and the unmistakeable smell of boiled sprouts. The latest creation from Chanel no doubt bound them all together, the smell of Christmas in all its glory.

"Well, now that we're all here, I give it you. Merry Christmas!"

"Merry Christmas!" four glasses were raised as one.

"I hope you remembered to put the little one in Gran's nativity this morning," Annie would never let him forget.

"He got there safe and sound, don't you worry." His Mum's smile suggested that she also had memories of carrying out that task.

"Come on then, let's get the bloody presents out the way. You know what Annie, I checked this morning and someone's made a great big hole in my pants and socks draw. Looks almost like they've got something to put back there later today. Ha ha." You could make a big hole in his Dad's pants draw just by taking out one pair.

The ritual was simple and quickly done. No searching for presents, each person having their own pile neatly made up for them, with no need for stockings or slippers to identify them. The presents were quickly opened and thanks quickly exchanged. Was it worth waiting another twelve months for the next time? Happy faces all round, just as it should be, as everyone found some pleasure within their pile. John showed a genuine interest in the autobiography of Kia Joorabchian and was quickly engrossed in the first chapter. Mary was puzzled by the variety in her hand care set and went straight for a Rose balm to smooth out the hardship of preparing the dinner, whilst Annie placed her new scarf next to her coat, all ready for the walk home. And what a great shirt for him. Just like the one he'd bought a few days before, but this time in white, his smile as bright as the coloured paper that he'd opened.

"It's in case they want to interview you again after the game. Though after your words of wisdom the last time, I doubt they will." Well at least it was his size.

Ritual over. No Gold, or frankincense or myrrh again, but gifts exchanged. Next on the order of service was the dinner.

They faced each other across the table, each determined to win the race. They were off, and well-practiced hands placed napkins, crackers, cutlery, plates and glasses exactly where they'd been taught, accompanied by the sound of heavenly choirs and turkey being carved. A hundredth of a second? She'd beat him anyway. Steaming plates and bowls arrived and were placed to within an inch of where they'd been the year before, crackers were pulled and hats placed on heads, a cork was forced out of a bottle and the silent fizzing of three filled glasses went unnoticed as they all took their places. Mary looked round with a satisfied smile and a brief silence passed as grace, even on such a holy day as this. All eyes went to the steaming slices of turkey and Big John took the serving spoon in his hands.

"Oh, hold on a minute. Haven't you forgotten something Mary?" What's he playing at?

"Oh yes, sorry," she got up and walked back into the kitchen. The smell, what was it? Fish, and pasta.

"That's a sportsman's dinner Danny. Ha ha ha. You've got a game tomorrow don't forget, so Mary organised with all of the mums and wives and girlfriends. We need you to be on form if you're going to win tomorrow. Ha ha, look at his face Annie." The rest of the team would kill him.

"But a bit of Christmas dinner won't do any harm. I've got lots of time before the game to walk it off. Yes, we can go for a walk up the park this afternoon, that'll help get it off me."

"It's not that Danny, I read about it in a book. I've got

to start boosting your energy levels now, if you're going to be at your best tomorrow. This, plus a few bananas and you'll be well on your way, and then a bit more of the same tonight. Anyway, our dinner's getting cold, so come on John, get serving. Don't worry Danny, I'll keep you a plate in the fridge for tomorrow night." What was it, anger, surprise? Helplessness?

"But can't I have at least a couple of roast potatoes, you know they're my favourites?" Pleading for roast potatoes?

"It's a sportsman's dinner son, roast vegetables aren't that good for you. All that oil and dripping. Like your mum said, she'll put you a plate aside and you can have it tomorrow. That's what we always used to do back in the day." And how could you question back in the day?

Resigned he pushed his fish and pasta around his plate, the handful of sprouts that they'd let him have joining in with the dance. They were boiled apparently, and not so bad for him. He wasn't sure how the mince pie passed Mary's health check, but it did, and with each mouthful of the sweet pastry his smile got bigger. Did people realise the sacrifices the Whites were making?

The slight drizzle that had cut short their walk on the green continued to fall as they sat there, surrounded by nuts and clementines and steaming cups of tea. The perfect lazy Christmas afternoon, and time for Danny to work through his last remaining questions about the team.

Attention! A drum roll startled him as the Grenadier band played the National Anthem.

"Oh look, it's the Christmas message. From the King too, it's his first one."

The anthem came to an end and the camera zoomed into the balding monarch, stood in a window at Sandringham, dressed casually in plain pullover on top of a checked shirt over a pair of dark trousers.

"They say he's doing it live too," the nervousness in

his Majesty's first words seemed to prove the point.

"For almost all of you this will be a strange sight. I can assure you that it is for me too, after so many years of my Grandmother delivering this message. I, also, used to pass my Christmas afternoon looking on as that fabulous woman would speak to us all. But now I find myself in her position, and I hope that you will afford me the same time and respect that you afforded her for more than seventy years." A shaky start, but there's confidence building. The Whites would be the same the next day.

"It'll be a tough one to follow. Like he said, most of us have only ever known the Queen, and now here he is."

"Shut up Mum and let us listen then," the King obligingly continued.

"These last months I have travelled all around our wonderful country. It will seem clichéd for me to talk to you of rolling greenery, wonderful pubs and village greens, cricket pitches and church spires. But it is these things that have captured my imagination, reminding me of my duties here as the King of the United Kingdom and Defender of the Faith, amongst other things. But the things I saw only remind me more that this message is given today, not to the people of the United Kingdom, but to all who can hear me. And that it is not given to the people of the faith that I defend, but to people of all faiths, as a gift from my own. This time of year is a reminder for many of the baby boy, born in a stable, the son of God. But it also shows us the power that belief has for all of us, no matter what we believe in. How people can be captured for centuries by a story from the Middle East. How they can celebrate in line with the Winter solstice from centuries ago, using the pagan symbols of holly, ivy and mistletoe. How they can reconcile their German trees with their American turkeys, their English cards with a Turkish Saint Nicholas. How they can combine all of these experiences into the most important festival in our calendar. And it is this diversity in us that makes us what we are, and which we must continue to fight for." The screen was now filled with an old familiar sight of children singing in a school assembly. It must be an archive shot? The King continued to talk, now out of shot.

"Some weeks ago I visited a school near Oxford, where the pupils were recreating an assembly from long ago. They sang a hymn, a folk song in its origin, of a Knight winning his spurs. At one point they sang of the Knights being no more and the dragons being dead." The camera came back to the serious face of the King. "Well, for all of their sincerity I believe that they were wrong. There may no longer be dragons, but there are many things that we need to fight. The intolerance within our society and the lack of understanding of others being prime examples. We also need to realise that we, yes every one of us, is a Knight. It is easy to expect others to solve our problems, Government, business, that man at the end of the street who always sorts things out for us. Everyone except for ourselves. Now I know that this world has far ranging problems, but we can only start to change these things if it is us who act, if we engage at the level we can do something about. Only by doing things differently ourselves can we hope to make things better." Wow, did he just say that? How on earth is he going to finish this one? The King continued in a calm, considered tone, determined to answer Danny's question.

"In the next few days, many of you will be considering giving things up, making your resolutions for a New Year," he paused.

"Well I ask you, please, do not," his voice raised, now controlled by his dedication to his message and not his Royal bloodline. "We have been giving things up now for far too long, and all of the wrong things too. Now is the time to start again," he subsided into calmed reason. "We must start again to talk with and know the names of our neighbours, to understand their stories and their hopes. We must start to spend money in our local shops and to use our local workmen." Building all the time in intensity and volume he continued. "We must join our local sports clubs and participate, we must visit our local restaurants and bars. To leave the quiet stillness of our bedrooms and our computer screens and to walk amongst real people and have real conversations. We must work together to make our villages and towns, our communities and neighbourhoods the magnificent places that they can be. We must forget our differences and appreciate all that we have in common." He was now at the peak of his powers, his years of waiting and standing by, his training and coaching finally being used. "Because this is what sets us apart. We are the ones who master what we do. We are the ones who see the dragons and take our shields and lances to protect ourselves, often not realising that it is those same spears that cause fear to others." This message had surely been written especially for them? In a whisper the King started up again. "And so I ask of you, not as my subjects or as followers of the faith that I defend, but as citizens of this earth and as people who live, side by side in our great country. I ask you to take this day and think of the sacrifices that would be made by that child, born in a stable. To take the next year, and to give up nothing, but to promise to start doing, or redoing, as much as you can. And with that we will start creating a World with no dragons, one that we can all be proud of." Thoughts of his nervousness were a long way away. All Danny saw was a confident King, safely arrived at the end of his first Christmas message. It was a message that people would remember for many a year. Would Danny look as good as he did after his team talk the next day? "And to finish, the words not of a real person, but someone who has touched the hearts of many in the past. Whoever your God may be and in whatever you may believe I wish you a Merry Christmas, God bless us, every one!" The screen cut immediately to old images of Christmas parties and people sharing their day. There was even one of a football game.

Full of a renewed energy he looked round the room. John snored and Mary was already gone, no doubt making another pot of tea. Well he'd seen it and the next day he'd play his part. The waiting was over, just one more sleep to go.

The next day was Boxing Day.

26 THE BIG DAY

What was that noise? Danny had heard it before, long ago, but couldn't quite place it. The strange, wooden rasping sound that had woken him from the short, shallow sleep that John had warned him about. He'd lay awake for most of the night, experiencing in his head the colours, the sounds and the atmosphere of the match. Whenever he thought he was finally ready to sleep he'd be presented with the padlock on the gates, the one that had for so long denied him entry. At first, shining like the knocker on Scrooge's door and then falling miraculously to the floor, letting them all in to the stadium.

There it was again, the wooden sound. It was coming from outside. He was pulled towards its strangeness and was quickly out of bed and in front of the window. His eyes clenched shut. The wonderful Winter sun that met him, shining brighter than any star that had ever guided three Kings, was already warming the ground. It was a perfect day for football. Looking round with his improving vision a small chuckle slipped out as he found the source of his wake up call. Across the street were two young boys from the house on the corner, old wooden rattles in hands and scarves around necks. He hadn't seen a rattle in years.

Too excited to eat he passed quickly through the kitchen and was soon showered and ready. Kit, boots, shin pads. Towel and shower gel. It was time. One last look in the mirror before he left. The features of the man looking back hadn't changed, but Danny knew more than anyone else that the person inside wasn't the same as the one who'd been there several weeks before. The smile that grew across the face said it all. Come on then Danny, you've waited long enough for it. Now get out there and enjoy yourself.

Cheering, for him? He wasn't the only one who'd been woken by his alarm call and there were already at least ten people in the road.

"Good luck Danny!"

"Do your best for us!"

He treated them to a small wave and walked on up the street to where he'd arranged to meet Statto and Richo. He was ten minutes early, but last to arrive. Everyone was keen.

"Hey up gaffer, I thought you'd bottled out," Statto was in a good mood. Richo looked as disinterested as usual. A sudden silence came over them. The moment had arrived and they all knew it. Danny slowly put his hand in the centre and the others joined him, hand on hand.

"One for all, and all for one," the cry went up and the musketeers set off.

Danny had hoped to talk of tactics and plans, hopes and fears. Not a chance. Every car that passed honked its horn, every street corner and shop had a 'You Whites!' helping them on their way. And still three hours until kick off. He'd expected fear, but every step brought nothing but warmth to his heart and a smile to his lips. They approached the King's Head, some hardy supporters already supping drinks outside, but now there were blue colours mixing with the white.

The sound froze him. Not today, surely? The high pitched wailing, but was it fire, police or ambulance? He ran instinctively, it was coming from the Lane. Not today, please. It was police, the car pulling onto the main road with no apparent urgency, the siren obviously on for effect, before it accelerated away into town. His heart rate slowed as he changed down into a walk, panic being replaced by helplessness. What had happened? Nothing looked out of place, the early arrivals mingling harmlessly together. What's that? Statto must've carried on running and was now talking with Benjamin and Ted Holmes.

"Walton," no need asking the question then, Statto needed no invitation. "She was here with a few cronies trying to cause trouble. Looked like she'd been on it all night, all wide eyed and wild so they say." Why's Holmes looking so pleased with himself? Benjamin was going to tell him.

"Ted and his dad seem to have solved the problem though. All over in minutes, without a shot being fired." Well they did start it all in the first place. Could Ted look any smarmier? "And so it looks like Ted's back on our team." Whoopy shit.

Panic over they all turned. In front of them the main gates, no padlock in sight but firmly closed in anticipation of the crowd. To the side the smaller door, now neatly signed 'Players and Staff Entrance'. That would be them then.

Danny raised his arm, returning Al's friendly wave. On another day they could've shouted a greeting, but the noise and presence of an army of volunteers made it impossible that day. Tea was being made, police officers were being positioned and the gates were being manned. Shaking his head was easy, truly understanding what they'd achieved was more difficult. Al was with Marsha, somehow orchestrating the hive of activity around them. How close were we to losing you my friend? He waved again, celebrating the fact that Al had come back. A battalion of stewards marched in front of him towards the pitch.

Following them he caught sight of Dilip and Reg, one putting the finishing touches to the patterns cut into the grass, the other making sure that all of the lines were neat and white. It couldn't have been any better.

"So you've got more bottle than I thought. I never expected you White shite to actually turn up," Benjamin had followed him. Was that a real smile? A hand was offered and they shook, Benjamin fighting not to drop on the floor the pile of brand new shirts that were in his other arm.

"There was never any doubt, my Blue bastard friend." Yes, he'd just called him a friend, and perhaps at another time it could be true. Benjamin opened out one of the shirts in front of him.

"Dropped off by Ted, this morning." Sponsored by the fucking Sky Bar? They must be having a laugh. "With these and the effect they had on Walton this morning, the Holmes' are forgiven. I don't understand the whole story, but for now he's back on the bench. Ted the Trainer returns, risen from the ashes."

"The bastard's been rising from ashes all his life." They would have to stop sharing laughter.

"But, the one certainty is that he won't be rising from the ashes with my little sister at his side. I just thought you might want to know. Anyway, must be going, I've got a team of wasters to rip to shreds, and need to make sure that I'm all ready and prepared." Benjamin walked off in the direction of the away team dressing room.

A feeble, but audible cheer floated in from outside, rewarded by a jolt from his muscles. Statto was walking towards him.

"Get them in the changing room when they arrive Statto, make sure they haven't forgotten any kit and keep them calm. We'll take a walk out on the pitch when there all here." Seeing Statto stare he followed his shocked look towards a long line of athletic young men, hurrying through the players' entrance. That must have been the cause of the cheer. The Blues had arrived.

"Look, they've all come together. That must have been one hell of a big bike."

"And a very little cheer, but you heard it didn't you? There are enough people around to make a cheer. It's starting Statto, it's starting."

Statto nodded behind him, Danny turning to see Tone forcing his way through the crowd of helpers. The Whites were starting to arrive.

"Hey up Danny. I'm all ready for them, bring it on." Tone could only look down on him, a bag on his shoulder and a glint in his eye. "The day we've all been waiting for, finally here." Statto showed him towards the dressing room, leaving Danny to walk onto the pitch and take a seat on the bench.

Had he ever imagined being so busy and so happy? The hustle and bustle of a match day was perfect, giving him little time to think about the match itself. All around him it was building, his own senses joining in. Was there a noise? He couldn't say, but there was certainly a lack of silence. Voices, feet, doors, a cacophony of sounds eager to witness the match. There was no turning back now, all that was left was to play the game. Ten o'clock already? Time flies and all that. Just thirty minutes until the gates would be open, so time to see the team.

'Home Team' announced the newly painted sign, so he pushed through the door into a beehive of activity. Where's Griz? Everyone else was there. Some sat quietly, reflecting in their seats, others stood in groups, talking and joking animatedly, designed to ease their nerves. Tone just walked around, seemingly locked into his own private world of preparation. The neatly placed white shirt behind each chair niggled him. Not new and sponsored, like those the Blues would be wearing, but each player had brought their own favourite. He should've organised something better. They'd always said that people would turn up just to cheer on the shirt, today they could choose which one they cheered for. The door opened, an exhausted looking Griz entering.

"Sorry I'm late."

"No problem. More babies to deliver yesterday?" Danny recoiled at the manic stare he received.

"No. I'm absolutely shitting myself and haven't slept a wink. Have you seen how many people there are out there?" Griz took the last remaining seat, silently muttering to himself.

"Right then you lot, we've got about ten minutes before things start to get even scarier. They'll soon be letting the crowd in, so we're going to make the most of it and take a walk on the pitch. Put your boots on, to make sure you get the feel of it, and then out we go."

The murmured comments were everywhere as they formed a rough circle on the pitch. Yes, he'd one last task to perform that would affect them all, to announce the team. In the stands he saw the odd steward or policeman, and around the edges were the volunteers, running around with last minute instructions and orders from Marsha and Al. Now wasn't the time, so they'd have to wait a little bit longer. The sounds from outside were now clearer. Groups of people chanting and singing, the faint sound of drums and horns, the slamming of doors and the chinking of glasses. The non-stop thud of feet, and perhaps hooves too? A flicker of his eyes gave the prearranged signal and Dick Sparrow stepped into the middle of the group.

"Now then, you all listen and I'll tell you how it works. This noise is going to get closer and closer and louder and louder, until you won't believe that it could be any worse. And then, all of a sudden things will become strange. Every notch louder will become more difficult to hear. It'll become smooth, really like a wall, and when it's smooth it doesn't stick out any more, you stop noticing it. Finally you'll be so far down inside yourself, concentrating, praying perhaps, that it'll be as if it wasn't there. And that's when we go, that's when we're ready." Danny saw every eye on Dick, staring in awe at the man who'd been there before. "And if, after that, it does come back it can only do you good, it can only drive you on." A cheer from the far stand roused them from their story. The crowd were coming in and the cheer wasn't for them, but for the Blues who were also out on the pitch. It was time to go.

Why did players clatter their studs? Was it boredom, nerves, both? Conversation and jokes died as they all got changed, replaced by the drunken cricket sound of the studs on concrete. Outside the noise increased, just as Dick had promised. Footsteps behind the stands merged with song and conversation, the occasional musical note drifting through to where they were. There was laughter too. What had they organised for the pre match entertainment? Was it just Ollie the Ostrich running up and down the touchline? One hour to go. It was time.

"Right everybody, I know you've all been waiting for this, so here's the team for today. Please don't forget, even if you aren't playing from the start, you've been just as much a part of this as everybody else. Without you all we wouldn't be here. We've got unlimited subs, so you'll all get a run out, but we can only start with eleven." Here goes. Keep it short and sweet and leave the tactics and stuff for the team talk. "Right, Tone you're in the pegs," the big keeper was surprisingly quiet. No threats or boasts, not even a defiant swear word. Is he alright? "At the back it's Dev, Rodders, Cooge and Smiler," a grinning quartet, happy to have their positions confirmed. "In the middle a flat four. Harish, Ling, Limm and Billy down the right." He'd expected a reaction, but still the momentary silence hit him.

"But, but what about you Danny?" Billy asked the question on all of their lips. Don't hesitate, get on with it.

"I'm here to win, for the White's to beat these Blue bastards one last time. For that we need the best team out there in the middle of the park. Whilst you lot were training hard and playing matches I was either injured, planning, on the telly or cleaning out the toilets," someone gave a sarcastic whistle. "I'm not ready, and the sight of Billy haring down the wing's going to cause lots more problems than the sight of my arse waddling around in the middle of the pitch. So it's Billy who plays," he'd done it, a look to the ceiling being his reward. It was a small sacrifice for the chance to win the game. "Now that just leaves the top two. Richo and Donaldo." Just the one surprise, now they could focus on getting ready.

"Well done Danny. It can't have been easy, but it's done. Use your eyes and brain on the touchline and we'll be fine," a comforting smile and a warm touch to the shoulder and Statto was gone.

His eyes followed Statto touring the room, talking, coaxing, comforting with every jest and word. Now to prepare for the team talk, the motivational speech yet to come. 'Once more unto the breach'? No, that'd been done already. The sound outside continued to build. The sound of a band playing was now clear, had Al organised communal carols?

"He looks like a fucking ghost Danny, look at him," Statto's voice contained no humour. Following the line of his finger Danny fixed on Tone. Shit, he's white as a sheet, just staring in front. It was certainly not meditation.

"Shit! Why him? We've only got Tone, otherwise it's Weeble between the sticks. Leave him for now, we've still got fifteen until we have to go out. It's all in his head. The roar of the crowd or the sight of Arnie'll get him going again." Did he believe or hope? A visitor arrived, forcing him to move on.

"Dad?"

"Danny, son. Can I just talk with them for two minutes? Nothing about tactics honest, I've got something to offer you?" Where on earth had he come from? Just when he wanted calm and peace everyone was deciding to pop in for a chat. He didn't even have time to answer. "Hey, boys. Listen up, I've got a proposition for you. In a few minutes you lot are going to go out there and prove to that crowd that you're willing to die for the shirt. I see that you've all got your own White shirt to wear, one that's special for you. I respect that, but look at these," he took a shirt from a pile in his arm and shook it out. "The very last shirts that were ever worn by the Whites in the league. I won't tell you where they came from, but they were worn on the 12th December 2020, when the Whites played at home to Coventry City. If you want them, they're yours." Everyone looked at Big John, bemused.

"But we lost three one didn't we?"

"That doesn't matter, look at them. Real shirts."

"Yes," said John, "real shirts for real footballers. If you want them, they're yours." John didn't have to ask again, half a dozen shirts were already gone, taken eagerly as if they carried the spirits of the players of before, releasing their magic abilities bit by bit throughout the game. Danny didn't believe in ghosts.

"Great, thanks Dad. Come on then boys, let's get changed again, we're out in five minutes. Tone, are you all right?"

Stretching and bending all around him as the team went through their last preparations, a tap on his shoulder made him turn. Statto.

"Annie wants to see you, outside." Annie? His face must have given him away. "I don't know what she wants, but she's your sister." Of course she was. Statto could manage without him for a minute. There she was, beautiful as ever.

"Thanks for coming. I know your busy and that but I thought you could find time for a last minute high five?"

"A fucking high five? It's twenty minutes to kick off in the biggest game in this town for five years and you want a high five?" If she was hurt nothing was visible. She fought back.

"Yes brother, a high five. It may've always been a game of football for you, but to me and the others it was always something more. Now the others might be busy and elsewhere, but I'm not, so stop being an arse and give me one," she stepped forward swinging her right arm and Danny raised his own just in time to connect. High five. A brief silence and a loving look his way. "Right then. Now you've lowered yourself, you can go and play your silly game of football." His grin returned as he pushed back into the changing room.

"There you are, we thought you'd given up. Come on, we're in the tunnel," Statto was alone to greet him.

"In the tunnel, but I haven't given my team talk."

"The ref came, and when the ref comes we obey." Damn. Everything had been so busy since the morning and he'd lots still to do. Statto rushed through to the tunnel leaving Danny to get quickly changed. Finally he went through the door into the tunnel himself, where he stopped dead.

His ears were ringing and movement was held back by the physical presence of thousands of sound waves, attacking him from the exit to the tunnel some twenty yards away. No longer filtered by the walls it was transformed from noise to sound. He picked each one out, cheers, songs, drums and trumpets. Clapping hands and stamping feet, names being announced over a microphone and fears being whispered between colleagues. Every shallow breath took in more of these sounds. In front of him a line of players in White, beside him a line in new and shiny Blue. Everything was in place, presumably being held back by the noise. At the head of the line of White was Tone, a good six inches above all the rest. Slowly Tone turned towards him. Why today? In the changing room he'd been very white, now he was fifty percent transparent.

A gentle touch on his shoulder and he turned.

"Not playing Danny?" It was the referee, Benjamin

being close behind, a surprised look on his face. "I always enjoyed refereeing here, it's a lovely little ground. As we agreed, as many subs as you want. The boys aren't pros and it's a big occasion for them." Almost as an afterthought he added "Oh, and by the way, from me personally thanks, both of you. Boy have I missed days like this for the last few years. I'm from Preston me, so battles with Bolton and Burnley and all…. Yes, come on, let's get on with it eh," turning the ref walked confidently towards the end of the tunnel, his linesmen falling in behind him.

A giant Ostrich passed the end of the tunnel, a packed Barkley Stand behind him a festival of White and Blue. How many could he see, two, three hundred? Preferred again because of the sound his eyes started to work. There was a Santa Claus, a Snowman and some sort of Super Hero. Of course, the fancy dress days had been the best, the magic of Christmas always hanging around for an extra day for the Boxing Day match. There was no detail in the faces, but he made out the replica shirts and he saw winter coats. He saw young and he saw old. He saw couples, groups and people on their own, not that you could ever be on your own when you shared such a passion. The line now started to advance, impossible as it seemed the noise increasing with every forward movement. A rhythmic beating, getting louder and louder with each step, floated in from the left. Fat Frank and the band surely, beating out the march of the gladiators, leading the Victory End in a ritual of clapping to greet the players. Pa rum pum pum pum. In front of him the first heads were suddenly lit up by sunlight. What on earth's that? He looked around him, as if someone would explain to him how the noise could increase so much further still. The lines stopped, those in the second row seemingly too scared to join their colleagues, as if they'd been mown down by machine guns at the top of a trench. 'Blues', 'Whites', 'Bastards', 'Shites', the cries filled the air, the clapping almost unbearable. And through it all, the drums, their rhythm seemingly the only way he could place one foot in front of the other. Shit, what had they gone and done?

Danny was one of the last to leave the tunnel, the steps becoming easier as he adapted to the noise. Free of the tunnel walls he could now see everything. To his right everything was Blue. Pockets of the stand jumped up and down as one, clapping and singing as they did, songs that had already started to disappear from memory, now saved like the folk songs of old. To his left there was something wrong, something missing. Where were all the people? There was just a large banner covering the entire Victory End, bigger than anything similar he'd ever seen. In the middle the club badge, below it the club motto and above it "Forever White", the saying of the supporters.

"Fuck me, they'll see that in the Space Station," Cooge ambled past him.

The banner moved in a thousand places as the hands beneath it pushed up. It made noise too, the drums and the band continuing to beat their rhythm as the noise got even louder still. To his side Statto was wiping a tear from his eye. It was Boxing Day and battle would soon commence.

"Right lads, over here, quick," Danny shouted as loud as he could, realising quickly that it wouldn't be loud enough. Some players came towards him, others continued with their rituals. Gradually the message was passed on and everyone arrived. It was time for his talk.

"Right then, two lines please. Tall ones at the back, short ones at the front. If you can chuck a couple of balls in then that'll help too."

"What? Who the fuck are you?" Danny snarled at the newcomer.

"Tim Candy, photographer for the Times. Team photos, didn't the ref tell you?"

"Yes, but we were just…."

"Come on, it's kick off soon, line up." The team took their places and Tim took his photos. Danny waited.

"Right then, Captains please!" No, Harish come back, we're not ready. Too late, like a faithful hound Harish was straight there in the centre circle, honoured to have been picked as Captain and eager to get the game going. Benjamin joined Harish and the coin was tossed. The Whites won and would kick towards the Tip End first half.

"I don't believe it. I didn't even get to do my team talk. Statto, what did you tell them earlier?"

"Oh, not much. Just to enjoy themselves, to not worry about making mistakes and to keep their shape. Oh, and to smash the Blue Bastards." Pretty much the same as Danny had planned, but in less words. He'd save his talk for half time.

Then it arrived, a hush falling over the ground. The banner was folded away and Fat Frank's raised hand silenced everyone around him. People looked eagerly towards the centre as if missing the whistle was punishable by expulsion. The ref slowly counted the players and checked that the keepers were ready, finally accepting Rodders' shouted yes on Tone's behalf. He looked at one linesman and then the next, raised his hand, placed the whistle to his lips and blew.

And the world roared.

27 MATCH OF THE DAY PART 1

The Blues kicked off, getting everyone comfortable with passes backwards and sidewards, despite the sound reaching fever pitch. Danny, stood on the edge of his technical area, looked on as the Whites were happy to leave them like that, no one in a hurry to start too quickly. How could the morning have passed him by so quickly? He hadn't even given his team talk. Look at them before him. Oddjobbers who'd have got no nearer to this ground on a Saturday than they would have Anfield or Stamford Bridge. But not today. Here they were, accompanied by drums and cheering, by the singing and clapping of seventeen thousand people. The sounds and the colours were back, for a day at least.

He was roused by a cheer, Limm leaving a Blue player rolling on the ground. The referee's outstretched arms indicated 'play on', the Whites had the ball. A quick ball in front of Billy and a break was on, Richo and Donaldo searching for space behind the Blues back line. A skip past the left back and an early ball, finding Richo running on. Arnie slid in for the Blues but was already too late. Richo struck the ball well but it was comfortable for the Blues keeper to take and hold. The supporters behind the goal jeered and gesticulated as Richo put his head in his hands. The Whites supporters oohed and aahed as the sound of the drums got louder and faster, cheers coming down from the stands. 'Richo! Richo! Richo!' It didn't take long to become a hero.

"Not a bad start, eh Gaffer," Statto had joined him.

"Very early yet Statto. Our speed will make us tricky on the break, but look at them. They're just playing around at the moment, testing us out." The Blues tried to prove his point, upping the pace. A quick exchange in midfield found Benjamin breaking through on his own, thirty yards from goal. He looked up quickly, trying to find movement around him. Seeing something else he extended his step and let loose a vicious shot towards the goal.

"Fuck me, he's stood there like a statue. He isn't even going to move the daft bastard, frozen with fear. We're fucked Danny." Shit, Statto's right. Tone, transfixed as the ball moved towards him and the goal. Danny almost sensed the internal conflict as Tone's motionless legs did battle with his heart. The crowd saw it too, their thoughts and hopes being added to the ethereal battle taking place before them. Too late, though, look. Statto was right, they were fuc…

Danny's fist shot up towards the pale clouds. You beautiful bastard, where did that come from? With the ball already on him and traveling at speed towards the top corner, Tone's legs won the battle and returned to service. Propelled to his left, his arms followed like Superman. The very edge of his supersize gloves stroked the bottom of the passing ball and deflected it up slightly from its flight, diverting it from the back of the net to the inside of the upright. The bouncing ball was hacked away by Cooge with a swipe of his left leg. Tone sprung up from his position on the floor, his arms open as he cried out in homage to Tiw, Statto's god of combat. The fans in the Victory End joined him, realising the importance of the battle they'd just witnessed. Fat Frank and the rest of his drummers went into overdrive and Benjamin held his head in disbelief, denied first blood by a miracle of biblical proportions. Tone was back, and the crowd were alive.

"Well that's one less thing to worry about!" Statto was right, but there were plenty more left.

Danny barked out orders. Good, at least they were listening. The pattern had been set though, the Blues moving the ball confidently around and the Whites holding on as best they could. Tone made another comfortable save, cheered again by the crowd behind him. Somewhere behind the stands an unheard church bell chimed the quarter, fifteen minutes gone. Tone looked up, saw some space and bowled the ball out towards Harish.

Danny's hands clamped even tighter together. Harish turned his marker and opened up a bit of space, then floated a forty yard ball over the heads of the midfield. Billy again beat his man to the ball and again Richo and Donaldo darted into the space between their markers. A cut back, hard and low towards Richo who dummied leaving the advancing Ling all alone, with just the keeper to beat. Ling picked his place and put his trusty left foot through the ball, sending it on its trajectory towards the keeper's right hand side.

"Shit!" the ball beat the keeper's outstretched hand, only to bounce off the post and past the onrushing Harish, whose lost marker moved the ball quickly to Benjamin. He passed quickly to the space between Cooge and Smiler where a boot on the end of blue socks got there first, leaving the two White defenders to collide, falling into a heap on the floor. Tone made himself big, the ball striking his outstretched arms and ballooning into the air. Why did it fall there? All White eyes looked pleadingly at the linesman as Marlon buried the ball into the empty net from two yards out. The shrill sound of the ref's whistle announced the first goal as Marlon was mobbed by his Blue teammates, in front of a silenced Victory End.

"Double shit and triple shit. Get your bag out, Smiler

looks hurt." Danny stared intently as Statto ran slowly out to where Smiler lay on the floor, motionless since the collision. There was no need for him to look behind to know that the Tip End would be celebrating like mad men. How could you explain it? Ten seconds between hitting the post and conceding. They always said that football could be a cruel game and that cruelty was confirmed.

"Get warmed up and ready Weeble, you're on." Smiler was finished. "Keep going lads, you don't deserve this. There's a long way to go still." Did they believe him? He didn't think so, the pressure had been intense. Did he believe himself? Of course he did.

"Unlucky Smiler, but at least you heard them singing your name eh." Danny tried to comfort his player.

"Did they? I don't remember them singing my name, are you sure?" He was sure.

The game restarted. After the shock of the goal against them the crowd were back in voice. They were well used to Whites teams going behind at home after all. Danny was conscious of his movements. They could surely see him? Playing every ball and making every tackle under his track suit bottoms. Behind him Statto was talking, most probably to him, but he could hear nothing. The sound of Fat Frank and the band successfully covered up the church bell marking the half hour, the game now wave after wave of Blue attacks and a desperate White rear-guard. He sipped a bottle of water, hoping that his face was as invisible to those in the crowd as theirs were to him. He'd picked his team and he'd prepared them to play, the Blues were just better, full stop. How could he change the game? Just keep on doing what we're doing. At one nil there was always a chance.

"Just under fifteen to go Statto. If we can hold it until then we're right in this. They look like they're starting to get a bit cocky to me, that's a sure sign they'll start making mistakes." What was he saying? There was just confidence, not cockiness. They were better and knew it.

The Blues won another corner which Benjamin set up to take from the left. Arnie and the other big lads were up from the back, lined up around the edge of the area. Just defend it like you have the others and we'll be okay. They've changed their routine, the bastards. As Benjamin ran up to take the kick they scattered, like the Red Arrows on exercise, and the ball floated towards the penalty spot.

"Keepers!" Tone claimed the ball for himself as Cooge also jumped to make the clearance. Oh no, why does it only happen to us? As Tone closed his hand around the ball Cooge's head knocked it away. Tone flustered, claiming a foul off his own player. Arnie just picked up the pieces and blasted the ball into the empty net, roaring his delight to the heavens and stepping forward to shout into Tone's face as he lay on the floor. Danny couldn't look, turning from the pitch as players from each team stepped in to calm things down. His reward? Looking up, there was Winston on his feet in the Directors box, clapping enthusiastically and beaming out a smile. John was next to him, seated and silent. He turned back quickly, before either of them could catch his eye.

"Fuck," he had no other words.

The Whites kicked off again, and as they did the crowd again got into voice. Neither crowd nor players had given up yet, and for the first time in the game the Whites enjoyed a period of pressure. Would they have time to make the most of it? The fourth official came to the touchline, raising the board announcing a single minute of additional time. Almost immediately the board revealed itself as cursed. A wayward pass caught them out of position and Benjamin intercepted, playing a quick ball forward for Marlon to chase. Rodders got mugged, the only word for it, and his panicked lunge was an opportunity too good for Marlon to turn down. Their legs clashed and down he went, a yellow card and a penalty. The board was cursed.

"Did the bastard dive, couldn't see it from where I

was?"

"I don't know, I don't know." Would Marlon dive? He knew him for many things, but being a cheat wasn't one of them, but it didn't matter. What did matter was that the Blues now had a penalty and would be going in at half time three goals up. What a disaster. The ball was placed and Ali Hassan, a senior league striker with over twenty goals already that season, breathed deeply as the entire ground went silent. Danny couldn't watch, turning away and preferring instead to look at Reg, Dilip and an old man dressed in an ostrich costume, eagerly watching from the end of the tunnel. The shrill sound of the whistle was followed by the thud of boot on ball and then the most almighty roar of the day. Turning so quickly that he almost fell over he saw it. Tone was holding the ball up towards the heavens whilst behind him, and almost everywhere else, people in white went absolutely crazy. It was half time and they had a let off. Three nil had threatened, but instead they were still at two, and with the crowd on their side.

Get down that tunnel quick, this game isn't over yet, is it?

28 MATCH OF THE DAY PART 2

It was a pity. The empty changing room had been fresh and free, a good place for Danny to think. It had only lasted a few seconds, but it had been enough. The trickle of players became a flood, and the silence turned to noise. It was a good noise, they were far from beaten, each one offering the others tips and advice, things they could do together to become better. Tone beamed a smile towards him, now back in full colour version, a person of the ghost he'd been just before kick-off. Good old Statto, moving amongst them, checking them out physically and applying sprays and creams where needed. In the background he could just about make it out, the noise of the crowd brought back to life by the excitement at the end of the half.

"Right then lads, listen up. Come on quiet," his hands were held high, pleading for calm and a few moments of attention. They had to keep believing. "Tone's save's kept us in it," everyone nodded in appreciation, "but you've all had a great half. You've never given up and you've stuck to the plan. Yes, they've had lots of possession, but we always knew they would. But they're only two up and we've had a few chances of our own. Now this second half's going to be a bit different. People are going to get tired and that means more space and more chances. We just need to make sure that it's them that give up more space than us." Were they nodding in agreement or simply from tiredness? Give them some time to think. He met their eyes, one at a time as the noise of the crowd crept back in. A tap on the door gave him his cue, the ref announcing that it was already time to get back out. "Last words boys, give me another minute. I'm proud of you all, and that lot out there are too, you can hear it. Yes, we're against the wall, but we're still in this. Don't forget, today we're all Whites!"

"Whites! Whites! Whites!" they took up the chant as chairs were dropped, walls and lockers banged and doors slammed as they left the changing room and went back into the tunnel. All fear and apprehension was gone and they ran out into the wall of sound as if they'd done it a hundred times before. Tone, the ghost of an hour before strutted down in front of the Tip End revelling in the abuse thrown at him, finally bowing in front of the main Blues crowd as the inevitable invitation to 'fuck off' was delivered. The rest of the ground was also alive, no doubt still talking about the penalty save from the end of the first half. 'The Great Escape' was being belted out by Fat Frank and the band as the banner was once again being packed away. Kicking towards the Victory End would be a pleasure, but there were just forty five minutes left as the whistle blew to start the second half.

His new position in the technical area was carefully chosen so as not to risk wearing away the grass that Dilip and Reg had carefully nurtured. Of course, Benjamin would've given the Blues a good talk too and it showed as they attacked from the start. They were after that third goal, the one that'd kill the game. The Whites had listened to Danny though and it made him smile. Quick, long balls out from the back were causing the Blues problems. It was them who were soon readjusting themselves, and after an initial period huffing and puffing the White house still stood and started to take control.

Harish intercepted on the left and quickly squared to the middle. No long ball this time though, as Richo received it to feet in space. His nearest marker was almost ten yards away, an invitation he didn't need to be offered twice. Picking up speed Richo forced the Blues back further, frightened by his pace and the neat runs made by the other White forwards. A quick one two and he was through, the desperate last challenges and a late surge from the keeper not enough as he calmly slipped the ball into the net. Then he was gone, swallowed up by Frank and the band as he dived into the crowd. Had Danny ever heard such a beautiful sound? It seemed to come from everywhere, though surely the Tip End was quiet. He danced a dance that he never knew he had in him, arms in the air, legs pumping up and down. As he turned in a tight circle he made out the blurred images from around him. The middle of the Victory End was now a human whirlpool, people swallowed up and spat out again moments later, each one with an arm waving or a fist pumping and an ecstatic smile. Reg and Dilip to his right were jumping up and down, arm in arm, trying not to knock over the small, sad looking man in the ostrich costume. Finally he saw behind him. Big John on his feet, both arms raised towards the heavens, and even Winston politely clapping and nodding in approval.

"What a goal eh? That'll be a dream fulfilled. He might even settle down a bit now," their hug was brief, hoping that no one else in the seventeen thousand would see them. Richo had finally been liberated by the stewards and had made his way back to the half way line. The teams got ready for another kick off, two – one, and just over thirty minutes left.

"Game on indeed my friend. Listen, you're in charge now," his time had come. Danny the manager was going to become Danny the player. "Billy's blown, so I'll be on in a minute. Give it until seventy and then get Griz and

Dick on for Donaldo and either Limm or Ling, the one who looks the most knackered. Hold Crock back a bit longer, but make sure he gets a run out. He deserves it just like the rest of us. Oh, and that means you're the Gaffer now."

His muscles eased into game mode as he ran up and down the touchline, the stress of watching disappearing with every acceleration. There were no twinges from the knock he'd taken, and finally he felt mentally ready to give his all too. The small cheers from small boys that didn't even know his name helped. Two minutes was enough and soon he was stood next to a couple of Blues also waiting to go on as substitutes. At last, a break in the game. Danny's hands warmed as he joined the whole ground in applauding a shattered Billy as he left the field. How does it feel to have people cheering your name? Billy's tired look said that the answer would have to wait until later. He sprinted now to the centre of the pitch, a ball of energy jumping up and down as he waited for the game to restart. This was what his Dad had felt so many times before. Had he been nervous? He couldn't tell, but a few tackles later he was already in the game, suddenly oblivious to the noise around him. Both teams were now finding themselves in good positions, but Arnie was as solid as a rock at the back for the Blues and Tone continued making good saves in front of the Tip to keep the Whites in the game. The crowd just didn't stop, old and young alike. Many households would be quiet that afternoon, the occupants too hoarse from shouting and singing to talk any more.

Hands on hips he breathed deeply, praying that the oxygen would make him feel better. What had it been, ten minutes since he came on? The general match day noise had been replaced with something else, something special. Over ten thousand people were singing in unison as Griz and Dick Sparrow took their places.

'He's only a poor little Sparrow' rang out from all corners of the ground, a blast from the past. How had anyone ever allowed all of this to disappear? The game restarted with no time to imagine an answer.

A White slip allowed Benjamin to pick up the ball. Danny tracked him back but was a spectator as Benjamin's shoulder dropped and he waltzed past a Griz still not in the game. He feigned a pass, accelerated past Weeble, finally prodding the ball under a diving Cooge. Stopping, then cutting inside and leaving Rodders stranded he finally slotted the ball into the corner of the net, Tone flailing, finally beaten by the exquisite placement of the ball. Continuing his run in front of a jubilant Tip End, he ended up in front of the corner flag, the rest of the Blues joining him in a massive pile on. The sound from the Tip End was explosive, the silence behind him he could only imagine. There was no time for pity. Around him heads were in hands, the Whites either looking to the sky or slouched onto the floor. He had no more words to offer, joining the others in the walk back to their half. He needed help.

What was that? The first one took him by surprise, a single beat on five drums simultaneously. Another followed and then another, and then the crowd joined in. 'Whites! Whites! Whites! Whites! they cried, clapping, stamping and jumping in time to the ever increasing rhythm of the drums. The crowd hadn't given up and neither would the players.

In the middle of the pitch Danny had lost the overview that he'd had on the sidelines. Around him there was no coordinated encouragement, captain Harish as quiet as the rest. It was there though, the looks, the nods, the little exchanges among colleagues. They were going to give these last minutes one hell of a go.

What happened to the Blues? It was difficult to explain, but from the kick off the Whites dominated, the Blue confidence and organisation evaporated. Dick

Sparrow's intelligence and what was left of Richo's pace was just too much for them. A long hoof forward from the Blues was recovered by Cooge and quickly played to Danny. Yes, he had space and knew exactly what to do, there was no need to even look. Dick had moved to the exact position that Danny had picked out and he turned on a fifty pence piece, only to be brought crashing down by Arnie. Yes! free kick, just on the outside edge of the area. They just had to get something from it.

Danny and Griz stood over the ball, all of the big men coming forward. As agreed Danny feigned and Griz curled it, quick and to the near post whilst all of the big men were at the back. Look at him move, no one could beat Dick Sparrow over four yards. Diving amongst the boots there was a firm head on the ball, sending it into the back of the net. He'd done it, two hundred and fifty goals for the Whites. Danny joined the rush of his team mates, each one wanting to be first to congratulate the legend that now stood before them, gently nodding at the mayhem that the Victory End had become. Two hundred and forty nine goals to pay his wages, one to show that he still loved his team. 'He's only a poor little sparrow!' was already echoing a round the ground by the time Danny arrived, jumping on the back of a player and joining in the celebration. Three – two with five minutes left to play.

How long does five minutes last? There always seemed to be more seconds to play. It was now just like his training sessions, Blues defending and Whites attacking. At least they'd practiced like this. Gloveless fingers in the Tip End were chewed to the bone whilst the White supporters sought guidance from the Great Redeemer. 'We'll support you ever more, we'll support you ever more!' ringing in everyone's ears. The repaired seats were useless, as no one dared sit down. Attack after attack from the Whites was fought back and finally the sign went up, there would be a minimum of four minutes of additional time played at the end of the match. Danny had the ball and everything was clear.

Destiny, or whatever it was called, had decided. He shrugged past a feeble Benjamin tackle, anything you can do and all that. A shapeless Blue team gathered around him, there were too many to go under and he couldn't go over, so he'd have to go through the middle. Every piece of skill and every trick that he'd ever had was put to use, just like his Dad against Villa all those years ago. Forward and backwards, to left and right, blocked out at every turn. Springing forward, there it was, a yard of space. There was no thought, everything was just perfect as he let fly with his shot. On target it fizzed over the ground. It was going in, squeezing in at the near post. Damn, how did that happen? A wonder save, a finger nail it must have been that tipped it onto the post. There was no time to think, just seconds remaining for a corner. Griz went over to take it and everyone came up, leaving no-one to defend the White goal. Danny placed himself on the edge of the box, perfectly positioned to see everything and ready for the ball falling at his feet. Behind the goal the Victory End held its breath, presumable saving it so that they could all suck in together at the same time if needed. Griz delivered and Cooge flicked on at the near post. Tone headed goalwards but the Blue keeper somehow kept it out. Dick and Richo both managed hits on target but desperate bodies thrown in the way prevented the ball from going in. Harish threw himself at the bouncing ball and it connected with his ear and looped dangerously towards the goal, only to be cleared away by a dramatic overhead kick from Arnie on the line. Danny was half way through his turn when he heard it, the three blasts of a whistle that told him that it was over.

The Blues had won.

29 MATCH OF THE DAY PART 3

Danny's eyes closed and a painful jolt greeted his knees making contact with the pitch. His hands were raised instinctively, but not enthusiastically as he tipped forward onto the floor. Motionless and sightless the sound of joy coming from the Tip End was the only thing he could identify. His heart was beating as if it would burst, the result of him giving his all for the short time that he'd been on the pitch. How must the others be feeling? It beat and beat, pounding in his ears as it pumped blood to wherever it was needed most. Slowly his eyes opened and he started to take in the sight around him. The rest of his troops were sat around dejected, either alone or in small groups. Statto walked between them, offering consolation and water in equal measure. With a few wounded horses thrashing around they could easily be at Towton or Waterloo, dejected losers who'd survived a definitive battle. He mustn't let the tears come. He squeezed his eyes shut and moved into a crouch. A tap on his head, Statto? No, it was Richo, offering water. Richo's lips moved, but only made a sound like the pounding in his head. Now Richo smiled, gesturing behind him. Concentrate Danny, concentrate. The pounding in his head slowly died away, replaced by another rhythmic beat, one that he could now see was coming from Frank and his band. There was singing too, the words still impossible to detect, but the tune came back to him from his time at school. 'H A P P Y. I am H A P P Y'. That was it, he remembered it now. He grabbed Richo's hand and pulled himself up, others around him doing the same. A line had formed in front of him, well there were six White players stood applauding and waving at the crowd. The Victory End were joined as one. No disappointment on their faces, just pride as they applauded and serenaded their team, the team that had stood up for them so defiantly that day. How could they lose when, for the first time in five years, people had pulled on the White shirt and given their all for the badge? Danny joined the end of the line, his hands moving together as he returned the applause.

"Did you see my finish Danny, the dogs wasn't it? I felt like Roy of the Rovers, scoring for my boyhood heroes. I think I can retire now," Richo had also joined the line.

"If your public let you. It looks to me like they might not want to let you go, look at them." They were singing their praises in their hundreds. Danny quickly wiped some unseen grass from his eye.

"I never thought I'd see it boys, and certainly not from this side of the wall, but I'm bloody glad I did," Danny winced as Statto's strong hand squeezed his shoulder. All they needed was Al and they were all there.

"Hey up losers, what was all that? While you were lolloping about on the pitch I've already run out of tea twice. I even missed our first goal nipping out for some more, who scored it?" Bingo.

The four musketeers, reunited again. Big John and Winston came to join them and eventually so did the victorious Blues. The tour of the pitch together followed, did he even see Arnie and Tone shake hands at one point? It was over an hour before the crowd started to leave, every one of them glad that they could say that they were there that Boxing Day morning, that they'd been witness to that game. Imagining that at some point it would be talked of in the same breath as the Christmas Day match during the First World War.

Scores had been settled and the Blues now held the advantage.

30 THE SIX O'CLOCK NEWS

The combination of the cold air and the feel of his fresh new white shirt was good. But where was the rest? The changing room had been a hive of stories and jokes as the tired limbs were cooled down and showers taken. They'd all been there like him and would surely tell their children, but Danny had never quite felt the occasion the same way. The stadium had also been busy, with volunteers sweeping away the rubbish and Dilip and Reg repairing the pitch. Had he felt the same pride as them for his contributions? And the supporters, the ones he'd passed, laughing and joking in the streets and outside pubs. The ones who'd seen an ordinary game of football elevated to a level higher than it deserved. Where was Danny's excitement? Finally the quick handshake with Benjamin. Of course he couldn't share the joys of winning, he'd lost, no matter what they all said. He searched for memories of Saturday evenings a long time ago. Had Big John ever come home miserable and sad, regretting his Saturday afternoon? He should have, he'd lost often enough. Danny's head moved slowly from side to side. Of course he hadn't. Why let the result of a game of football get in the way of your life?

"What's wrong? Can't you bear to go in?" here was the man who started it all a couple of months previously.

"But the Sky Bar Statto, how come everyone agreed to come here after the game?"

"Free food and ten percent off all night. Holmes knows how to pull them in all right," he could say that again. Danny hadn't seen hands go up that quick since the lifeboats came out on the Titanic. "So we shouldn't fight it, let's just drink, eat and be merry." Statto was right, as usual.

"And he did say turkey didn't he?" Yes, let's eat, drink and be merry.

They left the descending darkness and went into the airy lightness of the Sky Bar. The second floor was the largest, the players already there hardly making an impression on it. It would be fuller when the wives, girlfriends and other friends got there later.

"Ah, so the gladiators are starting to arrive," Ted Holmes and Benjamin hardly made the most welcoming of welcoming committees.

"We were all gladiators today Ted, all seventeen thousand of us," Statto was expert as ever when it came to taking the piss. Holmes seemed indifferent.

"It's the generals that write history boys, not the soldiers." God Holmes was a twat. "Anyway, the beer's on offer and the food'll be out later. I understand you all missed out on the trimmings yesterday," that sickly smile and a stare at Statto. "Except perhaps the big bloke at the back." Don't show too many teeth Ted, or Statto'll knock them out. "Feel free to talk about the game as much as you want. I knew you called it the Victory End for a reason." Benjamin stepped in, taking Danny's hand again.

"Well played. We were hanging on there at the end. Five more minutes and I think you'd have beat us." At least one of them talks sense. "And if you're interested I'll be talking you through my wonder goal every hour, on the hour, from now until midnight." Now until next year more like. "Anyway, enjoy the evening. Thanks all round to Ted eh?"

"Consider it my way of making things up to you, after all that trouble you had with the Council and all." Teflon Ted had well and truly landed, slipping through their fingers on his way to earth.

Reunited with a long lost friend he gulped from the pint pot in his hand. Despite the welcome committee things were starting to feel better. The initial White - Blue divide was weakening with every story and joke. Annie, Geeta, Gesine and to his surprise Laetitia were huddled in a group together, and the arrival of Al and Marsha signalled that all of the work at the ground was finished. What a team they'd been.

"Oi, Holmes, when's this snap coming out then? I'm starving here, been eating like a mouse for the last few weeks," Tone announced his arrival for anyone who may have missed it.

"Yes, come on Ted, get the turkey out for the lads," Arnie joined him. Perhaps they'd avoid bloodshed after all.

"It could've been worse Danny, we didn't do bad eh?" Nodding in agreement Danny greeted Richo, pint in hand and a wide grin on his face.

"You can say that again. Seventeen thousand people to watch us have a kick about. Who'd have thought it?"

"Seventeen thousand, three hundred and ninety seven to be exact. Not quite a record for Boxing Day matches at the Lane, but not been seen for at least a few years," Statto paused and Danny happily waited. "You know what, there were times when I was worried, but you dragged us through."

"I dragged no one Statto, I just went where you showed me to go. Being shown where to go makes things a lot easier."

"Yes, and so does walking behind someone else." They chinked glasses, knowing that no more words were necessary. All around them were people at last unwound, now enjoying themselves as the afternoon drew to a close. The adrenalin seeped out of their bodies to be replaced by the alcohol at ten percent off. Benjamin had already re-enacted his goal a number of times using beer glasses and bottles on a table top. He was now organising any willing people for a life size run out in the centre of the room, to loud cheers from the Blues as he skipped tackles again. Only Tone refused to play the game, cheering every time he managed to stop the rolled up paper ball passing between the two chairs that acted as goalposts. It was just like his Dad and the goal against Villa down the park.

"Hello Daniel, Jason," the voice that used those names could only mean one person. As expected behind them was The Fist, accompanied by the person they now recognised as Fat Frank and the old man who'd dressed as an ostrich. The Fist stretched his arms towards them and came forward, trapping them in successive bear hugs.

"Shit," wheezed Danny as he spilt beer on his new white shirt. The Fist stepped back, surveying them through moist eyes.

"Boys, on behalf of me and the rest of the gang I really do want to thank you. For several years now we had nothing to look forward to. Today you reminded us, and boy I swear that we were close to forgetting, what it's like to go to that ground and cheer on our heroes. And I promise you that, today, you were our heroes. Through the years we've seen some shit inside those White shirts, people who couldn't be bothered, people who were prepared to take the money without paying back in blood and sweat. Well today we saw sixteen players who cared, who would've died for that shirt," a fine finger was pointed at Danny and then waved in the general direction of the other players. "We also saw people who were prepared to organise the whole thing, to give their time and effort to make it all happen," the pointy finger now landed on Statto followed by the same general group of people that had represented the players before. "For that effort, once again we salute and thank you." Frank and Ollie nodded in enthusiastic agreement.

"Well we're really glad we managed to find you. Annie and the rest spent quite a lot of time trying to hunt you down. But it was definitely all worth it. Without you it really wouldn't have been the same," Danny's kind words were clearly appreciated.

"The only question is Daniel, when will we get to do it all again?" The Fist turned and left, his question not demanding an immediate answer, but hanging around as a threat in the background.

The food came and went, devoured by people who'd been on match rations for quite some time. The sight and smell of hot turkey pie had caused a most un English queue to be formed, though the sight of the second and third trays being brought out had avoided the potential riot. The food eaten and cleared away meant that everyone could get back to the main topic of the evening. Drinking, laughing and reliving the memories of that wonderful day.

"Fuck me Ted, can't you keep your tellies turned off for half an evening. There aren't any matches today, surely?" Tone was first to react as the TVs all came to life, the bright lights startling people already accustomed to the half-light of the bar. The evening news was just coming to an end and it was time for the daily sports round up.

"Just be quiet and watch, you never know what you might see," surprisingly it was Winston who spoke out, and the room quickly obeyed. People all round took seats and looked up at one of the many screens. Ted, or the person controlling the audio visual spectacular, obligingly increased the volume and the familiar face of the newsreader came sharply into focus.

"And now we go live to Kempton Park where Andrew will bring us up to date with today's sport. Andrew…"

"Yes, good evening Emma, and a very good Boxing Day eve to you, dear viewers. And what a day of sport it was. The King George meeting at Kempton gave us a race that will never be forgotten. Philip's Folly won a thrilling race by a short head from the Kuwaiti owned Abdin and gave the King his first winner of this classic race." Horse racing? A replay of the last furlongs of the race, the determined rider in the King's colours hanging on for victory blurred in front of Danny's eyes. His ears told him that Andrew was carrying on, a list of names and owners and starting prices, ending with the news that Eric Potter from Barnsley had won an extremely large amount of money in the roll over triple match. The white shirts of thirteen cricketers and two umpires then provided a further back drop as Ashes in Melbourne got to toss with a bat.

"Are you sure this is worth watching Winston? Gee gees and then public schoolboys. It'll be the egg chasers next. I think I'd sooner hear Al doing a duet with Cliff Richard than watch this." Winston simply raised his hand and Tone, his challenge heard, went back to his pint and another agitated demonstration of some save or other.

"So, a great day in the middle for England, who'll be looking to build on that great start tomorrow and try and get back into the series. Rugby has experienced record crowds today and provided them also with some wonderful entertainment..."

"I told you so," laughter drowned out the rugby scores, and seemingly so the sports report for the day.

Andrew was replaced by Kate and sport was seemingly replaced by nutters. The Tenby Boxing Day swim, a large group of people running past the camera waving and smiling before plunging into the icy sea. Cheese chasers in Gloucestershire, duck racers in Bilbury and barrel rollers in Grantchester all took pride of place in the wacky sports ceremony. Not even the sight of fishermen and firemen playing football on a beach could rouse him.

"Well thank you Kate. Isn't it wonderful to see our traditions in good hands. I do believe though that you've saved the best until last?" Danny's focus returned and he looked up at the screen.

"Indeed I have Emma. As you mentioned the World Series is currently in its Winter break, but we must remember that it wasn't always like that. From the 50s onwards games over the Christmas period were very common. Well, you wouldn't believe it, but two towns, rivals for ever, decided that this year they were going to revive this game. No one's quite sure how it started, or why they did it, but today at the old Cherry Lane ground over seventeen thousand people turned up to watch this match." The silence was absolute as the crowd outside Cherry Lane that morning filled the screen. It was beautiful. The noises, the colours of a match day all came back, the images overpowering the sound of Mayor Banks who was now talking to the camera.

"The lying bastard." What did he say?

"And so Kate, despite the enhanced community ties I'm sure that some of the thousands of people were also interested in the result?"

"Yes, Emma, they were indeed. We've no proper images but here is some spectator footage of the Blues scoring their third goal in a close fought three two victory." Benjamin, weaving through the Whites defence before scoring. It had to be him, didn't it.

"I told you it was left on the third tackle, not right. You can't even remember your own goal you tosser," more laughs drowned out the remainder of the commentary as the report and the news closed.

"We were on the news Statto, did you see it? Not so much fake news, as just slightly inaccurate, but we were there," Danny's heart raced as he turned towards his friend. "It may've been just after the ducks and the barrels and the cheese and the fishermen Santa Clauses, but we were there." They all had something new to talk about and more beers were fetched.

"Come on Danny, over here and join us for a while," Annie claimed her brother.

"Don't worry, I've got other friends. I'll go and offer Tone an arm wrestle or something," raising his glass Statto released Danny from his company. Taking his arm Annie steered him across the room towards one of the booths. It could even have been the booth that they'd been in when they'd graced the golden photo, all that time ago.

Looking from side to side as he walked, Danny recognised the typical pub three hours after a match. It was all laughter, jokes and friendly disputes. The notion of White and Blue had completely disappeared, no winners or losers, just those who'd one day say 'I was there'. The Fist was holding court, his listeners breathing in his every word as he no doubt recounted a story from long ago. Reg and Dilip were with Dave, surely passing on the secrets of their trade. Arnie and Tone were arm in arm, proving that beer truly does have miraculous healing properties. To top it all off Al was holding Gesine in his arms and Ted Holmes was alone. Danny's face was just one big smile. They entered one of the booths.

"Ha ha ha. Unbelievable Jeff I said to him and that was that. Hey up, here he is. Found time to finally join us have you?" the others all looked up. Winston, Benjamin and Laetitia plus Billy Holmes. Seeing a space he sat down between his Dad and Laetitia, immediately feeling the warmth as Laetitia moved closer.

"Well then, I'm sure that every one's already told you, but we're very proud of you all. What you've done today's above anything we ever expected, and I do mean everyone. When I saw old Marley ruffling out that flag I nearly fell off my chair. Ha ha ha."

"I'll be honest John it frightened me too. I'd already seen it, lying on the shop floor in pieces, but how it ever got turned into that I'll never know. It gives me something else to try and sell for next year though." Did Winston ever stop thinking about business? "Anyway, there has to be a winner and I think we can all agree that the best team won. I give you the Blues!" they all raised their glasses and repeated the toast as The Fist also joined them. "Anyway, there's just one last thing to clear up. What on earth was going on with Walton?" Winston's eyes stared at Billy Holmes, who looked up to tell his tale.

"Well it all started a while ago. You all remember Kylie from when she lived here before. She always had expensive taste for life and a poor taste for men."

"That explains why she chose you! Ha haha."

"Thanks John, I like to try and forget that bit. Anyway as she went through husbands and money she got a bit of an idea, about ten years ago now. She'd seen some local development papers that put serious doubt on Cherry Lane staying as it was. Even before all of the shit started there was a strong likelihood that the ground would be sold. For her it was a great opportunity to invest in the houses around the ground, knowing that they'd go with it, and that the owner would make a tidy little packet. Anyway, she needed a local presence, so she came to me." Holmes took a drink, winding himself up to finish the story. "Well, I had a bit of spare lying around at the time, so I joined her. When everything started to happen it just made the odds even better, so by the time the Whites went out of business we owned pretty much all of the streets around. Then it all started going wrong. The first sale fell through, the story of the Herberts came out and things stopped looking so good. I've been selling bit by bit, trying to cut my losses, but she came back up here, determined to make her fortune. So for a start she had me trapped, her partner in crime."

"And you did have a few dirty weekends in the smoke too eh, ha ha."

"Yes, thanks John, there was that too. She also had hold over Banksy, she must've found stuff in the accounts or something. Anyway, the game was the last straw. Laetitia was getting closer and closer to our mystery

Herbert, and she was frightened of the impact that a successful game could have on a potential sale. She was petrified that the Whites could one day start up again. In the end it just seems that we had more ammunition. I hear she's already got another job lined up, over near Hull, so that should be the end of that."

"And the houses?"

"All still bricks and mortar, but unlikely to be worth a lot more than we paid for them, if we can ever sell. I suppose you win some and you lose some," they all drank to that. Everything was clear when you knew the facts, even for Danny.

"So, to that long list of thanks we need to firmly add old Marley here and Laetitia. I give you thanks!" another toast and Danny felt a hand attach itself to his arm. Looking at his watch he saw that it was just after eight. There was lots of time left to enjoy the evening. And enjoy it they did, as more and more wives and girlfriends joined them and the music and people got louder. Even Annie and Richo were dancing together.

Just a typical Boxing Day.

31 WHAT ARE YOU DOING NEW YEAR'S DAY

There was a definite bounce in Danny's step, a sure sign that things were going well. Not so much going as planned, that would imply that he knew what he wanted, and that he'd put in place things that had made them happen. But in any case he liked what was happening, so things were going well. It was another mild, dry day. Perfect for a Sunday and perfect for a walk into town. Could it already be two whole days since the match? It was still there in his head, the sounds of seventeen thousand people from two rival towns, celebrating their differences. And as for making the news and being seen all over the country? His cheeks warmed, surely some sunshine breaking through. Talking with Laetitia had been easier than he'd ever remembered. Could they get back together? It was too early to rekindle the romance of their youth, she'd said so, but they were both free to spend time with each other. She'd said that too. Yes, things were going well.

Passing by Cherry Lane had always made him nostalgic, but today was something special. Could he still hear the echoes from the match two days before? The excitement of the crowd, the thud of the ball, the cries of the players. Everything had been well cleared up by their army of helpers and the local Council, almost as if they wanted to hide from those who weren't there the fact that the game had actually taken place. They were too late though. Seventeen thousand people had witnessed the game and the two towns had been talking of nothing else ever since. How many times had he been stopped on Saturday? He'd lost count. It was always the case. Football had never been just for those lucky enough to be in the stadium, it was for everyone and anyone who cared. The reaction of the whole town just proved it. The fans were united in the ground on a match day afternoon and that town was united throughout the year. It was still there, his padlock, but seeing it now was very different to that first time, over five years before. Now he believed he had the key.

He'd soon be there and his quickening steps took him across the Elizabeth Park. Unusually there was a group of people having a kick about on one of the pitches. He'd been there years before, pretending to be White against Blue. Would one of them be pretending to be Richo? Unlikely, but not impossible. Behind them was someone with a red windcheater, strange for such a day. Could it be Dave? No, he'd surely realised that there was no training for the Whites that day. He chuckled out loud. Waiting in the rain on a Tuesday night for someone, anyone to come along for the trials. And to think they'd played in yellow bibs, borrowed from the trolley handlers at the Co-Op. What would he have done that night without Statto's calm, Annie's bibs and Al's clipboards? The idiot he'd been. Danny had made friends that day, good ones. Tone and Dick Sparrow, heroes from the past and future, Ling and Limm too. And then there was Al. Breaking the bad news to him had been something he'd dreaded. He'd been saved from the situation, but nearly lost his friend anyway. Annie and Geeta had relieved him, adopting Al to join in their plans and in turn doing their part towards that whole mad event

. And he even ended up getting the girl, he'd never been so happy. In front of the changing rooms, breathing in the air he could see Lovers View at the top of Parson's Hill. Not majestic or distinguished, just higher than the ground below it. How close had he been to losing them that night? Statto struggling to get to the top, even on his motorbike. Tone and Arnie fighting and the rest just happy to still be alive after their exploits. And the Blues just running up like it was nothing. Yes, Danny was alive and living again, and he'd continue that way. He promised himself as he walked in front of the fire station and swimming pool. The places for the life savers, the ones who'd come to your aid when you really needed them. Around him he had plenty.

The end of the road, the door of the Bell was now in front of him, beckoning him in. Seven differences inside? Pushing the door he entered the place he knew so well.

"Here he is. We thought you'd found something better to do, some new friend or something like that." Change number one. Richo was no longer in a group with the lads, but was sat alone with Annie. Danny approved, they made a good couple.

"Says Romeo over there. Pot, kettle, kettle, pot. You two don't worry, we'll look after things for you." Change number two. Statto was always on his own when Danny entered, looking at some book or screen, devouring more information. Richo's little gang had joined him around his table, looking at papers spread out in front of them.

"You single men are all the same. One day you'll understand." Change three. Red Al had maintained his position at the bar, but was now accompanied permanently by his faithful German shepherd. She'd have to be a shepherd to stop Al getting in trouble. Not wanting to miss her turn she added in her sexiest German accent.

"Meine Entscheidung in England zu bleiben war schlussendlich vielleicht doch nicht so schlecht." The blank looks from everyone hadn't changed. Unperturbed she continued. "Anyway, I hope you lot haven't frightened Geeta off, going all soppy over those boys. No girl likes to be on her own." Change four, and one that worried him. Where was Geeta?

"She'll be here later, she just had to pop up to the factory for a bit. Winston wanted to have a word with her." Change five, Marlon was in the Bell. It had happened before, but wasn't normal. He should surely have been out somewhere with the rest of the Blues, planning their next steps to world domination.

"Turn the TV up a bit, it's the news in a few minutes." Change six. Why was there a telly in the pub and why had Statto walked over to listen to it? It was an old style flat screen, no more than thirty two inches, but it was in the Bell and it was switched on. A noise behind him and he turned.

"Oh, hi Laetitia." Change seven, lucky seven. Not that she was beautiful and not that her smile made his pulse quicken, but that she was there and that she was there to spend time with him. Or so he thought, as Annie whisked over, taking her to the bar, followed by Geeta who'd breezed in behind her. Never mind, seven changes was enough for one day. Walking to the bar he stood next to Statto, and ordered them both a pint.

"So what are you up to my friend, why the TV and why the interest?" His answer was a Statto stare, accusing him no doubt of being an alien, arrived from some far away planet.

"Where've you been the last twenty four hours? Has she really scrambled your brains that much in a day?" the stare changed into a grin. "Whilst you were away catching up on the sales, things have been happening. The country's woken up and things are moving," Danny still didn't understand. If there'd been any happenings then they hadn't happened in his flat. "Look, here we are," Statto pointed to the TV screen, the news just starting.

Nothing good would come here, just the normal long list of desperate events from round the world. Then his heart leapt.

"But that's the Lane. What's that doing there?" Statto hushed as news anchor Harriet Potter spoke.

"Welcome to the national news. Today we'll be starting closer to home than normal with what is now being called the Boxing Day effect. Just two days after the famous match at Cherry Lane it seems that the whole country is racing to join in. Short time scales and sometimes impossible logistics are not getting in the way of organisers up and down the country, in the race to put on this year's traditional New Year's Day game. Here's a report from our sports reporter Alan Spice."

"Thanks Harriet. You'll all remember that just two days ago now two local communities organised the famous Boxing Day Match." Did they really have to show Benjamin's goal for what must have been the thousandth time? At least they now had some good footage of Geeta's flag covering the Victory End and Fat Frank drumming enthusiastically. "Well it appears that many people saw the game and that almost all of them had heard the Christmas Day message from the King. Just yesterday, twenty four hours after the initial game, Swindon and Oxford played out a thrilling three all draw at a local ground, cheered on by just over two thousand people. Since then though the police have become more cautious, just as the organisers have become more audacious. Keys have been flying out of key cupboards up and down the country, just as local constabularies have strained to stay on top of all of the proposed matches. The result? Next Saturday, New Year's Day, promises to be a bonanza of football. Already confirmed we have the following matches: Darlington vs

Carlisle, Newcastle vs Sunderland, York vs Scarborough, Burnley vs Bolton and Preston vs Stockport," Alan paused, spots being lit up on a map of the country behind him. "Huddersfield vs Barnsley, we have two Sheffield derbies, Stoke vs Port Vale, a three way tournament in the Midlands between Derby, Leicester and Notts County. Ipswich will play Peterborough, Northampton vs Coventry, Wolves vs Walsall and a combined Bristol vs Yeovil. Bournemouth vs Portsmouth and Brighton vs Southampton. We've got Wycombe vs Gillingham and Fulham vs Chelsea. Brentford will play Charlton and Wimbledon against Millwall. These are all of the games confirmed and approved by the police so far, and there are many more still waiting for approval and others in the early stages of planning. All in all this is just a remarkable achievement," the map behind him was lit up like a Christmas Tree.

"I knew it Danny, I just knew it. All it needed was a spark and the fire would take hold," Statto was unable to hide his excitement and pride. We started all that?

"But how'll they organise the teams? It took us weeks."

"Yes, but we were the leaders. Following's easier. We know that anyone can turn up and play, what's important is that the crowds come along and enjoy themselves." Harriet wasn't finished.

"And so Alan, quite an amazing reaction up and down the country. But is that it, will it all end on New Year's Day?"

"Well Harriet, we all heard the King. This is a year for starting up, not giving up. There's already talk of a new league from next season, to accommodate this new interest. A series of games until the end of the classic season has been mentioned, and at present there is real interest from people all over who want to make this work. Whether it will work out we'll just have to wait and see, but for the moment things are looking good." Alan smiled, like all reporters do at the end of their reports and Harriet moved on to a new migrant crisis around the Mediterranean. The TV was switched off and change number eight walked through the door.

"Good afternoon Jason, Daniel and all," The Fist bowed in medieval style to those whose name he hadn't mentioned individually. "Jason, we've work to do I believe." Statto led him over to his table and The Fist took even more papers from his sports bag. Catching Laetitia's eye Danny waved apologetically before going over to listen in. The Fist was in the chair.

"So this is the proposal for the rules of the English Community Football League. It's mainly taken from the old existing rules, but I've taken a particular look at the sections on ownership and financial stability. Initial feedback from the others is good," Statto's hands rubbed together in excitement. "Then there's the first draft on player ownership, including the standard contract. I think we all agree that we need professional players for the long term quality of our offer. There's also the collective agreement for players rights which, if followed correctly by any new players union, should remove any need for agents," Statto's hands were in danger of being erased. "The last two are the most important. There's the ownership charter. Minimum of fifty one percent supporter ownership at all clubs and strict operational guidelines based on turnover. A maximum limit to make sure that the bigger clubs still have some advantage, but nowhere near as much as they had before. And finally the TV policy document," Danny's ears pricked up, surely not something to enslave them again to the TV powers? "As agreed we have the rights for highlights on all local news stations with two highlights packages each weekend, Saturday night and Sunday morning. For the league there'll be no live games, but the possibility for games to be shown in their entirety on a deferred basis. This is the one needing the most work, but it's less important than the ones relating to the league itself," Danny was nodding along, he approved.

"So how much interest have we got and what are the timelines?"

"So far we've fifteen serious enquiries, each with access to a stadium that would fulfil the requirements for matches. There are a further twelve showing an interest, though all of them have certain obstacles to overcome. I think we should seriously be targeting one league with a full programme, so a target of sixteen teams," The Fist's face melted into a large smile. "Gentlemen, and ladies," he nodded over to the group of girls in the corner, who were oblivious to the thanks he was about to give, "I think that we've only gone and bloody done it!" Everyone was smiling. Confused, unbelieving smiles, but broad, happy smiles none the less. All it had needed was a spark, and the fire was starting to take hold.

Danny and Statto shared a long look, they'd done something, anything, and it was going to work.

32 I DON'T LIKE MONDAYS

Danny parked his car yet again. The May sunshine could have made the journey easier, though he hadn't noticed too much that morning. Richo was never short of anything to say and their weekend in the Peak District had given him plenty of ammunition. The four of them had enjoyed the long days full of fun and the cold beer in the evenings. That and the company of two beautiful women had been more than the pair of them had deserved. He turned like a shot, his neck muscles burning. Statto, the idiot, banging on his window. The two of them got out, backing away in fear as Statto almost bounced around them, like an excited Saint Bernard.

"Three nil Danny boy, three nil against Liverpool," Statto was all energy and grin. "No Scouse bastard's going to look down at me again. You should've seen them though, it was a great game. The real gaffer's got them singing, I'll tell you." Danny joined in with the celebratory smile, even though he hadn't seen the game.

"It must've been a sight my friend. The first visit from Liverpool in half a century or more and we beat them. It's what it was all about though, isn't it. Were there many in?" Missing the game would've been impossible in the past. He had no regrets though, his priorities were right.

"Just over twelve thousand. Boy it was rocking towards the end. I bet poor old Frank's looking around for a new arm today." Now the sight and sound of the band at full blast must have been a wonder. To be honest Danny had heard it, in his head as they'd been navigating up Derwent Edge, desperately trying to get a signal in the hope that there was a message. He'd still cared, he'd still pined for the result and hoped for a victory. Living like all of the others, the butchers, bakers and candlestick makers. The ones who couldn't get to the games, but who still celebrated or had a quiet night in, depending on the result. Could he do it for a league match? Only time would tell. Statto continued. "Anyway, that's all of the friendly stuff over. The beginning of August we'll be running out in the first ever round of games of the English Community Football League. The ECFL," the pride on the face of the league co-founder and Chairman was a picture. Without him the eighteen teams ready to dispute the new professional league would never have been found.

"You've done an amazing job there. Five months of work and a bloody pro league back in place," Danny's hand stung as he delivered a slap on the back for the big man.

"We did an amazing job Danny, and the work started just over seven months ago, if I remember correctly," he smiled again. "Come on, or we'll be late."

They got changed and went out to the shop floor. The Management were already in place ready for the Monday meeting, the May light streaming through the high windows behind them, making them look like the cast from Close Encounters or ET. Everyone they passed was talking about the weekend results, the Blues having beaten Watford on the same day. The Monday morning banter was back.

"One nil against a real team lads. Watford have got a great young squad there and we beat them easy in the end."

"One nil easy eh, and they missed a penalty. We beat a team that's won five European Cups we did."

"Five European cups yes, just none in the last twenty years. Ha haha. Someone told me that Gerrard and Carragher were playing on Saturday."

"Gerard who?" they all started laughing.

"Well at least they had players who you've heard of. Elton John would probably get a game with that Watford lot you beat," Red Al had come over to join them, closely followed by Richo. "You're just a cuckoo team anyway, without your own ground. Borrowing the rugby club's ground, you're like bloody MK dons you are."

"Al, where were you this weekend? I thought you were coming with us?" Richo looked genuinely hurt.

"Well I had the game to go to, you know how dedicated I am."

"Yes, that and a trip to see the Mother in Law next week. I didn't realise you even had a passport."

"He certainly didn't need one to follow the Whites around on their European escapades," there was more laughter from everyone around.

"You make sure they let you back in Al. You know how tough they are these days. They're probably happy that Gesine's going so they can stop her coming back." Al did realise it was a joke, surely? Monday morning was fun again.

A loud bang announced that the meeting was starting and Benjamin stepped forward. At least he'd now stopped talking about his goal, having more important things to talk about.

"Right then everyone, please listen closely. We've got a lot of things to cover today, and some of it's very important stuff." The events of the last months hadn't changed his smooth style at all, though Danny now saw much more of the man that he'd shared a table with in the

Wheelwright's all those months ago. "First of all we've had a request from the Tarbuck Nursing Home in Liverpool. Apparently eleven of their elderly gentlemen had a day out in White shite country on Saturday, and two of them left their walking sticks behind," he continued to speak but his words were drowned out by the laughter of the Blues supporters in the group.

"Cuckoo, cuckoo," the riposte came back from the few Whites who were present and brave enough to show defiance. Benjamin raised his hand for silence.

"Please enjoy your childish bird noises while you can. Permission's been given for a new ground just outside town and the funding's all in place. In just one season's time you'll find that the best team in the area is sitting top of the league in its new palace, whilst the White shite's glad that there's no relegation as it sits in some old medieval shit house," more laughter and counter calls. "Anyway, on a different note I'm pleased to tell you all that the order book's overflowing. So overflowing in fact that we're going to start to look at ways that we can increase capacity in order to keep up. This will include looking at the current work patterns, so we'll be evaluating overtime and additional shifts, plus we'll be looking at opportunities to invest in additional machines."

"Not bloody German ones please," Al looked for the culprit, but his glare found no target. Benjamin continued, an air of true seriousness in his voice for the first time that morning.

"I don't need to remind any of you that this is absolutely great news for the company. There aren't many companies around here looking to grow, and certainly not in our line of business, one that was supposed to have died out half a century ago. Again thank you for the part that you play in that every day, whether you're Blue, White or any other colour," a strong silence as it sank in. Benjamin continued, his words becoming less and less clear. Danny took another look up to the windows, which had moments before been the entry point to the factory for thousands of beams of sunshine. A lonely cloud had taken position in front of the sun and he could now clearly see the window to Winston's office. Winston was there, looking down at what remained of his company, the one that he'd kept alive in times of trouble and helped grow in times of plenty. As their eyes met Danny saw the smile and a slightly raised hand. He returned a nod, to the man who may one day accept him into his family. Winston looked older than he remembered, but then he'd spent the last few months working harder than he'd ever done before. With a rejuvenated factory and a new football club to set up there was no shortage of things to do. He'd even asked John to be his manager. 'Fucking unbelievable Jeff, after the last time, really?' had been the reply over their bowls of tagliatelli. They'd both recognised the symbolic nature of the gesture. Supporter ownership hadn't been a problem for Winston and the funding for the new ground had been put in place and authorised early, but the search for a location had been long and hard. Like most hard things in Winston's life he'd just looked down after they were completed and gloried in the fun that it had been to complete it. A temporary ground share would be followed by a brand new stadium out of town. Another Winston success. Hearing the word 'Production' Danny rejoined the rest.

The sight that he was witnessing had taken him four months to get used to. The steps forward were elegant and assured, though they had been from the start. What had changed was the voice, and surely the confidence of the person behind it.

"Right then, we've got a bit of a busy week planned for this week, and you can see everything that should be going on in more detail on your huddle boards," the thick local accent was undoubtedly Geeta, as was the practicality of what she said. No words were ever wasted. "The highlights are the weekly cleans on 2 and 8, plus we'll be taking 3 down all afternoon today to give the new rollers a try out. If you've any questions then ask either your line leader or Dave, who's looking after all of the trials. For your information last week was another record for uptime, so thanks a lot and keep up the good work." Gone in sixty seconds, but nobody could have failed to notice the pride that being there in the first place gave her. Yet another battle that she'd fought and won. Marsha and Al rounded off the meeting with the late bank holiday Family Fun Day, worth the entry just to see Benjamin cooking hot dogs, plus a community project on the estate behind the White Hart. Everyone was welcome to come along and join in applying the paint that the company had kindly donated to the old playground equipment. The meeting over, the lines were started up and the day began.

Line 3 started up without protest and carried on that way. Danny had little to do, other than make sure that the people around the machine didn't let the line down.

"Hey Marlon, what are you doing round here? We thought you'd nothing to do these days, except sit around in the workshop, counting the days down to your retirement."

"What are you talking about, he can't count that high." Laughter all round as they all joined in.

"You must be joking. My new boss is a far harder task master than the old one. She's never satisfied, always finding new things for me to do. So don't you lot worry, I'll still be retiring at the same time as you lot." A few months ago he would've said Marlon was alright for a Blue, today he was just alright. "Danny, Geeta was looking for you anyway, she should be over soon." Never a good sign. Looking across the floor he found her in conversation with Winston, Benjamin and Dave. Pointing here and there, nodding her pretty head when needed. His walkie talkie crackled.

"Rubber Duck calling the Gaffer, Rubber Duck calling Gaffer, do you read me," did Statto really believe that this made the day go faster?

"What do you want Statto? Have we got a problem?"

"Not at all, just wanted to know if you were coming to the meeting on Thursday? It's the last one before the close season, so we'll have quite a bit of business to get through." How had he ended up on the supporters committee for the newly formed Whites community team? He didn't do anything, it was almost a ceremonial post, a reward for managing the team to its only defeat in the last five years. The mystery de Lisle-Hubert owner and Statto organised most of the business. Danny and the rest turned up mainly for the tea and biscuits at the end.

"Of course I'll be there, wouldn't miss it for the world. You just tell me what to vote for and I'll do it."

"It's not like that Danny," there was genuine hurt in Statto's voice. "I don't mind working on the detail of the proposals and all that, but every member's needed in order to make sure we don't make the same mistakes as before. You've to always vote how you want, always."

"I hear you Rubber Duck. Yes, I'll be there, but make sure they've got some Rich Tea this time. The Digestives get too soggy too quickly for me. Over and out." How did people like Statto manage to work as they did, and where would the World be without them? He wasn't after power or publicity, he just wanted to make things better. With him and The Fist the future of the Whites was guaranteed. They even had Big John as honorary Chairman.

"Danny, here you are. Bad news I'm afraid," Geeta looked serious and her bad news was often very bad.

"What is it, how long do you need the line for?"

"Not that sort of news. It's Harish. He twisted his ankle in the nets last night. Cricket training's already started, so he can't make 5-a-side tonight. Sorry it's late, but you should be able to get a replacement?" Damn, that was all he needed. Neck and neck in games since the New

Year and only a couple of weeks before the holidays started. There was only one thing for it.

"Rubber Duck, come in please."

"What is it now, you after Jammy Dodgers or something, Custard Creams?"

"It's worse than that Statto. Have you got your kit, we're one short for tonight."

"What, another chance to give those Blue bastards a kicking? I'll be there, don't you worry, I'll be there."

Everything was just how it should be.

ABOUT THE AUTHOR

Paul Bullimore grew up in Leicestershire and now lives in France. Travelling a lot with his job gives him lots of time for reading, writing and searching for football results on the internet.

Printed in Great Britain
by Amazon